VITAL LIES

Also by Ellen Hart

An Intimate Ghost
Immaculate Midnight
The Merchant of Venus
Slice and Dice
Hunting the Witch
Wicked Games
Murder in the Air
Robber's Wine
The Oldest Sin
Faint Praise
A Small Sacrifice
For Every Evil
This Little Piggy Went to Murder
A Killing Cure
Stage Fright
Hallowed Murder

VITAL LIES

Ellen Hart

 St. Martin's Minotaur 🐾 New York

www.minotaurbooks.com

ISBN 0-312-31766-2
EAN 978-0312-31766-9

First published in the United States by The Seal Press

First St. Martin's Griffin Edition: July 2004

10 9 8 7 6 5 4 3 2 1

*For Mary, Allen and Jo,
dear friends.*

Acknowledgments

Many thanks to Mary Trone for her energy and sound editorial comments. Her deep love of the mystery—and of those who write and read them—has been a constant source of delight. Thanks also to Allen Simpson for reading the manuscript at a critical stage and offering not only encouragement, but insight. And finally, my deepest thanks to Kathy Kruger for reading each page along with me—agonizing over every nuance of character and plot. As always, her patience, humor, and love made the crucial difference.

CAST OF CHARACTERS

LEIGH ELSTAD: Owner of The Fothergill Inn; old friend of Jane Lawless.

VIOLET SVENBY: Leigh and Ruthie's aunt; sister of Inga; helps Leigh run The Fothergill Inn.

INGA SVENBY: Leigh and Ruthie's aunt; sister of Violet; helps Leigh run The Fothergill Inn.

STEPHEN LAPORTE: Financial advisor for a large brokerage house in St. Paul; living with Leigh.

RUTHIE SVENBY: Leigh's cousin; Violet and Inga's niece.

JANE LAWLESS: Owner of The Lyme House restaurant in Minneapolis.

CORDELIA THORN: Artistic director at The Allen Grimby Repertory Theatre in St. Paul.

BURTON MARCH: Head chef at The Fothergill Inn; father of Dylan.

DYLAN MARCH: Burton's five-year-old son.

WINIFRED VINSON: Feminist witch; old friend of Leigh's; life partner of Tess; half owner of a bookstore in River Falls, Wisconsin.

TESS INGMAN: Winifred's life partner; half owner of a bookstore in River Falls, Wisconsin.

PER GYLDENSKOG: Writer staying at The Fothergill Inn.

HENRY GYLDENSKOG: Father of Per, retired.

MICHAEL PAGET: High school student in Repentance River; works part-time at The Fothergill Inn.

ELMER LAPINSKI: Handyman at The Fothergill Inn.

BO DIERDORF: Owner of a small grocery in Repentance River.

PETER LAWLESS: Jane's younger brother.

SIGRID MUNSON: Peter Lawless's girlfriend; attending medical school at the University of Minnesota.

RAYMOND LAWLESS: Jane and Peter's father; defense attorney.

DANIEL SVENBY: Ruthie's deceased father; Violet and Inga's brother.

HARLAN SVENBY: Ruthie's deceased grandfather; Violet, Inga, and Daniel's father.

RANDY WILLARD: Per's ex-lover.

BERYL CORNELIUS: Jane's aunt.

*The only thing that ever came back
from the grave . . . was a lie.*

Marilla Rickler
The Philistine
Vol. XXV
1901

A Scene From the Past

What's past is prologue.
The Tempest, Act II, Scene I
William Shakespeare

The clock on the mantle ticked off the minutes. Two burning eyes stared intently out the window, watching the cold, gray daylight sink into night. That's the way it was on this island, he reminded himself. Blackness fell like a thick curtain. There were no in-betweens. No comfortable street lamps to ease a person into the dark. None of the noises of a living, breathing city. Just stillness.

He pulled the gun nearer.

It was out there all right. He could feel the hate right through the walls. If it wasn't for the deafening sound of his own thoughts, he was certain he could hear it creeping toward the house. Stalking him. Nobody believed him, but that wasn't unusual. Behind his back, they were all laughing. Wolves didn't come this far south. Not even in Minnesota. Yet they had all misunderstood. This was more than flesh and blood. This was fate inviting him out into the snow to play hide and seek.

He took another gulp of whiskey.

They could smirk if they wanted, it didn't matter. He knew what he had to do. A dark, sinister image floated in front of his eyes. A solitary wolf in sheep's clothing. He contemplated the vision for a moment before shaking it out of his head. If only the guys down at the hardware store could see it, they might finally understand.

1

Taking one last swallow from the nearly empty bottle, he gripped the rifle and stood. It was now or never. He weaved unsteadily into the front hall and switched on the outside light. As he opened the door, snow blew hard against his thin body. For a moment, he closed his eyes and struggled against the irrational fear about to overtake him. This had to be done. He owed it to those he loved to protect them. Running a hand over his face to clear his vision, he strode purposefully out into the drifting snow. By morning, he or his prey would be dead.

Raising the rifle, he waited.

PART ONE

Portions and Parcels

All things are taken from us and become
portions and parcels of the dreadful past.
The Lotus Eater, 1842
Alfred Lord Tennyson

1

Monday Morning, December 21, Winter Solstice

"Twin Cities Weekly," said a young man sitting behind a grimy reception desk. He held the phone precariously between his shoulder and ear as he unwrapped a sticky caramel roll.

"I'd like to speak with one of your staff reporters," said a soft voice.

"Just a minute." The sound of computers whirred in the background as the call was routed up to the third floor.

"Editorial. Can I help you?"

"Hello," said the caller. "I understand you're doing a feature article on The Fothergill Inn in Repentance River."

"Yes, that's right. We've heard it's a great place for a vacation."

"Yes, it is," agreed the voice. "But I have some information I doubt you were given. It's something you might want to include in your article."

"Oh? And what would that be?" The reporter leaned forward in her chair and looked out the window. From her vantage on the fifth floor she could see traffic backed up for blocks along Hennepin Avenue. It was all that new construction on the basketball arena. Just what Minneapolis needed. Another sports facility.

"Do you have a pencil?" asked the caller.

"I do."

"I assume you'll be telling your readership what a wonderful place the inn is for a little rest and relaxation. That will not be entirely true. Has anyone told you about the bomb scare that occurred there in early November?"

The reporter flipped open a notebook. "When was that? Can you give me an exact date?"

"The night of November the fourth. The entire house had to be evacuated. The police were called but found nothing. It was a highly distressing experience for the guests. I'm sure you can appreciate that."

"I can. Anything else?"

"Many things." The voice grew confidential. "A dead raccoon was found in a guest's bedroom. It was rotting. I'm sure I don't have to paint you a picture. Broken glass was scattered in the parking lot and caused a fair amount of damage to some tires. Several pieces of expensive leather luggage were slashed. And three days ago, cow manure fertilizer was scattered over the dining room floor before breakfast. All of this and much more is documented in the police reports if you want to check."

The reporter wrote quickly.

"If you care to follow the events of the next few days, you may have even more to add."

"How do you know that?"

The caller was silent.

"Who are you, anyway?"

"Let's just say I'm someone who doesn't want to see any of the guests hurt."

"Is that right?"

"If you don't believe what I've said, call Leigh Elstad. Or talk to Dale Freeman. He's the chief of police in Repentance River."

"I need your name," said the reporter. "Where can I contact you if we have more questions?"

"No names. Just this information. It's up to you to report the truth. I'm sure it will make an interesting addition to your story."

Damn straight, thought the reporter. "But what's behind it all? Who's doing it?"

"I don't know. I just know being at that inn right now isn't safe. Warn your readers."

The line clicked.

2

"What am I going to do with you?" asked Leigh, smiling down affectionately at her aunt.

"What do you mean?" said Violet. She knelt next to the Christmas tree and draped tinsel on the lower boughs.

"You have tinsel stuck to your sweater, in your hair, on your shoes. . . ."

Violet examined herself briefly, her smile sheepish. "Well, I guess you could say I take my work seriously. You better get busy yourself. We've got to finish decorating the parlor pronto. If we don't, we'll never be able to get everything done before the solstice gathering tonight."

For a moment, Leigh let her eyes travel around the large, richly decorated room. She loved looking at what she had created out of a huge, run-down Victorian house. She'd even received an award from The Minnesota Trust for Historic Preservation. It had come as a complete surprise and added to her sense of accomplishment.

"Get going," prodded Violet. "You need to straighten that star on top of the tree."

Leigh climbed a rickety stepladder she'd brought over from the barn. The stately Fothergill home had been rental property since the late thirties. Back in the fifties, her grandfather had rented it after his retirement from teaching. As a child, the lofty ceilings, spacious rooms, majestic fireplace and intricate carvings had made a big impression. When she came up to look at it three years ago—shortly after her mother had died and left her a sizable inheritance—she knew exactly what she wanted to do. She'd been working in hotel management for seventeen years, learning the business from the bottom up. At the age of thirty-eight, opening this inn was a dream come true.

"I remember spending Christmas here once," said Leigh, cocking her head at the star. "I must have been about five. That was before Uncle Daniel quit college. I guess I always thought it was really great of Grandpa to let his son move back in. Especially with an infant daughter."

"Your grandfather loved children. Ruthie was his pride and joy."

"I know," groaned Leigh. "Ruthie keeps telling me that."

"Be nice to your cousin," frowned Violet. "Her life has not been easy. Now that she's living here at the inn, she really wants to be your friend."

Leigh didn't feel like another lecture on Cousin Ruthie. She decided to change the subject. "How long did Grandpa live here before he died? I can never remember."

"Almost ten years." Violet's voice grew wistful.

While they were speaking, a middle-aged man had entered the parlor, hastily stuffing papers into a briefcase. Physically, he was slight, with thin, clipped features and a small, shrewd mouth.

"Stephen! I thought you'd already left for work." Leigh

climbed down the ladder and stopped as the man brushed a kiss across her cheek.

"Not yet." He approached the carved oak mantel and tossed his cigarette into the fire. "I wanted to remind you to have someone pick up the station wagon at the garage in town today. I'll be needing it tomorrow."

Stephen Laporte was dressed expensively in a black pinstripe suit. At his side was a hand-stitched Italian leather briefcase. His hair was slicked back, revealing a wide, intelligent forehead and piercing blue eyes. Turning from Leigh, he glanced at Violet, who was still kneeling next to the tree.

"Shall we wrap you in red ribbons and tell everyone you're part of the decorations?" He grinned, a mischievous glint in his eye. "Perhaps you could hang some of that tinsel over your ears. It's the only part of your anatomy that isn't covered."

Violet attempted a hurt look. "Just because I throw myself into my work, I've become the target of abuse."

Stephen laughed, turning back to Leigh. "Try to take it a little easy today, sweetheart."

"I'm fine," said Leigh. "Really. By the way, the solstice festivities officially begin at seven. I hope you won't have to work late."

Stephen's smile dimmed. "Don't worry. I won't be late." Turning briskly, he left the room.

Leigh felt like a nag. Yet it had been a pattern lately. Promises broken again and again. Stephen seemed angry and preoccupied about something. At times, it was almost as if he tried to pick fights. No doubt it had to do with his pending divorce, yet he never seemed to want to talk about it. He was under a lot of stress right now, and Leigh knew she had to be patient. If only they could get away for a few days. Spend some time alone together. But around the holidays, there was never enough time. Perhaps after Christmas they could drive up to the North Shore. Relax and

unwind in front of a roaring fire with a bottle of Stephen's
favorite . . .

Violet cleared her throat.

Leigh realized she had been staring into space.

"Work, remember? Plenty of time for pondering later."

Leigh nodded. "Yes, ma'am."

Violet pulled a box of gold Christmas ornaments across
the floor and began hooking them onto the lower branches.
"Stephen doesn't seem very excited about the solstice gathering tonight."

Leigh sighed. "Unfortunately, that's pretty accurate. He's
also not thrilled to have Winifred's coven here again. But
since I'm so irresistible, he puts up with my quirks. Even
my quirky friends."

"Is that right?" Violet arched an eyebrow.

"Is what right?" asked a plump, white-haired woman
standing in the archway. Slowly, she jingled across the floor
holding a small brown paper parcel in one hand. Her clothing, makeup, and jewelry—gold and silver chains, brace-
lets, handmade rings and other assorted pins—as well as
her general aura, were more rococo than the parlor's ornate
furnishings.

"Aunt Inga!" said Leigh, her voice delighted. "You have
to see what we've done to the tree! Isn't it beautiful?" She
put her arm around her aunt and drew her close.

Inga put a finger to her cheek and pretended serious consideration. "Yes. Definitely a masterpiece *à la* . . . who
shall I say . . . Jackson Pollock?"

"Pollock?" Violet winced. "Surely not. What's that in
your hand?" She pointed at the parcel her sister was holding.

Inga handed Leigh the package. "This just came in the
mail, dear. I thought you might want to look at it right
away."

"I'm such a sucker for presents." Leigh grinned. "Do

you think I have to wait for Christmas Eve to open it?" Without waiting for a response, she began to unwrap the small parcel, slipping out a brightly colored red and gold paper box. Lifting it to her ear, she shook it gently.

"There's a note," said Inga, pointing to a small card inside the brown wrapping.

Leigh unfolded it and read out loud:

> "For a joyous solstice celebration!
> A traditional herb tea. Try some
> right now and see if you like it. If
> you do, perhaps you'll want to prepare
> it for your guests on Monday evening.
> See you soon."
>
> Jane Lawless

"How lovely," exclaimed Leigh, opening the box. Inside were dried leaves and roots, orange peel, and lemon verbena. It smelled wonderful. "Isn't that sweet of Jane? This is such a nice idea. What do you say we try a cup right now?" She handed the box to Inga. "Would you mind asking one of the kitchen staff to brew us a pot?"

Inga took the box and left, delicately sniffing the contents.

"You know," said Leigh after she had gone, "I don't know what I'd do without you two. I'm so glad you agreed to move out here to the island."

Violet plunked down on the floor and brushed off her sweater. "Tempting us with that beautifully renovated gatehouse didn't hurt. Inga and I have lived quietly in our little cottage in Repentance River for over forty years. It was time for a change."

"What kind of joke is this!" boomed a deep voice from the doorway. A short, stocky man with mounds of curly brown hair and a thick mustache entered the parlor. He was wearing a white chef's uniform and holding the box of herbs in front of him like an accusation. "This is sick! Who gave you this?" he demanded, shaking the little box under Leigh's nose.

Leigh blinked uncomprehendingly. "What's wrong, Burton?" She offered him the note.

He grabbed it and studied it for a moment. "Preposterous," he grunted, flinging it into a chair. "Jane would never have sent you this."

"What do you mean? Why?"

"It's pokeweed!"

"What?"

Burton brushed past her and tossed the entire box into the fire. Flames licked the fragile contents, turning it quickly to smoke and ash. "I'm doing you a favor, Leigh. That is, unless you want everyone around here to have a bellyache the size of the Grand Canyon!"

3

At one end of a long mahogany bar, Jane sat huddled over a cup of strong, black coffee. Since it was still early morning, the cozy downstairs pub was completely deserted except for a young man polishing glasses at the other end of the counter. Jane liked the morning quiet in this room. She liked the emptiness before the noisy lunch crowd descended. It was one of her favorite places to think. And this particular morning, she had plenty to think about. Last evening just after dinner, she had received an overseas phone call from her aunt, Beryl, in England. Jane knew her aunt had been in the hospital for almost a month. The doctors had diagnosed her illness as acute hepatitis. Jane was unclear how she had contracted it, but Beryl was now back at her cottage and from the sound of her voice, extremely depressed. Her words still echoed in Jane's mind.

"Jane dear," she had said, pausing just long enough to make sure Jane was giving full attention. "I need to ask you something." The strain of trying to sound chipper had made her normally resonant voice into an aging parody of itself.

"Sure," Jane had said. "Ask away."

"I know this may come as a surprise, but I was wondering how you'd feel about having a house guest for . . . oh, I don't know, maybe a few weeks? A month at most. I guarantee I won't overstay my welcome. A month and a half would be the very longest."

It *had* come as a surprise. Jane tried hard to form the right response, but Beryl could hear the hesitation.

"That's all right, dear. Perhaps I should call you in a few days. Give you some time to think about it."

Jane quickly agreed. Yes, a few days. That was good.

As they continued to talk, Jane could clearly hear the loneliness behind each word. Beryl's husband, Jane's Uncle Jimmy, had died less than six months ago. It had been a close marriage. And even though her aunt had many friends around Lyme Regis, her low, normally cheerful voice spoke of a growing sense of isolation and of her need to get away. She wanted to be with family. She wanted to come for a visit.

Jane knew Aunt Beryl very well. Too well. A visit was a fine idea. But once here, she might never leave. So the question was, did she want to live with and take care of an aging aunt. And if not, how could she say *no*—gracefully.

Aunt Beryl and Uncle Jimmy had opened their home to her shortly after her own mother died. She was thirteen at the time and had stayed with them for over two years. The decision to go back to England had marked the beginning of her deteriorating relationship with her father. Jane knew he felt she had deserted him. But she'd had to go. In England, where she'd spent the first nine years of her life, she knew she would feel closer to her mother. At the time, that was all that was important. Her mother was English. Going back was the only way she felt she could truly mourn. In many ways, Beryl had become a second mother, and now she was asking for a similar kindness. The same open door Jane had found so many years ago. How could she refuse?

As she sat quietly sipping her coffee, her mind wandered to those early mornings she had spent sitting in her father's favorite café in Lyme Regis. She was six years old again and watching him drink his tea while paging through the morning paper. Occasionally he would look up and smile at her, reaching across under the table and squeezing her knee. She'd loved those times, remembering the smell of salt air and the way the sun filtered through the lace curtains, spilling light onto the small wooden table where they sat. Those memories were so important to her that she had even named her own restaurant after that little town on the southwestern coast of England. The Lyme House. The art nouveau panel in back of the bar had been a present from her father when the restaurant first opened eight years ago. Even though the south shore of Lake Harriet wasn't much like Lyme Regis, it didn't matter. She loved them both for different reasons.

Jane checked her watch. It was almost ten. Cordelia would be arriving any minute. She'd have to come to some conclusion about Beryl soon, but not until she'd had a chance to talk it over with her old friend. Jane had known Cordelia ever since her junior year of high school. In almost every sense, they were a marriage of opposites. Cordelia was bombastic and impatient, quick to make friends and quicker still to dump them if they didn't live up to expectations. Jane, on the other hand, was quiet, liked to take her time—especially when it came to making friends and thinking things out. Yet she and Cordelia had formed a strong bond over the years. Jane knew her friend to be a kind, generous, and acutely creative person, but one who was often difficult to be around. Like sisters, they often rubbed each other the wrong way. And like sisters, they put up with each other's quirks and still remained close.

Glancing up at the shiny brass tooling on the back of the bar, Jane caught a glimpse of herself in one of the side mirrors. Not too bad for someone nearing forty. Round, blue-violet eyes, generally hidden behind a pair of wire-rimmed glasses. A nose that was straight and well formed, albeit a bit too large. A full mouth with relatively straight teeth. And the smile. A nice smile. Definitely her best feature. The hair was long, chestnut colored—starting to gray. So what. She was liberated. Gray was good. Although she lingered a bit too long these days around the hair care section of the drugstore. It didn't mean anything. She was just browsing. And thankfully, her body was reasonably robust. All in all, a pleasant image. She knew she could lose a few pounds, but what the hell. Nobody's perfect.

Slipping off the stool, Jane walked to the other end of the bar and refilled her cup with fresh coffee. On her way back, she spied a small table in the back near the fireplace. It had been Christine's favorite spot from which to observe life. She and Christine had been together for almost ten years. Jane realized her sense of time had slowed since her lover's death four years ago. Some days it didn't seem possible Christine had been gone that long. But most of the time, it felt like centuries.

Jane sat down again and pulled out the brochure her friend

Leigh Elstad had sent several weeks ago. The full-color picture of The Fothergill Inn on the front cover was pure gingerbread. It was a tall, gabled house painted in cream, rose, green, gray, and black. The open spandrels above the porch arches gave it an almost carousel quality. The large screened porch that circled the entire structure opened up onto a garden in the back. Even though Jane knew Victorian houses were often considered architectural embarrassments, she loved the peaks and towers, the open balustrades and floral carvings above the doors. Just like modern Americans, the Victorians were always redecorating. They liked new things and cheap reproductions of old things all mashed together in one room.

The inn boasted twelve guest rooms, each one furnished differently. Leigh had done her homework. The building was truly a showpiece. Jane thought back to the hysterical letter she had received several years ago, shortly after Leigh had closed on the property. Someone had tried to burn it down, and Leigh was worried the insurance wouldn't cover the damage. Thankfully it had, and the rest of the renovation went smoothly.

When Jane received the invitation to spend Christmas week there, it felt like a godsend. It had been years since she'd allowed herself a real vacation. The restaurant provided a perfect excuse to turn down unwanted invitations. Yet lately the city had begun to close in around her. Perhaps the silence of the country, the bleakness of a winter landscape would help her unwind.

Leigh and Jane had been close since college, even though life and work often separated them. Jane had been delighted to recommend Burton March for the job of head chef at the inn. He had worked at The Lyme House several years ago, and she'd been very impressed with his culinary ability. By all reports, he was doing a great job. One of the reasons she'd been invited up for the week was to look at

an old summerhouse he wanted to use to extend the seating
in the restaurant. For the time being, he had set up tables
in the library as well as the dining room. Since people were
driving the fifty miles from the Twin Cities just to eat at the
inn, more room was desperately needed. Burton wanted
Jane's advice on how they could best utilize their available
space. She was looking forward to helping them out.

"I'm all packed and ready to hit the bricks," called a
deep, throaty voice from the doorway. "How about you,
Janey? Where are your six completely stuffed steamer
trunks?"

Jane turned to find Cordelia leaning casually against the
door frame, eating from a bag of beer nuts.

"A nutritious breakfast as usual," said Jane.

Cordelia grunted.

"And as far as the steamer trunks go, I believe you have
us confused. You're the one who travels with a ton of
clothes. If you remember correctly, *I'm* the one you accuse
daily of thinking jeans and an old hunting jacket suit every
formal occasion."

"I forgot." Cordelia popped another nut into her mouth.
"Actually, I was referring to your penchant for dragging
along a plethora of weighty tomes."

"Are you doing a Victorian play right now? Your choice
of words is a little stilted."

"Too erudite for the *hoi polloi?*" Cordelia grinned.

"No doubt." Jane pointed to the bar stool next to her.
"Have a seat. I don't want to leave just yet. Peter said he
was going to stop by sometime before ten."

Cordelia checked her watch. "Good thing your brother is
punctual. I want to get an early start up to Repentance
River." She scrunched up the empty package and tossed it
with perfect precision into a tall wastebasket behind the bar.
"Thank you. Applause is not necessary." With a languid,
leggy walk, she approached the bar stool, her bearing re-

flecting the total ease with which she lived in her large-framed body. Jane envied her confidence.

"Who did you finally get to stay with your dear little beasts?" asked Cordelia, fluffing her auburn curls with one hand.

"Adrienne Vee. You know her? The pastry chef here at the restaurant. She really loves dogs."

"Of course. But not enough to forsake her condo for the joys of home ownership."

Jane sipped her coffee and smiled.

"I've brought along lots of warm clothes. Heavy socks. Wool sweaters. And, unfortunately, three new plays I've promised to read before I get back."

"Oh Cordelia, you haven't? This is supposed to be a vacation. You remember what that is, don't you? Relaxation?"

Jane knew Cordelia was constantly bombarded by young playwrights wanting her comments on their work. And truthfully, Cordelia rarely turned anyone down. She had been instrumental in helping many new talents get their plays read at theatres around the Twin Cities. She considered it paying her dues. This was Cordelia's second season as artistic director at the Allen Grimby Repertory Theatre in St. Paul. Lots of people had helped her over the years. She simply wanted to return the favor.

"Don't worry. I'm a fast reader. There will be plenty of time to lie around—no doubt in front of a roaring fire—and sip sherry. Isn't that what one does in an old Victorian mansion?"

Jane nodded. "I believe you have the agenda down perfectly. By the way, do you remember Winifred Vinson?"

Cordelia cocked her head. "Vinson. Now that you mention it, yeah, I think I do remember her. Wasn't she one of Leigh's good buddies in college? Right! She was the crazy one who got that body paint and . . ."

Jane held up her hand. "That's the one. She and her

lover are going to be up at the inn for Christmas week too. Actually, Winney is now a witch. She's going to be guiding the solstice ritual tonight."

"I wonder if we're going to be doing anything unusual with body paint?" mused Cordelia.

"Jane?" called the young man from the other end of the bar. "You've got a phone call."

"Thanks, Johnny." She got down off the stool and walked over to the opposite end of the bar, picking up the receiver. "Jane Lawless. Can I help you?"

"Janey, it's Peter."

"Hi! I thought you were going to stop by."

"Can't, sis. Something came up at work. One of the other cameramen is out sick, so I got drafted for an assignment. But before you left, I wanted to make sure you and Cordelia will be coming to the lodge for Christmas Eve."

"We'll be there," Jane assured him. "Don't worry. It's less than a mile from where we'll be staying. Unless there's a blizzard or a typhoon, I'll see you then. Is Sigrid coming too?"

"Yeah, she'll be there," said Peter, adding, "we've got kind of an announcement to make. I really shouldn't be saying anything at all, but I wanted you to know how important it is to me that you come. Dad is driving up with Marilyn. Oh Janey, I'm so happy I think I could burst. This is going to be the greatest Christmas ever!"

He sounded more than happy. He sounded like he was in love.

"Worry not, Peter. We'll both be there if we have to rent snowmobiles."

"Seven o'clock, okay?"

"Seven," said Jane. "And give my love to Sigrid."

"Will do. Gotta go. Have fun up at the inn. And try to relax, Janey. You work too hard." He hung up.

Jane put the receiver back on the hook and turned to look into the fire.

"The moving van is double parked outside," said Cordelia. "I think we better get going."

Jane groaned and shook her head.

"Well, you wouldn't want me to start out this vacation with a parking ticket, would you?"

4

"Sorry I'm late, honey," called Stephen as he entered the front sitting room. He flipped his briefcase onto a chair. "Leigh? Are you up here?" Slipping off his heavy top coat, he walked over to the front closet and carefully hung it on an old wooden hanger. Christ, everything in this house had to be antique. Even the hangers. It was like living in a museum.

When he'd first discovered the third floor, before the house had been renovated, he'd at least had some hope. It wasn't difficult to imagine the entire space gutted and turned into a lovely, spacious living area. But those hopes were dashed when Leigh decided to turn the top floor of the inn into four separate suites. At the time, he'd agreed it did make sense financially. Two of the sections would be guest apartments. The rest would be divided into living quarters for Burton and his little boy, and a small apartment for him and Leigh. Lately, that decision was beginning to feel like a complete disaster. Their apartment might have made an adequate kennel for a small poodle, but that was about it. Stephen dreamed about owning a spacious, modern condo overlooking downtown St. Paul. And commuting fifty miles to and from the Cities every day was starting to wear pretty thin too.

"Leigh? For pete's sake, where are you? Answer me!" A few minutes ago, as he was coming through the downstairs foyer, Aunt Violet had mentioned that her niece hadn't been around all afternoon. That was unusual since there were no doubt lots of last-minute things that needed attending to. People were already beginning to gather in the front parlor. Leigh should be there to greet them.

"Stephen, is that you?" called a voice from the bedroom.

Loosening his tie, he headed into the room and switched on the overhead light.

"Please!" said the voice. "Turn it off."

A little surprised by the request, Stephen nevertheless did as he was asked. "What's wrong, Leigh? What's going on?" He waited a moment while his eyes adjusted to the darkness before approaching the bed.

Leigh gripped his arm. "Hold me for a minute. That's all I need."

Stephen sat down and drew her into his arms. "What's wrong, sweetheart?" He stroked her hair softly.

Leigh allowed him to turn on a small night light next to the bed. "I feel so ... embarrassed. Give me a minute." She ran her hand through her hair, shaking her head to get rid of the cobwebs. "I'm a little confused. I just woke up. What time is it?"

"About six-thirty. How long have you been lying here?"

"I don't know. Let me think a minute." She leaned her head back against the pillow.

Gently, Stephen traced the curve of her neck up to her chin. She was a lovely woman. Hair the color of straw. Features delicately carved in an arresting, irregular face.

And she was competent. Strong. A sense of sadness over-
whelmed him as he watched her lying there, so quiet, so intense. He didn't want to hurt her. God, he'd never wanted
that. But what he'd done couldn't be undone. He hated being at the mercy of other people's decisions. If only he
could be sure. But that was the problem, wasn't it? He
couldn't. Leigh was resilient. In the long run, she would
survive even him. "Tell me what happened," he said tenderly.

Leigh took his hand in hers and squeezed it tightly. "After Winifred and Tess arrived around two, I was feeling
kind of tired so I excused myself and came up here for a
nap. I'd already helped Jane and Cordelia get settled in
their suite, so I figured I had a good hour to relax before
I needed to get back downstairs to supervise the last-minute
preparations. I set the alarm for three o'clock, but I must
have slept right through it. I didn't wake up until a few
minutes ago. When I tried to get out of bed, this heavy
wave of exhaustion just rolled over me."

Stephen brushed the hair away from her face. "It's stress,
honey. It's gotten to both of us. All these crazy things happening around here. I hate to say it, but I think you may
have made yourself an enemy somewhere along the line. I
know you don't want to hear this again, but maybe we
should sell the place. I mean, who needs this crap?"

"But Stephen . . ."

"Now you just rest and listen to me for a minute. I may
have the perfect solution. Remember I told you about this
friend of mine who talked to me about a partnership in his
firm? Well, I found out today that, with a certain amount of
seed money, I could buy into his company. It's the chance
of a lifetime! I've been a financial advisor for Jackson,
Byrne, and Mulmquist for almost twelve years now. He
knows the kind of clients I could bring with me, and he
knows my reputation. If I could offer him the right capital

up front, I'd be pulling down six figures in less than a year. Think of it!"

"That's wonderful," said Leigh. "I'm really happy for you."

"It's just . . ." He hesitated. "With the financial particulars of my divorce up in the air right now, I don't know how long my assets will be tied up or what I'll have left after everything is said and done. I've got that mortgage on the house in Arden Hills and my two kids to think of. You understand, honey. And now Marjie is insisting I pay her way through school. She says she worked to help support me while I was getting my MBA and it's only fair that I reciprocate. I hate it, Leigh. I hate all these demands. I wish I didn't see her point, but I do. I just don't know what it will mean for me financially. Now, consider this for a minute." He paused, feeling a rawness in his throat.

"What are you saying?" asked Leigh.

He continued. "If you were to sell this place, we'd have plenty of money to invest in my partnership—with a percentage of my income going directly to you in repayment of the loan *with interest*—and still we'd have money for you to invest or start a business of your own. Have I ever steered you wrong?"

"No," said Leigh.

He could hear the tentativeness in her voice, and it hurt him. But he went on. "Remember that import business I suggested you invest in last year? You made a bundle on that."

She nodded.

"When we're married . . ."

"Stephen! I . . . don't want to hurt you, but I never said I wanted to marry."

He looked away. "I just thought . . ."

She squeezed his hand. "You of all people should know what this place means to me. We worked on it together! It's part of *us*. Remember our candlelight dinners in the parlor? Just the two of us sitting amidst the dry wall and plaster. Or our trips into town to look at wallpaper samples or to pick up an antique? I can't sell. All my life I've wanted something like this. I would never have been able to afford it if it hadn't been for the money my mother left me. This place is like her last gift. I can't just give something like that away. What's left of my family lives here now. I won't leave and turn them out."

"But you wouldn't be giving anything away. Don't you see?" He gazed down at her, his stomach churning violently. "Look, of course I understand how you feel. But I'm not so sure your aunts have the same loyalty to you as you do to them. Remember? Just last week they were trying to get your crazy cousin Ruthie to take a long cruise with them. If they'd actually gone, they would have been away for months. And yesterday I overheard Violet talking to Ruthie about moving to Arizona. She said the winters in Minnesota were getting too cold for her. I'll admit it would take dynamite to get your cousin out of here. Sometimes I think she's more attached to this place than you are."

Angrily, Leigh pulled back her hand. "You don't believe for a minute Aunt Violet actually meant that? It's just talk. Wishful thinking on cold days. Everyone says things like that when it gets below zero. They don't want to leave any more than I do."

"That's not the way it sounded."

Leigh shook her head. "They just want to make it easier on me in case I do have to sell. Which isn't going to happen." She rose and walked into the bathroom, turning on the faucet and splashing water into her face.

"Okay," said Stephen. He decided to try another approach. "If you won't consider selling the place to a stranger, how about Burton? He's mentioned to me several times that he's sure he could get a bank loan based on the restau-

rant business here alone. He thinks the inn is a gold mine.
Or how about Henry Gyldenskog? He salivates at the
thought of owning this house."

Leigh emerged from the bathroom wiping her face with
a towel. "No. Let's just drop it, okay? I feel much better
now. Really. And besides, I have to get dressed."

Stephen got up and walked over to her. "Okay. We'll let
it drop. But I want you to promise you'll at least think
about what I've said. I'd never hurt you, Leigh. I love you.
You know that." He took her in his arms, burying his face
in her hair. God, what a mess he'd made of his life. He
closed his eyes against the pain.

Leigh whispered softly in his ear, "I promise, Stephen.
I'll think about it." Pulling away, she smoothed his lapels
and straightened his tie. "Now, since you look presentable
and I don't, will you go downstairs and make sure everything is going all right? Introduce people. The ritual will
begin at eight."

"You'll be down soon?"

"Just as soon as I change." She gave him a kiss on the
cheek.

He wished it didn't feel like she was dismissing him.
Like she had promised to consider what he'd said only to
get him off her back. He wanted to take her in his arms, to
tell her the truth and *make* her understand. And after she
knew the truth, he wanted her still to love him. It was all
crazy. Why couldn't they just forget that silly solstice gathering downstairs and lock the bedroom door? Shut out the
world. But instead of saying the words he didn't dare
speak, he simply smiled and said, "If I don't see you in the
parlor in fifteen minutes, I'll be back up."

"I'm fine," said Leigh.

Her voice was firm, but in her eyes, Stephen could see
the strain.

5

Jane stood alone in the curved archway and scanned the crowd of people gathered for the evening's solstice celebration. The first thing on her agenda was to locate Leigh. She had hoped they might spend a few minutes together at dinner, but for myriad reasons, Leigh was probably too busy to eat. No doubt she was attending to last-minute details. Jane didn't need to be reminded how much work a large function like this was. Standing on her tiptoes, she searched the faces. Once again, Leigh was nowhere to be found.

A few minutes earlier, as Jane was combing her hair, Cordelia had hollered from her bedroom for Jane not to wait for her. She would be down *presently*. That, of course, meant something specific to Cordelia. In reality, it could mean just about anything. A young woman floated through the archway holding a silver tray filled with champagne glasses. Jane helped herself, taking a sip before diving into the crowd. The inn's parlor was just short of cavernous. On one end, a number of people were gathered around a string quartet. In another corner, the richly decorated and lighted Christmas tree towered over the heads of the guests. Across the west wall was a series of large windows overlooking the circular drive in front of the house. Above them ran a long panel of stained glass. Tonight all the windows were hung with pine boughs and red ribbons. Obviously, by the number of people in attendance, some had come just for the evening and were not staying overnight.

"Jane!" called a short, freckled woman with a narrow face and bright blue eyes. "Come on over and join us." To-night, Winifred Vinson was wearing a green velvet robe studded with silver sequins. Her long red hair fell around her shoulders and looked as soft as lamb's wool. Standing next to her was her lover, Tess, a tall woman, with dark, short-cropped hair and sleepy, dreamy eyes. Her perpetually serious expression suggested a thoughtful, somewhat mel-ancholic nature. Jane had enjoyed their conversation at din-ner. Winney had changed a great deal since college. Jane doubted body paint figured very prominently in her life anymore.

"This is wonderful, isn't it?" said Winifred, beaming proudly as Jane approached. "People are really into this cel-ebration!"

Jane smiled, continuing to sip her champagne. "Do you have something special planned for tonight?"

Winifred nodded. "We're going to do an old Scandina-vian ritual called Tying Down the Sun."

"That's quite an image," said Jane.

"I agree. It's part of an ancient tradition. Hundreds of years ago, our northern ancestors were practicing this ritual on the night of the winter solstice. At this time of year, the sun was at its farthest point away from them. The earth's light and warmth were thought to be in great peril. If the sun didn't return, the earth would become darker and colder until eventually no one would be able to survive. Hence, the ritual to tie it down—to prevent it from moving further south. Of course the sun is also a metaphor for spiritual light and insight. That, too, can often be far from us during the darkest part of the year."

Jane was fascinated. She wanted to continue the conver-sation but saw Stephen heading their way accompanied by two men she had not yet met. One was of medium height and build, with platinum hair parted in the middle, and an impeccably clipped ginger-colored beard. The other was an older, beardless, and graying version of the first.

"A merry solstice to you all," said Stephen as he stepped out of the way of a young woman carrying a tray of krumkaka. "I'd like each of you to meet our longest running guests, Per and his father Henry Gyldenskog. They have the other suite on the third floor." He smiled at Jane.

Jane had first met Stephen when he and Leigh moved in together two years ago. She found him intriguing, albeit a bit too consumed by the time-honored American dream of financial success.

Per nodded formally, shaking each person's hand. Jane studied him for a moment. He was dressed immaculately in a gray tweed suit and pale yellow tie. His father, Henry, was attired more casually in sweater and slacks. As she continued to watch them, Henry drew out a pipe from his pocket. Immediately, Per leaned over and said, "Dad? Dr. Hemple said you weren't . . ."

Henry's look was full of exasperation. Slowly, he stuffed the pipe back into his pocket. "You're not my keeper," he said under his breath.

"Per is a writer," continued Stephen. "His fourth novel was just published this fall. And I believe he's already at work on a new one."

"May I ask what the next book is about?" asked Jane, a little surprised to find one of her favorite new authors in attendance tonight. "I've read your last three books and enjoyed them very much."

Per was clearly delighted. "How very kind of you," he said, accepting a glass of champagne off a tray. "And yes, of course you may ask what my current book is about. However, I'm not sure I can answer your question other than to say it's . . . a mystery of sorts."

"I like mysteries," said Tess, beginning to warm to the conversation. "Winifred and I own a bookstore in River Falls, Wisconsin. I always take care of the mystery section. What's your book about?"

The question appeared to make Per uncomfortable. "I guess you could say it's about my life. The mystery of my life."

Jane noticed Tess's smile fade. Perhaps she felt he was playing with her?

Stephen continued. "Per and Henry lived in this house a long time ago."

"Is that right?" said Jane.

Henry answered: "I had accepted a job over in Cambridge. Per was about sixteen. Believe it or not, in 1964 this house was one of the cheapest places we could rent. I think by then the rental company was almost *paying* people to get them to stay here. It was terribly run-down."

"In case your mind doesn't whiz along with the speed of a calculator," smiled Per, "that makes me forty-one years old."

Henry laughed. "And how old does that make me? None of your damn business, I always say." He began to cough. "Actually, I knew this house could look the way it does now. But in my younger days I never had a pot to piss in."

"Dad!" Per no longer hid his annoyance.

"Well it's true. Thank God my luck finally changed. For the last fifteen years I've been a general contractor in the Twin Cities and done pretty well if I do say so myself. I'd always had it in my mind that I'd buy this place one day. Live in it after I retired. Well, I retired last fall and wouldn't you know someone beat me to it." He nodded toward Leigh who had just entered the parlor carrying a tray of small goblets filled with eggnog. A stocky, round-faced young man followed closely behind talking loudly into her ear.

Jane was surprised by how pale and drawn Leigh looked tonight. She wondered if something was wrong.

"Eggnog anyone?" asked Leigh, walking up to them holding the tray in front of her. The glasses shook ever so slightly.

"Thanks," said Tess. She handed a cup to Winifred and then took one for herself.

"I'd like you to meet Michael Paget," said Leigh, introducing the young man standing next to her. "Michael is a high school student in Repentance River. We're lucky to have him as a part-time employee here. He helps in the kitchen, waits tables, and even lends a hand when Elmer—that's our full-time handyman—needs a strong arm."

Michael's grin was infectious. And his eagerness to please Leigh was quite apparent. Jane's eyes traveled to Tess, who seemed more than interested in the young man.

"How old are you?" asked Tess.

Noticing her intensity, Winifred stopped her conversation with Stephen to listen.

"I'm seventeen, ma'am. A senior this year."

"Seventeen," Tess repeated softly.

"Would you like some dessert?" His voice was shy. He nodded to a buffet table against the far wall where Burton stood serving guests from a tempting array of creations. "I helped make some of them."

"What?" said Tess. He had caught her off guard.

"Over there." He pointed to the table.

"Sure. I'd love something."

A look of puzzlement passed over Winifred's face. "Well, that's a first," she said, watching them blend into the crowd. "Tess hates sweets."

As the string quartet switched from Bach to Mozart, Jane could see the two of them over by the fireplace, deep in conversation.

"What gives here?" asked Winifred, speaking to no one in particular.

"Oh my God, will you look at that!" cried Leigh, handing the tray of eggnog to a young woman from the kitchen staff. "I don't belive it."

Cordelia stood framed in the archway, about to make her grand entrance. She was wearing a flowing burgundy satin Renaissance gown with rhinestone-covered sleeves and bodice. Draped casually over one shoulder was a multicolored shawl. And worst of all, sitting precariously on top of her head was a large, pointed hat. She winked at Jane.

"Good evening," she said in her most theatrical, Elizabethan voice. Maintaining an air of great solemnity, she arched an eyebrow at Winifred.

Leigh was the first to recover. "I suppose I should explain to everyone that Cordelia asked me earlier what was considered appropriate attire for a solstice ritual. I recklessly suggested that she wear anything she liked, as long as she was comfortable. Little did I realize . . ."

Cordelia interrupted. "This was my favorite costume from a production of *The Duchess of Malfi* we did recently at The Allen Grimby. I asked one of the seamstresses to let it out just a wee bit here and there. After all, we're certainly savvy enough to realize *all* clothing is essentially costume. And," she added, adjusting her hat, "I *am* completely comfortable, thank you very much. Now, where are the Christmas sweets?" Her eyes darted around the room. "Ah," she said, spotting the buffet table, "catch you all later."

Jane shook her head and grinned as she watched Cordelia remove half a dozen cookies from a tray with one hand while grabbing a glass of champagne with the other. Cordelia had done it again. At the last party they had attended together, Cordelia had worn an old military uniform. Chekhov perhaps? Or Strindberg? Of course. That had to

be it. It was Strindberg's Captain from *The Dance of Death*.
Next summer The Allen Grimby was doing a special adap-
tation of *Dracula*. Jane tried to imagine Cordelia dressed in
a tuxedo with an enormous bat cape attached to the back.
It was a truly terrifying thought.

"Excuse me," said Leigh, laying her hand on Winifred's
arm. "It's almost eight. Should we start?"

"Yes, I suppose," said Winifred. With her eyes still glued
to Cordelia, she continued, "These events certainly do take
on a personality of their own." She glanced back at Leigh.
"Now would be fine. We'll begin by casting the circle."

6

"I call on the powers of the East to be with us this night,
to bring forth the sweet abundant air we breath and join us
in our journey." Winifred lit a long white taper and handed
it to a woman standing next to her. According to plan, all
electric lights were turned out just as the ceremony began.
A few minutes before, Winifred had taken a broom and cast
a circle by holding it out in front of her as she spun around,
calling on the Goddess to create a holy space for the solstice ritual. People had gathered around the edge, holding
hands and silently calling on their own vision of the Goddess to bless the evening. Groups of candles burned
brightly in each corner of the room, symbolizing the four
directions.

"I invoke the powers of the South," said Winifred, closing her eyes and raising her head, "to help us tonight, to add the passion and light of the southern fires to our journey." She lit another candle and handed it to a woman standing near the fireplace.

Silently, Jane watched, acutely aware of the settling sounds of the old house. For some unknown reason, she felt a sense of uneasiness as she stood in the darkness and listened to the rafters creak and sigh. Brushing the feeling away, she returned her attention to Winifred.

"I call on the powers of the West to be with us this night, to carry life-giving waters on the wings of the wind and join us in our journey." Winifred lit the third candle and handed it to Per. Jane noticed his hand tremble as he took it from her.

"And finally, I call on the great powers of the North to join us this night, to bring us all the true richness of winter hope. Blessed be the powers of the North. Blessed be our hope. Blessed be." The last candle was lighted and handed to Cordelia.

Jane's eyes traveled slowly around the circle. With the exception of Stephen, who had seemed preoccupied all evening, and Henry, who looked totally bored, everyone had their eyes glued to Winifred. Gracefully she moved into the center of the circle. Dipping her hand into a bag, she drew out ball after ball of brightly colored yarn.

"I'm going to pass these out," she said, walking slowly around the group, handing a ball to each person. "As I explained before we began, the name of the ancient ritual we're going to recreate tonight is Tying Down the Sun. I'd like each of you to toss your ball—being careful to hold on to the cut end—to someone across from you. That person will then toss the ball to another, and on and on until we've created a web from the strands of yarn. This candle," she continued, lighting a tall white taper and placing it in the center of the floor, "represents the sun. Once the web is

formed over it, we'll spend a few minutes raising energy. I
have some guided imagery we may want to do, as well as
chants and songs. Before we finish, I'll cut the threads and
you can each take home a piece of the web. All right," she
said, stepping back, "please, as the spirit leads, you may
begin."

Cordelia was the first to toss her yarn. Jane caught it and
threw hers to Tess. After that, everyone seemed to get into
the spirit and balls began flying thickly through the air.

"Remember to think of the sun as you're doing this,"
called Winifred. "Make your request felt. Ask the sun to
come back, to fill the earth with the warmth of its fire."

The strands were quickly becoming an intricate maze.
Many of the participants were not only creating the web,
they were becoming *part* of it by winding the yarn around
various parts of their bodies before tossing the ball on to
the next person.

In the candlelight, Jane was awed by the lovely simplicity of the idea. Directly across from her, a woman began to
sway and hum softly. Others watched for a moment and
then followed along. Closing her own eyes, Jane held on
tightly to the strands of yarn in her hands. Everyone was
physically bound together by the web. She could actually
feel the energy of the group flowing together.

And then, someone screamed.

Jane blinked open her eyes as a flaming ball of fire
crashed through the front window, landing almost at her
feet. Without stopping to think, she let go of the yarn and
pulled off her jacket, tossing it over the flames.

Immediately, others began to back away from the circle.
Some were finding it difficult to extricate themselves in the
darkness and started to panic, becoming even more entan-
gled as they tried to escape.

"No!" called Winifred, helplessly watching the growing

pandemonium. "Please! Don't break the circle. Don't let go. Nothing will hurt you."

"Look," shouted Stephen. He was standing by the shattered front window, looking outside. "What on earth is that?"

Jane finished smothering the fire. "What do you see?" she called, brushing ash off her pants. Before she could reach him, people began crowding in front of her. Standing on her tiptoes, she caught a glimpse of a huge fireball rolling down the hill out of the woods.

"It's a snowmobile," called someone. "I can hear the engine. My God! The rider is on fire!"

Frozen by the terrifying sight, everyone watched in stunned silence as the burning figure came to a stop directly in front of the house.

"We've got to help him!" shouted Jane. Others began to cry out in fright. As she tried to back up, a heavy hand gripped her arm.

"No," whispered Cordelia close to her ear. "You stay put."

A second later an explosion sent chunks of flames hurtling into the black night sky. Guests began scrambling backward as several of the windows shattered from flying debris. Jane could see their frightened faces twisted into strange expressions by the firelight. Outside, burning pieces began to drift down into the front yard. Fire and brimstone, she thought to herself. Breaking free of Cordelia's grip, she backed out of the crowd and headed into the front foyer. Burton was already on his way outside. Before she joined him, she switched on the outside porch light.

"The gas tank on that thing must have gone up," he shouted over his shoulder. A few feet from the door he bent down to examine a burned piece of the machine. "God, I can't believe this," he kept saying, over and over.

Twenty feet further out into the yard, Jane found a man's

glove. It was relatively untouched by the flames. Inside was a stuffing of thick cotton. That was strange. She walked over to the spot where the snowmobile had come to a stop. The packed snow underneath had melted from the intense heat. Very little was left other than the singed ground. Looking up toward the woods, she noticed something sticking out of the snow. "Look over there," she called to Burton. "Do you see it?" Without waiting for him to answer, she ran to the spot and yanked out a leather boot with part of a charred cotton form attached. "What gives here?" she said under her breath.

Leigh and Stephen reached her a moment later, followed closely by Burton.

"I don't think anybody was riding that thing," said Jane, holding up the boot.

"What do you mean?" demanded Leigh, her breath swirling like steam in the frigid air.

Jane glanced back at the woods. "If you want my opinion, I think someone set this whole thing up. It was supposed to look like the rider was on fire, but I'll bet we find it was just old clothing stuffed with some kind of heavy material. See for yourself."

"But what's the point?" asked Burton, his exasperation growing. "This is the worst yet. These pranks are getting out of hand."

"Pranks?" said Jane.

Burton looked away.

"Well whatever, I think the intent is pretty obvious," continued Jane. "Someone wanted to ruin the solstice celebration tonight."

"Can we talk about this back inside the house?" asked Stephen, blowing on his hands and stamping his feet. "We're going to freeze to death out here with no coats or boots."

"Good point," shivered Burton. "We better get back and calm everyone down before all our guests pack their bags and leave. I can't believe this is happening!" Together, he and Stephen started for the house.

Jane couldn't ignore the strain on Leigh's face any longer. "What's going on, Leigh? There's more to all of this, isn't there? Burton seems to think you've had other problems. Is that true?"

Leigh walked a few paces away. She turned, searching Jane's face a moment. "Yes," she said finally. "This isn't the first. I don't know what to think anymore. I suppose if you're really interested, maybe we could talk about it. But in the morning, okay? This is about all I can take for one day." Her eyes returned to the house. "I've got to get back there. I have to find some way to salvage this evening. Janey, I could really use a friend right now."

"Of course," said Jane. "I'm here."

Together they crossed to the shoveled path, moving past a large retaining wall. Both were oblivious to the figure pressed hard against the bricks, watching them intently from the darkness.

7

Tuesday, December 22

"I look like a kitchen mop," snapped Cordelia as she squinted into the bathroom mirror. "To quote Gloria

Steinem, 'this is what fifty looks like.' Except I'm only thirty-six."

Jane stood in the doorway cleaning her glasses. "Are you saying you didn't sleep well?"

"I'm saying," said Cordelia, leaning toward the mirror and pulling down one of her lower eyelids, "that I should never have allowed you to talk me into going back outside with you last night after everyone had gone up to bed." She squeezed some toothpaste onto a toothbrush and began lethargically brushing her teeth.

"But if we hadn't looked around, we might never have found the broken wire used to stop the snowmobile right in front of the house. Who knows, by morning it might have been gone. The whole thing was really quite clever. It took some know-how. I mean, stringing that thin wire between two trees at just the right height to prevent the riderless machine from going any further . . ."

"That wasn't the problem," sniffed Cordelia, spitting into the sink. "Christ, this toothpaste tastes so fucking cheerful. Pardon me. It's simply too early to be out of bed on a Tuesday morning. No, what I objected to was tramping around in the woods looking for footprints. How am I supposed to know what footprints look like in a partially frozen swamp?"

"It wasn't a swamp."

"Whatever. And what did we find? Zip."

"Well," said Jane thoughtfully, "I think we did find the spot where the snowmobile had been rigged up. It seems pretty clear to me this was a two-person operation."

"What do you mean?"

"Well, one person had to toss that flaming rock through the window while the other—someone out in the woods, close enough to the house to see what was happening—sent the snowmobile on its way. And whoever did it was very careful to cover their tracks. It almost looked like the snow had been swept."

"Ah," smirked Cordelia. "Another tasty little mystery." She sat down heavily on the edge of the old claw-foot bathtub. "How delightful. You're building up quite a case load lately. Let me think. Sherlock Lawless, catering and detection. No no, this is better. Miss Jane Marple-Lawless. You can hyphenate it. It's all the rage these days anyway. You could get testimonials. How about this: 'Jane Lawless is my kind of guy,' signed, Mickey Spillane. What do you think?"

"I think you should go back to bed." Jane backed out of the doorway.

"Well, if you want my honest opinion," said Cordelia, following her out into the sitting room, "this house seems kind of creepy. We should leave well enough alone."

Jane pulled a heavy wool ski sweater on over her flannel shirt. "I'm going for a sleigh ride this morning with Leigh. I want to get away from the inn for a while. She and Burton both said this wasn't the first problem they've had. She promised to tell me the whole story."

Cordelia sneezed. "See? It's pneumonia. What did I tell you?" She dragged herself over to a chair and flopped down wearily.

"Maybe you really should go back to bed," said Jane. "How about if I meet you for lunch downstairs at one o'clock?"

"I suppose." She waved her hand limply. "Say, since you're up, will you bring me some of those tissues? Thanks Janey, you're a peach."

"You'll be fine," said Jane, disappearing into the bathroom and reappearing a second later. "I'll ask Burton to send up some breakfast on a tray." She dropped the entire box into Cordelia's lap. "Let's see, what about fresh orange juice, a mushroom and Gruyère omelet, and some of that wonderful cardamom bread I smelled baking yesterday?"

Cordelia coughed weakly. "And hot Russian tea with lemon. I'm feeling ecumenical."

"Of course," said Jane. "And don't forget. One sharp, down in the dining room."

"I shan't forget. I'll no doubt spend the morning in bed reading scripts. It's my fate."

"Right. Don't strain yourself. At lunch we can plan the rest of the day. What do you think about getting in a couple hours of cross-country skiing before dinner? I've heard they have some wonderful trails here on the island."

With a look of concentrated disgust, Cordelia got up. She pulled a tissue out of the box and blew her nose loudly. "I do not think you appreciate the acuteness of my condition, Jane." Without further comment, she hobbled pathetically into her bedroom and fell facedown onto the bed.

After a quick breakfast of fresh fruit and toast with some of Burton's homemade apricot jam, Jane stood on the front porch in the bright morning sunlight adjusting her wool cap. It was a beautiful winter day, the temperature in the mid-twenties. The sky was an intense cobalt blue. She looked out toward the river, listening to the sound of the wind high in the trees. The inn sat on the island's only hill, allowing visitors a magnificent view of the surrounding countryside. The town of Repentance River was just across a narrow bridge connecting the island to the mainland.

"Are you ready for the grand tour?" shouted Leigh as she rounded the corner of the building, driving a freshly painted red-and-black sleigh pulled by a huge brown horse. She stopped directly in front of the porch. "This is Dudley. Isn't he wonderful? We have three other horses, but he's my favorite." She slid over in the seat. "Come on, get in. I want to drive you out to the point. The view from there is breathtaking on a clear morning like this."

Jane climbed in beside her. Leigh lifted the wool blanket

over her legs. A second later, they were off in a cloud of
snow and heading toward the woods.

"It's really lovely up here, isn't it?" said Leigh, unable to
hide the sadness in her voice. "If I ever had to leave, I
don't know what I'd do."

"Why would you have to leave?" asked Jane, watching
the sun peek between the pine trees.

Leigh shrugged off the question, launching instead into a
discussion of the various flora and fauna on the island. A
few minutes later she brought the sleigh to a stop on a high
cliff overlooking the river. Both women sat silently for a
moment, admiring the view.

"I suppose the inn has really changed a lot since you saw
it last," said Leigh. "When was that?"

"About a year ago."

Leigh shook her head and sighed. "Has it been that long?
You know Jane, I know that restaurant of yours keeps you
very busy, but one might almost think it's less a place of
business than it is a hideout. Does the term workaholic
mean anything to you?"

Jane laughed. "Yeah, I hear you. I guess I like to think
of myself as indispensable. Being away for an entire week
should cure me of that little insanity."

Leigh turned her head and gazed out at the river. "That
was pretty awful last night. It wasn't a very auspicious beginning to your stay with us."

"You said it wasn't the first crazy thing that's happened."

Leigh inhaled deeply and held her breath for a moment
before slowly letting it out. "You're probably just going to
laugh. I mean, it's all so bizarre."

"I won't laugh," said Jane. "I doubt you really think last
night's episode was very funny. When did this all start?"

Leigh's smile faded. "About two months ago. It was the
first week in November. I remember because Stephen had
just started putting in a lot of overtime." She glanced at

Jane. "At least, that's what he says. It's my theory that he's been spending some of that time at his wife's house. He misses his kids terribly. For a while she didn't want him around. The first year they were separated was a pretty bitter time, though things have eased a bit now."

"I'm glad for him."

"Yeah. But still, he's under a lot of pressure. He's trying to organize a career move, juggle lawyers and property settlements, and not lose his kids or me in the process." She paused. "He'd like me to sell the inn."

"Oh?"

"I'm not going to," said Leigh. "Don't worry. But I have the feeling he's not going to give up easily. Last night he even mentioned something about marriage. That really took me by surprise. You know me, Jane. I've always been too independent. I love being in a relationship. I'm willing to live in mortal sin with a special someone for the rest of my life. I simply don't want to be married. It's not that I have some adolescent fantasy of perfect freedom. That doesn't exist unless you don't mind inflicting pain. What I've always craved is autonomy. Do you understand?"

Jane nodded. "I do."

"The thing is, I thought I'd made that quite clear to Stephen. Lately, he's been so . . . I don't know. One minute he's up, the next he's depressed and withdrawn. I guess I've just got to be patient."

Jane could tell Leigh was more upset than she was letting on. She waited, not wanting to rush her.

"The first incident happened shortly before Stephen got home one evening. It was a Friday night, and we were full up. Someone called the inn and said a bomb had been placed in one of the guest rooms."

"That's awful!" said Jane.

Leigh laughed. "I know. Why am I laughing? At the time I figured it was just somebody playing a practical joke.

Aunt Inga took the call. She said the voice sounded serious. No, that wasn't the word. *Menacing*, I believe she said. Anyway, so I called the police in Repentance River, and they came out right away. Checked the whole house. In the meantime we had to evacuate all the guests and staff. It was an inspiring sight, everyone milling around on the front lawn."

"Did they find anything?"

"No. Nothing. But it didn't matter. Most people simply checked out. Financially, it was a disaster."

"Did your aunt say if it was a man or a woman's voice on the phone?"

"She couldn't tell. The person whispered. She said she felt like it was a woman, but she couldn't be sure."

"What else has happened?"

"Well, about a week later someone poured acid into several of Burton's best copper pots. It must have happened in the middle of the night. He had a fit the next morning. Then, about a week after that, one of our guests found a dead raccoon in the middle of her bed. She'd just come back from dinner. In ten minutes she was packed and out of here. Word got around and some other guests checked out too." She rubbed her sore eyes and looked away. "I can't even remember everything now, so many things have happened. Several days ago, Burton came downstairs to start his breakfast preparations and found cow manure fertilizer tossed all over the dining room. God it was a mess."

"One might almost think someone had it in for Burton. Did you call the police?"

"Sure. Many times. But what could they do? They come and look around, but whoever is responsible is being careful."

"It sounds like this person may have access to a master key. How many are there and where do you keep them?"

"I have one on my key chain. It's usually with me or in

the top drawer of my desk. My aunts share a second. And the third we keep downstairs on a hook under the front counter. Several days ago we found it missing. I talked with everyone on the staff. No one has seen it. I just can't believe any one of them is responsible. A few other things have happened that I suppose I should tell you about. Broken glass was scattered in the parking lot. Some tires were slashed. A dead garter snake was found on the dresser in one of the guest rooms. The main breaker switch downstairs was shut off during dinner one evening. It plunged the entire house into darkness. Truthfully, Jane, the police are sick of hearing from me. I really can't blame them. Something has happened out here almost every week since the beginning of November. I even hired a private detective. He stayed here for three weeks and all he did was get fat on Burton's cooking. I fired him two days ago. But the police force in Repentance River is so small, I don't know what they can do."

Jane shook her head. "Somebody really has it in for you. I wish I could help."

"Me, too, Sherlock. Cordelia told me about that sorority business last year."

"Uhm," said Jane. "She usually says she solved it single-handedly. I'm surprised she mentioned me at all."

Leigh smiled. "She did. Briefly. But I read between the lines."

Both women laughed.

"Listen, Jane, maybe you could help! Why not? You've got more brains than that P.I. I hired. At least you could keep your eyes open. Who knows? You might get lucky."

Jane drew her head back and looked across the river. "I suppose I could try. What happened last night was serious. People could have been hurt. I think you have to face the fact that you've got more than a simple prankster here. Have you told me everything?"

"No," said Leigh. She hesitated a moment. "Yesterday morning I received a small box in the mail. It was addressed to me personally."

"And?" said Jane.

"It was a box of herbs. For tea. And there was a note. It said this particular tea was a solstice tradition. It suggested I try some right then, and if I liked it, I should serve it at the party before the ritual last night. It was pokeweed, Jane. It would have made anyone who drank it violently ill. Thankfully, Burton realized what it was and prevented a tragedy. The note was signed."

"Who was it from?"

Leigh grimaced. "You."

"Me! Are you serious? I would never send you anything like that! You couldn't possibly think . . ."

"No, don't worry. I knew you had nothing to do with it."

Jane felt a chill. "Where is it now?"

"Burton threw the box into the fire."

"That wasn't smart. How about the note?"

"I looked for it later but couldn't find it. I even asked Aunt Inga if she'd taken it. Apparently my cousin Ruthie had been doing a little last-minute tidying up in the parlor and she must have thrown it out with the brown paper wrapping. When I asked her, she didn't remember seeing it."

Jane was silent, intent on gathering all the threads of the conversation together in her mind. "Okay," she said, "and then last night there was the snowmobile incident."

Leigh nodded. "At first, I found all of it terribly upsetting. Then I think I almost got used to crazy things happening all the time. I started to expect them. But now, I can tell it's really getting to me. It's even upsetting my sleep. I've never had to take naps before and now I take several a day. I'm embarrassed to say it's interfering with my work. Last night was the last straw. I can't live like this any more. But what can I do?"

Jane was quiet for a moment. "Do you remember anything unusual happening around the beginning of November? Something that might explain this?"

"No. Nothing comes to mind. Well there is one thing I guess. My cousin Ruthie quit her job in town in late October and moved in with my aunts at the gatehouse. To be quite honest, my aunts weren't very happy about it, so I put Ruthie on the payroll just to calm them down. She tries to help, but most of the time she just gets in the way. I feel sort of bad about it. She's been so intent on becoming my friend. The thing is, she overdoes it and then backs off, acting hurt when you aren't pleased. And she has no sense of boundaries. The first week she was here, she walked into my bedroom without even knocking. Stephen and I . . . well, suffice it to say, she won't do that again. Lately, she's been spending more and more of her time in her bedroom or wandering around the island. I don't know what to do with her."

"How well do you know your cousin?"

"Not very well. Just between you and me, Jane, I think she's kind of a nut case. She doesn't like to talk about herself. She gets tongue-tied when you get too personal. I don't think anyone knows her very well, not even my two aunts. They raised her from the time she was a little girl. She's like their daughter. Neither Inga nor Violet ever married, you know. It must run in the family." She winked.

"Right," smiled Jane. "Biology is destiny. But think now. Did anything else change at the beginning of November?"

Leigh shrugged. "I don't know. No. Not really. That was about the time we started using a new greengrocer, but I hardly believe that's of any significance. So where does that leave us?"

"I think it's pretty clear someone wants you out of here.

Why, I don't know. Has anyone expressed an interest in buying the inn?"

Leigh's expression grew a bit more guarded. "Yeah. Well, only one really. Henry Gyldenskog. You met him last night. He made me an offer on the place last August. I told him no thanks, so he and his son moved in as guests and have been here ever since."

"Anyone else?"

"I suppose Burton has mentioned it a few times. If I should ever sell, he'd like the first crack. I think it's mainly wishful thinking on his part. I doubt he could come up with the financing."

"And Stephen? You said he wanted you to sell? Why?"

Leigh looked away. "At first he said it was because of the daily commute to and from St. Paul. He also hates the small space we're living in up on the third floor. It makes him claustrophobic. Lately, he's been talking a lot about these strange pranks. He keeps telling me I don't need the hassle. Maybe he's right. But yesterday, he really took me by surprise. He asked if I would consider investing some of the profits from the sale of the inn in a business venture of his."

"I see."

"Yes. I'm sure you do. But I feel pretty sure it's on the up and up. He's meticulous about his finances. Money is terribly important to him. Oh Jane, don't get that look on your face. Stephen isn't behind any of this. He's put so much of his own time into this place, I can't believe he really means for us to leave. And deep down he knows I won't, so the whole thing is moot."

"You're sure of that?"

Leigh seemed uncomfortable with the question. "Yes. I'm sure. At least I think I'm sure." She smiled. "This is too ridiculous. I can't believe we're discussing my friends and family as if any of them could be responsible. It's got

to be some wacko from town. They'll eventually get tired
of their games. You'll see."

"For your sake," said Jane, looking up at the cloudless
sky, "I hope you're right."

8

"Are you going to completely ignore that pickle?" asked
Cordelia as she sat eating her lunch of linguine tossed with
fresh scallops and sweet peppers.

"Be my guest," said Jane.

Cordelia reached across and snatched it off her plate.
"So," she continued, "is that all Leigh said? No dead bod-
ies in closets? No death threats from Norwegian terrorists?
I'm sure the woods around here must be filled with them."

Jane shook her head. "No, that was it. But I don't like it.
She's concerned, but she's still minimizing things. These
pranks, as she calls them, may have started out with no real
intent to harm, but as far as I'm concerned they've already
turned into something quite dangerous." She glanced up at
a table near the bay windows where Winifred and Tess sat
silently eating their meal. Neither looked happy. Every so
often Tess would steal a peek at Michael Paget, the young
man she had talked with last night. Today he was waiting
tables.

"Well, I intend to enjoy *my* stay," said Cordelia, taking a
sip of her sparkling water. She sneezed into a napkin. "As
much as humanly possible, that is, since I'm on the verge

of a complete physical breakdown. Did I tell you what I'm going to do this afternoon, Janey?"

"I thought you were coming cross-country skiing with me."

Cordelia ignored the remark. "Look at this." She picked up a tall white chef's hat from under her chair.

"You'll look kind of funny sailing through the woods on your skis wearing that."

"Very amusing. No my dear, Burton has asked me to join him this afternoon. We're going to make gingerbread men for the Christmas tree. Actually, it's Aunt Inga's recipe, and she'll be supervising. He said he's learned a lot from her. You remember those fattigmanns we had last night at the party?"

Jane nodded, taking the last bite of her cold pheasant salad.

"It was another of Aunt Inga's recipes. She helps him out all the time. I guess she's a great cook."

"That sounds fun for you. But why the chef's hat?"

"Burton insists everyone in the kitchen wear one. He's very fastidious. Hair has to be covered at all times."

"Of course," said Jane distractedly, glancing again at Winifred and Tess. "Where is my mind? I run a restaurant. I should know that." Jane had noticed Tess looking in their direction several times. She seemed to be focusing on something just above Cordelia's head. Leaning back, Jane examined the bare wall but saw nothing unusual. Very strange.

As a waiter came by with more coffee, Jane heard a little voice in back of him say, "There's Cordeel!" It was Burton's son, Dylan.

"Oh no," whispered Cordelia. "He's found me again." She held the chef's hat in front of her face as she turned her head to the wall.

The little boy ran up and crawled uninvited into her lap. "Will you and Jane go ice skating with me today, Cordeel?"

"That's Cordelia, Dylan. Remember? *Cordelia!*"

Dylan blinked. He turned to Jane. "I have new skates!"

"That's wonderful," said Jane. "I'll bet you can go really fast in them."

Dylan nodded, grabbing Cordelia's fork and zooming it through the air. Cordelia pried it out of his hand and laid it back down on the table, all the while smiling through clenched teeth.

"Dylan, we've got to get going," called Aunt Violet sweetly. She walked up to the table tugging on a hat. She was dressed for winter combat. Down jacket, wool scarf, and heavy mittens. "Remember, we have to get back in time for your nap. You promised Daddy."

"I'm a big boy," said Dylan, turning to glare at Cordelia.

"You're a lot of things," Cordelia smiled.

He stared at her a moment. "Yes," he said dogmatically. "I am."

Jane watched Aunt Violet gaze lovingly down at Dylan. She didn't look a thing like her sister. Inga was taller and at least forty pounds heavier; she dressed like a gypsy while Violet was a study in drab: gray eyes, gray skin, and a thin, nervous body. The only hint of color came from a rather bad choice of hair dye. After a moment's reflection, Jane felt the shade was decidedly apricot. Violet looked much like a dusty old rag doll that had been forgotten too long on a shelf.

"Promise you'll go ice skating with me," said Dylan, pointing at Jane.

"I promise. On my honor. Sometime before I go back home next week, we'll go skating together. Maybe we can even build a snowman. Would you like that?"

Dylan beamed. He hopped off Cordelia's lap and ran over to give Jane a kiss.

"Thank you, Dylan." Jane gave him a big hug. "Now you go with Aunt Violet before she dies of heat stroke. I'll see you later."

Violet winked. "Thanks." She took his hand, and the two of them walked together into the kitchen.

"I'll say this," said Cordelia, leaning confidentially across the table, "Burton sure has his hands full being a single father."

"With all the people around here willing to give that little boy love and attention," said Jane, "some day he'll realize he was living in paradise." She looked up as Winifred and Tess approached the table.

"And how are you two this afternoon?" asked Winifred.

"Frisky and feisty," said Cordelia, exuding postprandial well-being. "Roaring and snorting."

Winifred cocked her head. "Of course. Well. I don't suppose I could interest either of you in joining me for some cross-country skiing? Tess is trying to catch up on a bit of reading so I'm free until dinner."

"I'd love to go with you," said Jane, noticing Tess sneak another peek at the bare wall.

"Great! How about you, Cordelia?"

"Thanks, no. I'm going to be heavily into gingerbread men all afternoon. We might even break new ground. Make some gingerbread *gals*. Don't you just hate the word *gal?*"

"I've never thought about it," said Winifred. She turned to Jane. "I need an hour to get a few things done. How about if we meet at three by the front desk? We can rent everything we need right here."

Jane agreed, hearing the grandfather clock next to the library door strike two. She had just enough time to take care of something first.

* * *

The door to the tool shed was unlocked, so Jane let herself in without knocking. It was a small, heated room, located in back of the barn.

"Hello, anyone here?" she called, walking over to a long work bench and running her hand along the battered wood surface. All the tools hanging on the walls were perfectly clean and arranged according to size. The term *anal retentive* flitted through her mind. She decided to check out some of the bottles and tins on the shelf. Oil. Turpentine. Cleaning supplies. All neatly labeled. Nothing unusual. As she started to open one of the lower drawers, she heard a floorboard creak behind her.

"What are you doing in here?" muttered a deep voice from the entrance into the shed. "You've got no business." A heavily wrinkled old man with a crew cut and unusually large ears stood blocking the doorway.

Jane turned to face him. "I'm sorry." She gave a quick smile. "I was looking for something. A piece of wire, actually."

"Wire?" His rough voice was suspicious. "Why do you want wire? Are you a guest?"

"Yes," said Jane. "I'm an old friend of Leigh's."

"Fooey," he grunted. "What kind of wire?"

Jane pulled out the piece she had cut down from the tree last night.

He took it in his thick leathery hand and rolled it between his fingers. "I didn't catch the name."

"Lawless. Jane Lawless." Bond, thought Jane. James Bond.

"Lapinski," he said, brushing past her. "Now, let's see what we've got." He opened a cabinet and began rummaging through one of the small drawers. "Here you go. An exact match." He handed her the spool.

"There's hardly any left," said Jane, watching his response.

"So? I got eyes."

"Has anyone borrowed it recently?"

"No. What do you need it for anyway?"

"Oh, well, I guess you could say I'm working on a little art project." She tittered. She hated it when she tittered. She only did it when she was nervous.

"Sure. Like hell." He grabbed it back. "Try the local hardware store."

It seemed a politic time to leave. Halfway to the door she stopped. "Before I go, will you answer one question?"

"Depends."

"Have you worked here long?"

"Long? Lady, I been a handyman around this town since I was seventeen years old. Worked through the hardware store on Mill Street. I'm sixty-seven now, so I guess you could say I've made it out here a few times in my day. Got this full-time job at the inn right when they were starting to renovate it two years ago."

"You fix things when they break?"

"That's my job. Just replaced those broken windows in the parlor. Course, I take care of the horses, too. And I did a lot of the fancy work inside. That's my specialty. I acid-etched the front door. Did some of the stencilling. Some of the fine carpentry." He ran a hand over his prickly head. "Tomorrow morning I'm going to start work in the base-ment. Mr. March—he's the cook fellow—wants to put in a wine cellar down there. I got to break through a wall, build shelves—make it all look real nice. Gonna build those shelves outta oak. Expensive, but it'll stain up beautiful." He glanced away, obviously surprised by his own loquacity.

"Okay," said Jane. "So let me ask you something. The east wall of the dining room. Has it been altered in any way?" She had a hunch and hoped he could give her the answer.

He pulled on his wrinkled face for a moment. "The east

wall? Yeah, sure. There was a window there once. Miss Elstad wanted it taken out. It looked out on the old summerhouse. That place is an eyesore, if you ask me. They should tear it down."

Jane smiled. "Thanks. You've been a big help."

"Me?" he said, tossing the wire back into the drawer. "I just do my job. And keep my mouth shut. That's what I do."

9

In the growing twilight Jane and Winifred reached the front steps of the inn, lugging their skis and poles up onto the porch. The moon sat low on the horizon, casting its deep purple luminescence across the white landscape. Both women were pleasantly tired from several hours of brisk exercise. From their vantage on the hill, they could see the lights of Repentance River in the distance. "Funny how something as beautiful as this always reminds me of a postcard," said Jane, stamping off the packed snow on her boots. "So much for my poetic instincts."

Winifred smiled. "I think a place as rare as this island affects everyone who comes to it. It has to. I know when I'm here, I never want to leave." She pulled off her cap and shook out her long red hair.

They stood together for a few minutes, silently appreciating the bleak winter twilight.

"That was really fun this afternoon," said Winifred finally. "I love being outside in the winter."

"I couldn't agree more. Listen, Winney, before you head inside, I wanted to ask you something. You've been here a couple of times before, right?"

"Twice, no I take that back, three times. When the inn opened last March, it coincided almost perfectly with the spring equinox. My coven held its ritual here as well as a blessing of the house. Then in August, a group of us came up for a retreat. It was wonderful. We stayed a whole week. You know, Tess and I only live a couple of hours away. It's an easy drive. I should really try to get up here more often. And then, let's see. In November I came up for a couple of days. I was by myself that time. No celebrations. Just rest and relaxation."

"Did Tess come with you?"

Winifred shook her head. "No. She's never wanted to come. She would always say I should go whenever I liked. She'd stay home and take care of business."

"So she's never been here before?"

"No. Never. I was kind of surprised when she agreed to drive up with me this time."

"Is Tess from around here, by any chance?"

Winifred looked carefully at Jane. "What are you fishing for? No, she's from Madison."

"I see. Well, it just seemed to me she was kind of familiar with the house."

"Yeah, to be honest, I've noticed that, too. Yesterday someone asked for help carrying a bunch of wood into the basement. Tess picked up an arm load and headed directly for the basement stairs. I don't know how she knew where to go. We'd only just arrived a few minutes before. I thought at the time it was strange and was going to ask her about it, but in all the commotion, I simply forgot."

"How did you meet Tess?" asked Jane.

"We met at a book convention in Chicago seven years ago. She was working for a feminist bookstore in Milwaukee, and I'd just opened the one in River Falls. I guess you could say we met and fell in love almost right away. It was kind of a long distance romance for a while. But eventually she moved in with me and bought out fifty percent of the bookstore. We've been together ever since."

"Do you know much about her past?"

"Sure. Lots. She grew up in Madison. Had a pretty typical childhood. One brother. She left home in '69 to attend the University of Minnesota in Minneapolis. She still talks about how much she hated it there. Why are you interested?"

"Just curious," said Jane.

Winifred didn't seem satisfied. Leaning her skis against the wall, she kept her back to Jane for a moment. "Just curious, huh. If I know you, you've got a reason. What is it?"

Jane didn't want to be pressed on the point. "I don't know, Winney. Really. It's probably nothing."

Winifred turned around. "I'm not so sure. You know Jane, maybe I shouldn't say anything, but there's been something strange going on with Tess ever since we got here. I can't figure it out, and she won't talk about it. To be honest, I'm becoming pretty concerned." She looked out at the twinkling lights of the town in the distance and sighed. "But it doesn't seem likely I'm going to figure it out standing here. I better get inside and see what she's been up to all afternoon. Thanks again, Jane. This was great."

They entered the inn through the front double doors, their faces rosy from the cold. The dining room was already alive with guests. After promising to meet later for dinner, Winifred excused herself and disappeared up the stairs. Jane glanced briefly into the parlor. She couldn't help but notice Violet and the handyman, Elmer Lapinski, sitting together at the piano. Violet was playing a Christmas song rather badly, and he was singing along in a deep baritone. In the soft light from the fire, Jane saw a loveliness in Violet she'd overlooked before. Watching a moment longer, she was surprised to see Elmer slip his arm around Violet's waist. That was interesting. She wondered how long they had known each other. And how well. Not wanting to give into any latent voyeuristic tendencies, she turned quickly and headed into the kitchen. If things had gone as she estimated they would, Cordelia would still be up to her elbows in cookie dough.

After a dinner of grilled salmon in saffron cream finished off by a slice of Burton's famous maple-glazed cranberry tart, Jane left Cordelia and Winifred to their game of hearts and climbed the stairs to the third floor. She hadn't seen Leigh since their sleigh ride earlier in the day. Ever since their conversation, Jane had experienced a growing sense of foreboding. It seemed she should at least check in to make sure everything was all right.

Catching her breath as she approached the door, Jane knocked twice. No answer. She tried the handle and found it unlocked. Knocking once more, she stepped into a completely dark room. A radio was playing an old Buddy Holly song somewhere in the background. "Leigh," she called, "are you in here?" Standing in the darkness, she could hear soft breathing.

"I'm over here," said Leigh, switching on a dim light on a small table next to her.

"Are you all right?" Jane stepped further into the room. Leigh was stretched out on the couch.

"I'm fine. No, that's a lie. If you want the truth, I'm just slightly this side of hysterical."

Jane walked over and sat down in a chair opposite her. "Feel like talking?"

Leigh sat up, tossing a large brown envelope onto the

coffee table. "Sure. Why not whine a little? It always
makes me feel better. This afternoon I received last month's
financial report from my accountant. It's grim. We lost so
much business thanks to all the weird things happening
around here that our income is way down. December will
probably be worse. Until I saw the figures in black and
white, I didn't appreciate the tenuousness of our financial
position. If something doesn't change, I will be forced to
sell. I'm already mortgaged to the hilt. My operating capital's derived almost completely from the profit we make
each month. No profit means I can't pay my bills. It's that
simple."

Jane didn't know what to say. "That's awful, Leigh."

"Would you like to hear the latest?"

"What do you mean? Has something else happened?"

"Of course. It never stops. About half an hour ago, a reporter from *Twin Cities Weekly* called. She was here last
week to get some background on a feature article they're
going to do on the inn. She said someone had called the paper yesterday about the problems we've been having. I tried
to play it down, but she'd already talked to the police chief
in Repentance River. She knew everything. There wasn't
much I could say except I hoped she wouldn't print it. It
will ruin what's left of our business."

"And? What did she say?"

Leigh shook her head. "She got all self-righteous and
said she felt it was her duty as a journalist to print the truth.
Christ, that little twelve-year-old twit wouldn't know the
truth if it ran up and bit her in the ass. She's too stupid to
realize someone is using her. I only pray her editor won't
publish it."

"That's awful. Did she give you any indication who had
made the call?"

"No. It was anonymous. She wouldn't even say if it was
a man or a woman." She yawned. "You know, you'd think

all this stress would give me ulcers. I should be pacing the floor, tearing out my hair, running into my closet and screaming. But what did I do after I got the financial report this afternoon? I fell asleep. I made myself a cup of cocoa, read the report, and lay down on the couch. I didn't wake up until that reporter called. By the way, where are my manners? Would you like something to drink? Henry Gyldenskog brought me this lovely tin of English cocoa several weeks ago. Stephen hates sweet drinks, so I don't generally have to share. But in this case, I'd make an exception."

"No thanks," said Jane. She patted her stomach. "I just finished dinner. As my Aunt Beryl always says, 'I feel like a stuffed tick.' " Jane could hear the sound of footsteps in the hallway. A moment later the door swung open and Stephen entered. He looked exhausted.

"Hi honey," called Leigh. "Welcome to the land of the maimed and the bleeding. You look like you'll fit right in."

Stephen grimaced and headed straight for the kitchenette. "I need a drink. Would anyone care to join me?"

"Why not?" said Leigh. "Jane?"

"No thanks."

Stephen returned to the living room carrying two glasses and a bottle of Scotch. Setting everything down on the coffee table, he fell into a chair.

"A hard day?" asked Leigh.

Stephen poured the drinks. "A nightmare."

Jane took it as her cue to leave. "I'd better get going. I promised Dylan I'd play a game with him before he goes to bed."

"Thanks," said Stephen. He took a large swallow of his drink. "Perhaps we'll see you tomorrow at breakfast. I'm thinking about taking the day off."

"That sounds like a good idea," said Jane, stepping over to the door. "You look like you could use a break."

Stephen's lips parted in what Jane assumed was a smile. At least it was an attempt at civility. She could tell he was terribly upset.

"Good night," called Leigh. "Watch out for that Dylan. He likes to play poker for pennies. He'll clean you out if you aren't careful."

"And be careful of Ruthie," added Stephen, pinching the bridge of his nose. "She was really telling Elmer off down in the parlor. I've never seen her so mad."

"What about?" asked Jane.

"It sounded to me like he'd made some sort of comment about her father. Elmer needs to learn that, for Ruthie, her family is a holy topic. It's a subject he should avoid like the plague."

"See you in the morning," called Leigh.

Jane shut the door quietly behind her.

"You really do look beat," said Leigh, sipping her Scotch. She watched him lean back and close his eyes. There was something about him tonight. Something almost fragile. "What's wrong?" she asked.

For a moment, he didn't speak. With his eyes still closed, he said, "My wife came to see me today."

Leigh was surprised. "Marjie came to the office?"

Stephen nodded. He took another swallow of his drink. "She's very upset. At first I didn't understand why. Then it all came out."

Leigh waited, not wanting to rush him.

"She's been seeing this guy for almost a year. It's gotten pretty serious between them. A few days ago she found out she was pregnant. The guy doesn't want anything to do with it. He . . . wants her to take care of it."

"And?"

"Marjie's Catholic. It's out of the question."

"I'm really sorry," said Leigh. "But what's it got to do with you?" She could feel the muscles in her neck tighten.

"She's desperate. She's going to say it's my baby."

Leigh fought to control her voice. "It's not, is it?"

"Of course not. But what am I going to do? She wants me to pay child support for it even though it isn't mine!"

"I can't believe she'd do that."

"You don't know her. She's terrified it's going to mean she can't go back to school. She wants that desperately, Leigh. You can understand that, can't you?"

He was angry. It was no time to pick a fight. "What about a blood test," Leigh asked. "That would prove paternity."

He poured himself more Scotch. "God, I hope so. But she won't allow it until the child is born. That will be after the divorce is final. I can make the child support contingent, but what if the tests are inconclusive? What if I have the same blood type as the father? I called a doctor friend of mine. He said it happens that way sometimes. Then I'll be paying for three children plus alimony until Marjie gets through school. By then they can wheel me to the poorhouse." He put his head in his hands, shielding his face from her.

She could tell he was crying. Getting up slowly, she walked over and sat down on the edge of his chair. Gently, she took his head in her arms.

"What am I going to do? I feel like . . . my life is so screwed, Leigh. If I could get that partnership I'd be in a better position to pay all the bills, but without the money up front, I won't get in."

Leigh loosened his tie. "You need some rest."

"I know. All the way home in the car, all I could think of was crawling in bed and pulling the covers over my head. I just want to hide. But I'll never be able to sleep."

"Finish your drink. Maybe tomorrow you can talk to her.

Explain your situation. She'll see what she's doing is wrong."

He shook his head. "I already tried. It's useless." He stood, moving zombielike into the bedroom. "She's scared, too. That's why she's doing this."

Leigh helped him onto the bed and covered him with a quilt. It was hard to see him in such pain.

"Stay with me for a while," he said, taking hold of her hand. "I need you so badly."

"Of course," said Leigh. "I'm not leaving."

10

A few minutes before midnight, Jane switched on the bedside lamp. She'd said her good nights around ten and spent the next two hours tossing and turning, unable to get to sleep. Her mind kept coming back to what Leigh had said earlier in the day. There had to be a logical reason for everything that was happening. Yet none of the scenarios she'd toyed with seemed to fit. The motive seemed simple enough. Someone wanted Leigh out of the inn. How far that someone was willing to go was up for grabs. What may have started out as simple pranks had now escalated into something quite different. And that was the thought that had kept her awake.

Finding her slippers under the bed where she'd left them, Jane tied her robe snugly and shuffled into the sitting room.

Cordelia was still up, reading at a small table near the

door. She looked a bit like one of the characters from *The Wind in the Willows*. An old hedgehog attired in a green flannel bathrobe, a wool scarf wrapped snugly around her neck. "Is this a ... sleepwalker ... I see before me?" she asked, looking up.

Jane grunted, dumping herself into a chair. "If I was sleepwalking, at least I'd be *asleep*." The smell of Vick's Vapo Rub surrounded Cordelia like a fog.

"Ah," said Cordelia, wheezing into a tissue. "No rest for the weary. Or is it no rest for the wicked? I can never remember. Would you like me to sing you a lullaby? I could hum a few bars of an old Paul Anka song. That should put you to sleep in a matter of seconds."

"A Paul Anka song would not put me to sleep," said Jane testily. "It would merely upset my stomach."

"I see. I suppose you're still worried about the imminent arrival of your Aunt Beryl. That is, once you give her the green light. I thought we'd already solved that problem. You invite her to stay and then leave town before she gets here."

"Cordelia!"

"All right, all right. It's too late at night for that kind of humor. Besides, I've always liked Beryl. I think you should let her come."

"It's not that simple."

"No," said Cordelia. She reached over and patted Jane's hand. "I know it's not, dearheart. I'm not trying to make light of your anxiety. I just think it's the wrong time of day to be dwelling on it."

"Actually, tonight I was thinking about Leigh."

"Uhm. You do have an assortment of worrisome subjects."

"I seem to." Jane leaned forward, pulling the manuscript across the table. "What's this? *Audience for a Bride Doll*."

"It's an amazing piece of work. During tech rehearsal

last week, one of the actors—Annie Hastings—asked me to
read it. I don't even know who wrote it. I suppose she told
me but I was so preoccupied with the new third act blocking, I don't remember what she said. At least she never
mentioned anything about it being *meaningful*. I hate being
told I'm about to read a classic that happens to have just
been penned."

Jane groaned. "I sympathize."

"I'll say this much. After one reading it's certainly got
my attention. I was sitting here a few minutes ago thinking
how much I'd like to stage it. I doubt The Allen Grimby
would be interested. The Grand High Rodent, otherwise
known as the president of the board, wouldn't even consider something by a new playwright. But I could pull a
few strings at Theatre on West Bank. They'd love to debut
a new feminist play. Especially after I apply a little pressure
here and there."

"That's really exciting. I'd like to read it."

"In due time. First I have to do a second reading. Then
I want to find out who wrote it. Who knows. We may have
found another August Wilson."

Jane grinned. "Or even an *Augusta* Wilson."

"I think we are definitely dealing with an Augusta here."
Cordelia leaned back, lifting her feet up onto a chair. "So
now what? Do we jump in the car and find some place in
town to go dancing?"

Jane closed her eyes.

"No. Bad idea. Want to play twenty questions?"

"I want to go to *sleep*," insisted Jane. "But I'll go back
in there and just stare at the ceiling."

"That sounds like a good time. Say, I've got an idea. I
vote we head downstairs in search of a magic potion. Come
on, Janey. Burton must have something in the kitchen that
will send you to bed happy—and quickly."

"Cookies and milk? Brandy? An aspirin? Perhaps a hammer."

"Shhh," hissed Jane reaching the first floor landing. "Your slippers could wake the dead. You're clomping."

"I do not *clomp*. *Horses* clomp." Cordelia breezed past her into the foyer.

"I smell a wood fire."

"You look like a groundhog emerging from her hole. Stop sniffing the air. It's unbecoming."

Looking around, Jane noticed a flickering light coming from a small sun room in back of the main parlor. "Let's check it out," she said, motioning for Cordelia to follow.

"I am not up for another midnight reconnaissance mission."

"Shhh," said Jane. "And stop clomping."

"You're getting dangerously close to character assassination, sweetie. I advise you to watch it."

Jane moved through the room, past the grand piano, and stood at last in the doorway. A chair was pulled up in front of a small stone fireplace, its occupant concealed by the high back.

Cordelia elbowed Jane in the ribs. "My cookie detector tells me this room is an utter wasteland."

Per's head popped up. "What was that?" he said, eyeing them curiously.

"Hi," said Jane, feeling a bit like a child who had been caught up past her bedtime. "Cordelia and I came downstairs to find something to help us sleep."

"It's all this country quiet," said Cordelia, leaning on Jane's shoulder. Her voice sounded slightly adenoidal because of the stuffy nose. "The cows may like it, but we city folk need sirens, loud arguments, car backfires, and the occasional gunshot to sleep soundly."

Per smiled. "In that case, would you like to join me for a glass of sherry? That's about all I can offer."

"Dandy," said Cordelia, pushing Jane further into the room. "We'd be delighted. It's nice to know *someone* around here's got the agenda straight." She proceeded to drag two more wing chairs in front of the fire. Glowering at Jane, she pointed to one of them and said, "Sit."

Jane sat down.

"I've always been kind of a night owl," said Per, grabbing two more glasses off the sideboard. He handed each of them a filled glass and then refilled his own. Tonight he seemed a bit more disheveled than he had last evening at the solstice ritual. His clothes were less elegant. His hair uncombed. Jane found him more appealing because he didn't seem quite as perfect.

"And how are you two enjoying your stay?" he asked, adding, "other than your problem with a lack of city ambiance?"

"We've been here a day and a half," snuffled Cordelia, "and been besieged by stories of bomb threats, evil varmints in guest rooms . . . and then last night's little snowmobile extravaganza. . . . I'd say we're having a grand old time." She stifled a sneeze.

Per glanced at Jane. "I guess that means Leigh has filled you in. I suppose she would. You're old friends."

"Why do you stay?" asked Jane. "I would think trying to write in the midst of all this would be next to impossible."

A log shifted in the fireplace, sending a spray of sparks out into the room. Per brushed a cinder from his pants. "Yes, of course. The book. The problem is, I can't write it anywhere else."

"I see." She studied him for a moment. "You said you lived here once, in 1964, I believe."

"I was sixteen years old. The book is about that time in

my life. I thought staying at the inn would help me sort things out. It was the year my father found out I was gay."

Cordelia nodded her interest.

"You mentioned it was a mystery," said Jane.

"You listen carefully, don't you?" answered Per. "And you remember things. I better be careful. That's a dangerous combination. What I meant was that certain things happened during that time. Things I've never really been clear about. I'd hoped staying here with my father, getting to know him better, would help clarify some of it."

"And," said Cordelia, "has it?"

"No. It hasn't. I suppose if you're really interested, I could explain a little. To be honest, it's all I've been thinking about for months."

"Of course," said Jane. "I think we'd both like to hear it."

Per sighed. "Where do I begin? All right. When I was fifteen years old my mother died. Yes, I loved her very much. And no, she never knew I was gay. At least I don't think she did. It's my belief that mothers often intuit things from the minutiae of life fathers simply trample over."

"Hear! Hear!" said Cordelia. She held out her glass for a refill.

Jane glared.

"If my mother did know, she never said anything. Shortly after her death, my father lost his job. He worked for a radio station in Minneapolis and had started drinking heavily. I imagine it was to ease the pain of loss, but it eventually got him fired. After months of being out of work, he took a job in Cambridge. That's when we moved up here. This, believe it or not, was the cheapest rental house available. For some reason, no one wanted to live on the island. There were silly stories of wolves attacking innocent pilgrims who unwittingly entered the woods alone after dark. My suspicion was that it was a story used by the old geezers—pardon me, I know that is an ageist comment—down at the local hardware store to sell traps to the occasional unsuspecting city yokel. They would scare him with their stories and send them off with a sack full of traps. Dad was just the kind of patsy they were looking for. He bought the whole thing, including the traps. He set them all around the house. He wasn't taking any chances.

"Because of the furry threat, I wasn't allowed out after dark. Some days Dad would call and say he couldn't make it home. I'd have to stay by myself. Sometimes I figured he wanted to stay in town and drink. Or maybe he just couldn't face coming home. Anyway, I began to look forward to the nights he stayed away. If I knew he wouldn't be back, I'd walk across the bridge into town. About two months after we moved here, I met Randy. He worked at one of the local gas stations. He'd graduated from high school the year before and was saving his money so that he could get out of Repentance River once and for all. As you may have already guessed, Randy was gay. We struck up a friendship almost immediately. When Dad was away, he would stay with me sometimes. We'd build a fire back here, and he'd spend the night. I grew to care about him a lot, and I was sure he felt the same.

"Dad was becoming more erratic as time went on. Some days he wouldn't go to work at all. I'd come home to find him sitting in the parlor, drinking and playing solitaire. Then, for days he'd be gone. I knew it was his way of dealing with Mom's death. And also, with his crumbling life. Eventually I just felt disgusted. I was hurt and angry that he'd shut me out. The worst thing was, he never realized how much I needed him after Mom died. There wasn't any pain in the world except his.

"One night, Randy and I were lying in here in front of the fire, talking and laughing. Dad walked in. We were both fully clothed, but he probably saw him touch me or some-

thing. Before I knew what was happening, he had pulled
Randy to his feet and was dragging him toward the front
door. After he'd thrown him out, he refused to talk to me.
Days went by, and he ignored everything I said. Several
weekends later I was away at a gymnastics tournament in
St. Cloud. I didn't get home until late Sunday afternoon.
Dad was sitting in the dining room when I got back. He
looked really strange. I've tried many times in my mind to
define the look, but it still eludes me. He never even asked
how I'd done. Instead, he ordered me to go upstairs and
pack. We were leaving for Minneapolis right away. I assumed that meant he'd been canned again. Before I left the
room he stopped me. 'That other boy,' he said, nodding toward this room, 'he was your . . . girlfriend?'

"God, I hated the way he put it. I wanted to break him
in half. But instead of arguing, I just said yes. That I loved
him." Per finished his drink in one swallow. "Dad started to
cry. He wouldn't look at me. I can still hear his words.
'Per,' he said, pounding his fist on the table, 'you're never
going to see him again. I've taken care of that. I don't want
to hear another word about any of this, is that clear?' I remember standing there, shaking so violently it was all I
could do not to scream. I wanted to hurt him. To tell him
what I thought of his boozing. To make him feel how much
his endless self-pity disgusted me. But I couldn't. He was
my father. His tears and rage frightened me. Finally, I just
ran upstairs and sat in the corner of my room until I heard
him go outside. I packed my bags and brought them out to
the car. The only thing he said to me for the rest of the day
was, 'I never want to talk about this again, is that understood? I want to forget we ever came up here.' "

Per got up and walked over to a cart, bringing a second
bottle of sherry back with him. Jane declined the offer of
another glass, but Cordelia held hers out for a refill.

"What happened to Randy?" asked Jane.

"I wrote him many times—letter after letter. But I never got any response. One night I called his parents' house. His dad answered. I was stupid enough to use my own name, and believe me, that was all it took. He told me never to call there again and hung up. Next, I called the gas station where he worked. They said he'd been fired. The fact is, Randy was a loner. He rarely confided in anyone. There was simply no one left to contact, so I waited. By the next fall I'd earned enough money to buy my own car. One weekend I drove up here to look for him. At the gas station I found someone who said they were sure he'd left town. I didn't know where else to look. My search had reached a dead end. The thing is, to this day, it still bothers me. I've been staying here since the beginning of August, and every single time I go into town I think I'll see him. Deep down, I know that's not going to happen. Yet there's just something about all of this that doesn't seem right. Why didn't he get in touch with me before he left? It doesn't make any sense."

"You think something might have happened to him?" asked Jane.

Per hesitated. "No, of course not. What could happen? You don't hide much in a small town. He was young. Headstrong. He must have had his reasons. Someday I'll find out what they were. It's just, lately I've been thinking about him a lot. I can't seem to get his face out of my mind. What he did feels like rejection, and I hate him for that. But maybe it's all just part of growing up. Learning to accept the past. I suppose we all have to come to terms with unfulfilled dreams. We tell ourselves a lot of lies when we're young. I was sure Randy and I would be together forever, but I know now that was pure, adolescent romanticism." He looked up, studying the painting above the mantle. "Sometimes those past lies are more comfortable than present truths. Do you know what I mean?"

"I do," said Jane. She turned to look at Cordelia, who hadn't said a word since Per began his story.

"Is she asleep?" asked Per.

"She's snoring. I think that means she's asleep."

Per shook his head and sighed. "It's curious, isn't it? How unattractive pain is in real life. In art, it's always so appealing."

Jane lifted the sherry glass out of Cordelia's hand. "I think it's only fair to tell you I'm the one suffering from insomnia. Not her."

Cordelia let out a snort.

"That's quite apparent," smiled Per.

Jane set the glass on the floor. "You seem like you're on such good terms with your father now."

"You know," said Per, stretching his legs and sinking down further in the chair, "I hadn't seen him in almost twenty years. I left Minneapolis when I was in my early twenties. I moved to New York and put myself through college. Dad and I never called or wrote. It just seemed like there was never anything to say. I came back to Minneapolis last spring as part of a book tour and decided I should at least look him up. I didn't even know if he was still alive. I found him living in Kenwood. You know the area?"

Jane nodded, raising an eyebrow.

"Yeah, I know. He'd really come up in the world. When I'd seen him last, he didn't have a cent to his name. Right away he invited me to stay with him. I was a bit surprised by the warm welcome, so I told him I had to finish the book tour and then we'd see. In late July, I moved in. That's when I found out about his heart condition. He's not well. One afternoon he left a note saying he had to go out of town, and then two days later he returned with the story that he'd driven up to Repentance River. That surprised me even more. He said the place we stayed at all those years ago was now an inn. He'd rented a suite on the top floor and was going to drive back up the next day. If I wanted, I could come with him. I thought about it. We were getting along pretty well, and I felt it might be my only chance to get to know him better. Before ... you know. I suppose none of us knows how long we have left. Anyway, on an impulse I said yes. As we were packing, he even mentioned something about wanting time alone with me to clear the air between us. The thing is, we could have done that in Minneapolis. Why did we have to come all the way up here? He's always had a sense of the dramatic. I suppose that could be it. But ever since we've been here, he's never once broached the subject of our past. Our relationship seems to have settled into a comfortable rut based on mutual disinterest. In some ways I suppose that's all right. He's supposed to avoid stressful situations. He's a gregarious man, so he's made lots of friends here—especially with Leigh's two aunts and that old handy man, Elmer Lapinski. I don't think he was lying when he said he wanted to clear the air. But something stops him. I guess whatever it is must stop me, too." Per finished his drink. "My father is a more complex man than he lets on. The truth is, he's the mystery I'd like to write about. But I'm no closer to being able to do that now than the day we arrived. If I weren't his son I think I'd have a better chance of getting him to open up about his life. As it is, that parent-child relationship sits between us like a minefield."

"He may be afraid of you," said Jane. " 'Children begin life by loving their parents. As time goes by they judge them. Rarely, if ever, do they forgive them.' "

"Did you make that up?"

"No. Oscar Wilde did."

Cordelia's head snapped back against the chair. Her nose twitched violently as she mumbled the words, *bluf flub*.

"I'm glad we're not boring her," laughed Per. "I'd hate to think I was responsible for keeping her awake."

"You've heard of religions where people speak in tongues? Cordelia *sleeps* in tongues. I better get her upstairs before she falls on the floor and breaks something."

"Ah, the sleep of the innocent," smiled Per.

"In Cordelia's case, that hardly applies."

11

Wednesday, December 23

Winifred sat cross-legged on the unmade bed. A huge, hand-embroidered bag lay open in front of her.

"What are you doing?" asked Tess as she entered the room, briskly rubbing her short, damp hair with a towel. Dylan sat on the floor in front of the TV set, playing with a deck of cards.

"Did you have a nice shower?" Winifred smiled.

Tess walked behind the closet door and began dressing. "It was fine. Not too many people up yet." She glanced at the candles, incense, and small vials of scented oil Winifred had scattered on the bed. "Are you looking for something in particular?"

"An herb," said Winifred, her voice distracted.

Dylan slapped his small hand over a king and cried, "I won! Winney? See? I won!"

"That's great." She glanced up at Tess. "Are you going somewhere, honey?"

"I promised Michael we'd go for a walk before breakfast. Why?"

"Nothing." Winifred chewed her lower lip thoughtfully and looked down.

As Dylan continued to sputter about his card game, Tess finished buttoning her sweater and then sat down on the couch to pull on her socks. "He wants to show me around the island. He really loves it here, I can tell."

Dylan crawled across the floor and hopped up next to her. "What's that?" he asked, pointing to a birthmark on her hand.

Winifred stood and grabbed her own bath towel. "My turn. Will you stay with Dylan until I get back?"

Tess looked up. "Winney? I . . ."

"I won't be more than a couple minutes." She breezed out the door.

Tess stared uncomfortably at the little boy, inching her body away from him.

Hoisting himself up on his knees, Dylan plopped happily down onto her lap. "I wear socks, too," he said, pulling up his pants leg. "I like pink. Jimmy DeGidio says that's bad. Do you like pink? Daddy says he likes pink."

"I do," said Tess, not knowing quite where to put her hands.

Dylan looked up at her curiously. "You have pretty eyes."

"Thank you," she smiled, lightly touching his hair.

"Wanna play cards?"

"I'm sorry. I don't have much time right now."

"Okay," he said cheerfully. "My dad plays with me a lot."

"Does he? That's nice. You like your dad, don't you?"

"Yup. And Aunt Violet and Aunt Inga. And Leigh and . . . well, I kinda like Ruthie. I asked Daddy if I can have a dog. A black one."

"I have a dog," said Tess.

"Is he black?"

"No, she's brown. Her name is Custard."

Dylan wrinkled up his face. "I want to name my dog Barnacle. Isn't that beautiful!" He snuggled close. "What's that?" he asked, feeling a lump in her pocket.

"It's a Swiss Army knife. I always carry one when I go out into the woods."

"Can I see it?" he asked, poking at the lump.

Tess shrugged. "Sure. Why not." She pulled it out.

"Ooh!" said Dylan. "Neat!" He took it from her hand. "It's really neat! Can you pull this out?" He pointed to the longest blade.

Tess placed her hand over his and held it firmly. With her other hand she pulled out the blade.

"Wow! I could kill a bear with this! I saw a bear once. I wasn't scared." He looked up at her defiantly.

"Not even a little?"

"Nope!" He hopped off her lap. "See? If a bear came here now, I would save you."

"Dylan, a bear wouldn't—"

"See? Watch!" He climbed up on the bed and began jumping up and down, holding the knife like a dagger.

The door opened and Winifred entered, her towel slung over one shoulder. She smiled a smile at Tess that said, See? It wasn't so bad after all.

As her eyes danced to Dylan, her expression froze. "No!" she called, running to him.

Dylan flopped on his knees.

"Tess! How could you?" She pulled the knife away and threw it on the floor. "He's five years old. You can't let him jump around with a knife!"

Tess stood, a deep flush climbing her cheeks. Grabbing her coat and boots, she flew out the door without looking back.

* * *

After breakfast, Jane needed some fresh air to clear her head. Lack of sleep had made her mind sluggish. Once out in the woods, she began to feel a bit better. Unlike yesterday, this morning's sky was an angry gray. The temperature had risen overnight into the high thirties.

Unzipping her green-and-black plaid hunting jacket, she gazed up into the bare tree branches. Many hours ago, long before the first light had reached her window, she had awakened from an intense dream. It must have been about Beryl, though it had been so confused, she couldn't remember much of it now. Yet it had left her missing her aunt terribly. She knew she'd have to tell her father what Beryl was proposing sooner or later. The problem was, he and Beryl had never gotten along. He'd always refused to talk about why. Jane had sensed an animosity between them ever since she was a little girl. Though she didn't consider herself a coward, it had been one family closet she'd never wanted to unlock. Her aunt's arrival would no doubt rekindle a few sparks.

As Jane walked down the winding trail, her boots squeaking on the snowy path, she began to wonder what it would be like, living with someone again. After several intensely lonely years, she'd finally gotten used to being by herself. She'd even begun to enjoy it. If Beryl came, would she want to take charge? She was a strong woman, with strongly held opinions. Yet Jane knew she could hold her own. It might even be fun. She lived only a few blocks from her restaurant, so Beryl would occasionally want to take her meals there. The next question seemed to be, what room should she have? The house was certainly big enough. Three bedrooms on the second floor and a third floor she and Christine had made into a loft, complete with bathroom, kitchenette and skylights. Christine had used it partly as an office for her real estate business, and partly as a stained-glass studio. The entire house was filled with the evidence of her craftsmanship. Christine loved the traditional windows of Victorian England. She'd reproduced many of them quite faithfully. People often inquired whether Jane would sell this or that piece. The answer was always the same. She wouldn't part with a single one. She hadn't touched the third floor since Christine's death. She'd merely closed the door. Most probably Beryl would find it too removed from the activity of the house for her liking. No, one of the small rooms on the second floor would do quite nicely.

Jane could easily envision herself and Beryl together in the evening, sitting over a tea tray. She vividly remembered the teas she'd enjoyed as a young girl at her aunt and uncle's cottage. Delicate sandwiches. Anchovy toast. Little frosted cakes. Long ago she realized that she remembered her entire life in terms of the food she had eaten. People often found something vaguely suspicious about that. Perhaps, it was a bit too hedonistic. Who cares? Jane shrugged, smiling up at a squirrel sitting in a barren oak tree.

Rounding a bend in the trail, Jane entered a clearing. About fifty feet in front of her she spied a young woman sitting on a rock, bending over what looked like a notebook. She was writing furiously.

"Hello," called Jane. She hopped over a fallen tree trunk and walked towards her. "Beautiful morning."

The woman looked up.

Jane thought she noticed a flicker of fear in the woman's eyes before her face arranged itself into a tight smile.

"May I sit with you for a minute?" asked Jane. She watched the woman tear out a page and fling it down into a small ravine in back of her. It landed in a patch of melting snow.

"Why not," said the stranger.

"My name is Jane Lawless."

"Ruthie Svenby."

"Oh," said Jane, breaking into a delighted smile. "I've been wanting to meet you. You're Leigh's cousin."

The woman nodded.

"She's told me a lot about you."

"She has?" Ruthie's thin voice was immediately defensive.

Jane realized she had said the wrong thing. What Leigh had told her wasn't particularly flattering, and it seemed Ruthie must know. She tried to cover her mistake. "Yes. She's so happy to have her family living with her. She mentioned you'd moved in a couple months ago."

Ruthie nodded. "She said she was happy I was here?"

"Of course." Jane cleared her throat.

"Don't bother lying. I know what she thinks. I try too hard. I'm a pest." She looked away.

Jane took a moment to study her. Ruthie Svenby was a small woman with wispy, light brown hair and a pale, oval face. She looked a bit like an old photograph, vintage 1920. Jane noticed the nails on her right hand. Ruthie was obviously a nail biter. Though outwardly calm, Jane could feel a certain rigidity in the way she held her body. "Do you spend a lot of time out in the woods? It's so . . . quiet out here. I like that."

" 'Tis an unweeded garden," said Ruthie, her eyes shifting to the ground.

What an odd thing to say, thought Jane. It's the middle of winter.

"I should go," said Ruthie. "I'm supposed to sit at the front desk during lunch." She stood but didn't move away. "It was nice meeting you, Jane. I don't really socialize much, except with my family. Some people around here think that makes me odd. Do you think so?"

"No," said Jane, her voice gentle. In a strange way, she

found Ruthie touching. "I'm kind of a loner myself. But I think it's important to have friends. People you can talk to."

"I don't have many friends. Oh, Henry Gyldenskog is a nice man. We play checkers in the mornings. And I'd hoped Leigh and I would become close if I moved out here, but this stupid inn keeps her so busy she never has any time. I think that's awful, don't you? Sometimes it makes me so angry. She's my only cousin. Our whole family is a dead end. Leigh doesn't want children, and I'll never marry. My aunts have been good to me, but they don't understand. No one does. If you could have only known our grandpa . . . he loved me. I remember him so clearly. Especially now that I've come back to live on the island. I stayed here with my dad and him until I was five. I remember some of it real well, but other stuff . . . well, how could I remember? I was so little. Anyway, that's all gone now. But I think Leigh should have more time for me. It's wrong to ignore family. She's going to regret it one day."

"What do you mean?" asked Jane, turning to stare at her directly. It almost sounded like a threat.

"Oh," she laughed, "don't listen to me. No one else does. I'm just ranting. Maybe Aunt Inga is right. She says if you never expect anything, you'll never be disappointed."

"That's rather cynical."

"Do you think so? Aunt Violet thinks so, too. But then, she's gotten so chummy with that awful Elmer Lapinski. Maybe she should take Inga's advice. Anyway, you've been kind to listen."

"Anytime," said Jane.

Ruthie faced her for a moment. "How long will you be staying?" Her voice was oddly expressionless.

"A week. My friend Cordelia and I have to be back in Minneapolis next Monday."

"I see. Well then, I hope you have a nice time while you're here." She turned to go.

"Me, too. Thanks." Jane didn't want the conversation to end just yet. "But you know, I'm kind of concerned about all the strange goings-on around here. You don't have any idea who could be behind it, do you?"

Ruthie turned away, her profile stoney. "No. Why would you ask me?"

"Well, you've lived here since the beginning of November. You might have seen something."

Ruthie seemed startled by the suggestion. "You aren't accusing *me*, are you?"

"No," said Jane. "I'm just interested in any theories you might have."

"Theories?"

"You know? Why someone might want Leigh to sell the inn?"

"I don't have any theories." Tucking her notebook under her arm, she headed quickly across the deep snow and disappeared into the woods.

Jane sat for a moment, staring at the empty spot where Ruthie had just been standing. Leigh was right. Her cousin was a strange woman. Life in a small town could be a rich experience if a person had the right temperament. Yet for some, it must feel like a prison.

Checking the trees to make sure Ruthie was out of sight, Jane made her way carefully down the side of the ravine to retrieve the piece of paper Ruthie had thrown away. As she unfolded the soggy note, she could see that water had managed to obscure most of the writing. Very few words were still clear enough to read. Yet it was quite obviously a poem.

"_____ *solid* _____

_____ *dew*

_____

His cannon _____

Fie _____
_____ "

Jane stood for a second trying to make sense of it, then she patted the limp paper dry with a tissue and folded it, slipping it into her coat pocket. Cordelia might be able to shed some light on the origin of the poem. Most likely, it meant nothing. Then again, it might prove of some interest. Besides, it would give Cordelia an opportunity to feel gloriously superior when she was able to recite it verbatim.

On her way back up the steps into the inn, Jane bumped into Stephen, who was carrying a large brown plastic garbage sack stuffed with something soft.

"Would you believe it's my lunch?"

Jane stared down at it curiously.

"Actually, it's a bunch of old clothes. I hate to keep them around. I take a load every now and then to a Goodwill Center close to my office."

"Good idea," said Jane, catching her reflection in his mirrored sun glasses.

"Well, I'm off to a meeting. See you later." Quickly, he lifted up the sack and disappeared around the side of the house.

That was interesting, thought Jane. She wondered if the sack really contained old clothes. Or . . . ? Stop it! You're becoming paranoid, she told herself. Besides, it's almost lunch time. She could feel her stomach growling. Perhaps Cordelia would be back from her jaunt into town and ready to have lunch.

Standing before the door to her suite, Jane fished in her pocket for the door key. She entered the small sitting room and called Cordelia's name several times. No response. As she pushed open the bedroom door she shouted, "Anybody hungry in here?" The room was quiet. A funny smell tickled her nose, lodging in the back of her throat. It was almost a taste. Sweet, yet foul. What was Cordelia up to now?

Jane backed out of the doorway and pulled off her hunting jacket, tossing it over a chair. The smell seemed to linger in the room. It was too cold to open a window for very long, but Jane decided it might be smart to open the one in her own bedroom for just a few minutes. As she reached for the doorknob, she noticed a small stain on the carpeting. That was strange. It wasn't there when she'd left several hours ago. Sensing the need for caution, she slowly opened the door. A whiff of something vile reached her nose. A heavy object of some kind was preventing the door from opening all the way. She wedged her shoulder against it and pushed hard. She could feel her foot slip on something wet. What on earth was that? She switched on the overhead light and peeked carefully into the room. A deer head lay face up on the floor, it's dead eyes staring lifelessly at the ceiling. A sticky liquid oozed from the back where it had been severed from the body.

Jane could feel her stomach begin to churn. Above the door, several nails jutted out of the wall. Someone must have tried to hang it there. The heavy head probably fell to the floor after the intruder had gone. Written in blood on the wall next to the dresser were the words, *Leave Now*. Jane held her breath as she allowed her eyes to examine the sickening scene. Every drawer had been dumped on the floor. The bedspread and sheets were bunched together in a ball and stuffed into the closet. The rest of the contents of Jane's suitcases were scattered here and there. Slowly, she inched out of the room, holding her hand over her mouth. Out in the hallway, she could hear footsteps coming toward the door.

"Jane? Are you in there?" called Leigh, knocking softly. "Come here!"

Leigh opened the door. Jane's expression told her everything she needed to know. "What is it? Show me!"

Jane pointed to her bedroom.

Silently, Leigh crossed the room. "God!" She steadied herself on the door frame. "There's blood everywhere. And pieces of . . ." She turned away.

Jane shook off her nausea and grabbed Leigh by the shoulders. "It's all right. We'll deal with it."

"Are you okay?" asked Leigh.

"I'm fine. I just got back from a walk. Someone must have been in here while Cordelia and I were gone. We've got to get someone up here right away to clean this. Okay? Can you do that, Leigh?" Jane bent down and looked up into her friend's face.

"Right."

"And we've got to keep this quiet. I don't think your other guests would be very happy if they found out. As few as possible of the staff should know. Only the ones you trust not to talk. Okay?"

Leigh nodded.

"I have to go back in there to see if anything is missing. You look pretty green. Why don't you sit down for a minute."

"Good idea." Feeling dazed, Leigh dragged herself over to a chair.

Jane took a deep breath and re-entered the room. The first thing she checked was her clothing. Most of it seemed free of blood. Her shoes were scattered around, but looked undamaged. "I suppose I should check my wallet," she called, noticing it on the bed. She walked over and picked it up. "My money is all here," she said, "but . . ." She stopped.

"But what?" called Leigh.

"I don't believe it. My family pictures. They're gone."
Jane felt a shiver pass through her body.

Leigh appeared at the door. "Are you sure?"

"They're not here." She turned around, a look of revulsion on her face.

"Are you going to leave?" asked Leigh, her voice quivering.

Jane's expression hardened. "No. That's what someone obviously wants. But now, more than ever, we have to find out who's doing this. This is sick, Leigh. Don't kid yourself. This is no game anymore."

12

"He's dead!"

Michael Paget emerged breathless from the basement stairway, his face flushed with emotion. "Call someone! Please, somebody help me!"

In the dining room, Jane had just finished her late lunch with Cordelia and was sitting quietly, sipping her last cup of tea. As soon as she heard Michael shout, she jumped up and ran to the top of the stairs, catching him in her arms. "What did you say?" she demanded, trying to get him to speak more slowly.

"I don't know what to do! I tried CPR, but he's still not breathing. We need to call someone! It's Mr. Lapinski!" He grabbed her arm and pulled her down the steps. "You've got to see for yourself. He's not moving."

Burton appeared at the top of the stairs. Per stood peering over his shoulder. Both were motionless, unable or unwilling to move. "What's going on?" called Burton tentatively.

Jane motioned for them to follow as Michael dragged her further into the cellar. "Look," he cried, pointing at a body lying on the floor next to a pile of bricks. A sledge hammer leaned against the opposite wall.

"I tried to help him, but I couldn't get him to breathe!" Jane bent down to take a quick look. Elmer felt cold. She laid her ear close to his mouth. He didn't seem to be breathing. She shouted at Burton, "Call 911! Right away!"

Burton turned, bumping past Per, and ran up the stairs. Per hesitated a moment and then walked further into the room. All the color had drained from his face as he stood with his eyes fixed on the lifeless body. "I'll go up and try to keep everyone out of here."

Jane nodded her thanks. Immediately she felt for a pulse at the side of Elmer's neck. There was none. His face bore the look of a struggle. It told her very little other than he had not died peacefully. "Is this how you found him?"

"No," said Michael, kneeling down next to her. "He was over there around the corner. He'd been vomiting. I pulled him in here. Then I tried the CPR. Do you think he's going to be okay? I know people can go for a while without breathing."

Jane looked up and saw that Violet had come down and was standing next to them. "Is he dead?" she asked, covering her mouth with the back of her hand.

"I'm afraid so," said Jane.

"But I just had lunch with him less than an hour ago! He was fine. He's a strong man. How could this happen?" She backed up a step.

Jane heard the shock and pain in Violet's voice. There was nothing she could offer in explanation. Standing up, she gave the room a quick examination. The air was heavy with the smell of brick dust. And something else. She knew she was missing something important. She gave it a few seconds more but nothing connected. "Let's go back upstairs, Violet. We can't do anything else down here."

After a few weak protests, Violet agreed. "But it seems so awful to simply leave him lying here on the floor. So cold . . . so terribly cold." She covered her eyes.

Jane took off her sweater and laid it over the body. Gently, she helped Violet back up the stairs. Before she could get her seated at an empty table, Burton burst out of the swinging kitchen door, his face rigid with frustration.

"They're sending a paramedic team from the fire station in town. They'll be here any minute. Is he . . . ?" He didn't finish the sentence.

Jane nodded. "We better find Leigh. I think she may be in my suite."

"Sure. I'll get her."

Jane seated Violet at a small table near one of the bay windows. She sat down next to her, struggling for the right words to say. "You were good friends, weren't you?" she asked. The image of Elmer and Violet sitting together at the piano flashed through her mind.

Violet put a shaky hand over her eyes and began to cry.

Bingo, thought Jane. You sure have a way with words.

Michael walked hesitantly over to the table, his eyes red and swollen. He looked very young fidgeting with his belt buckle. "May I sit with you?" he asked.

Jane nodded to a chair.

He eased himself down, shyly watching Violet's quiet sobbing. "I was helping Elmer before lunch," he said softly. "Around eleven I had to leave to wait tables. I got back a little late because Burton asked me if I'd like to help him make this new sauce. He's teaching me about cooking, you know." Again, he stole a furtive glance at Violet. "The roux broke, so I was even later than I expected. I keep thinking, maybe if I'd found him sooner . . ."

Jane put her hand over his. "It's not your fault, Michael. Get that out of your mind right now. You did nothing to hurt him, and you did everything you could to help."

Michael's expression was full of gratitude.

"He was a good man," said Violet, taking a handkerchief out of her pocket and wiping her eyes. "Kind. And lonely, like me."

As she was speaking, Inga came rushing in from the front desk, her fringed shawl jerking with each heavy step. "What happened?" she asked, bending over her sister.

"I'm afraid it's Mr. Lapinski," said Jane, her voice gentle. "He's dead. I'm sorry."

Inga steadied herself on Violet's chair. "How can he be dead?"

Jane glanced up just as Ruthie peeked out of the kitchen doorway. Her eyes looked wide and frightened. A second later Burton and Leigh entered the room followed by two young paramedics. Leigh walked past the table, her fists thrust deeply into a long gray sweater. Jane was unable to read anything into her expression other than worry.

"I think I should walk you back to the gatehouse," said Inga, taking hold of Violet's thin hand. "You need to lie down. This has been a terrible shock."

"That's a good idea," said Jane. "We'll let you know what the paramedics have to say."

Once again, Violet allowed herself to be led away. She dabbed delicately at the corners of her eyes with a white linen handkerchief.

"Maybe they'll be able to help him," said Michael, nervously biting his lower lip. "You never know. I've read lots of stuff about near-death experiences. Would you like to hear some of it?"

Jane smiled, but shook her head.

They both waited in silence until Leigh emerged from the basement a few minutes later, her face full of defeat. Michael stared down into his lap, knowing instantly what the look meant.

Leigh came and stood next to him. She put a hand on his shoulder, looking tenderly down at his sad, young face. "There's nothing they can do." Her voice was just above a whisper. "Is Violet all right?"

"I don't know," said Jane. "She seemed pretty upset. Were they very close?"

"Yes," said Leigh. "They were. She and Elmer and Inga and Henry played poker over at the gatehouse almost every night after dinner."

Burton and one of the paramedics entered the room talking quietly.

"Do you have any idea how he died?" asked Jane, unable to wait any longer.

Both approached the table. "It's hard to say," said the paramedic. "He'd been violently ill. My guess is it was something he ate or drank. I suppose it could be food poisoning."

"Food poisoning!" cried Burton. "Not from *my* kitchen! God, why don't you just shoot me right here. My career is ruined!"

"Or it could be the flu. He may have aspirated something as he was vomiting. Did you notice the bluish cast to his skin? It—"

"Please," said Burton holding up his hand. "I don't think we need details."

The paramedic stared at him curiously. "All right. Whatever. Bottom line is, I think we can be fairly sure the death was accidental."

"Of course it was," said Leigh, her voice a little too defensive, "what else could it be?"

"We found a glass down on the work bench with a small

amount of liquid left in it. We haven't been able to identify it yet. We'll want to take it in for testing."

"Will you do an autopsy?" asked Jane.

"Probably. I'll have to talk to my supervisor before I can give you a definite answer. Now, I need someone to answer a few questions about the deceased."

"Of course," said Burton. "I can help you. I'll get Mr. Lapinski's file from your office, Leigh."

Leigh nodded. "The door's not locked."

The paramedic followed Burton into the other room. As Leigh watched them go, her entire body seemed to crumple. "This has turned into a complete nightmare," she said wearily. "Cordelia is out there preventing people from wandering downstairs just to take a quick peek at the body."

"Is Stephen back yet? I saw him leave around noon. I thought he was going to take the day off."

"He had a meeting with the man who is offering him that partnership. He couldn't get out of it. And that's another thing. We had a bad fight this morning. He's really pressuring me to sell. I'd pretty much come to the conclusion last night that I was going to stick it out and hope this craziness would end. But now, I don't know. Jane, what if this wasn't an accident? I can't stand to even think about it."

"Listen," said Jane, turning to Michael. "Could you go out and give Cordelia a hand? I'm sure she could use it."

"Sure," he said eagerly, glad for something to do.

Once he was gone, Jane leaned her head back against the wall; she took off her glasses and rubbed her sore eyes.

"This hasn't been much of a vacation for you, has it?" said Leigh. "What did Cordelia say when you told her about . . . about what happened to your bedroom?"

Jane shook her head. "She wasn't thrilled. I got a ten-minute lecture on my stubbornness. She said we should pack and leave. I explained that *that* was just what someone wanted. She said fine. She believed in giving people what they wanted. Then I got another ten-minute lecture on stubbornness in general, after which she pretty much gave up. She'll stay as long as we get that room cleaned before she actually sees it."

Leigh sat down at the table. "Thanks. But now with this—what if Elmer was . . . ?"

Jane shook her head. "If it really was a murder, I think it's pretty clear one of your friends or relatives has gone over the edge."

"No!" insisted Leigh. "There's got to be another explanation."

"Why can't you admit that someone around here is responsible?"

Burton popped his head into the dining room. "The paramedic has a couple of questions I can't answer, Leigh. Could you deal with it?"

Leigh got up. "I'll be right there." Turning her back on Jane, she walked to the window and looked out. A light snow had begun falling. The woods to the south looked indistinct, as if seen through thin gauze. "It's so beautiful." She put her hand to her forehead and rubbed her temple, closing her eyes and leaning her head against the cold window pane. "I better go," she whispered. "I just want this day to end."

13

Inga bent over the ironing board, pressing one of Ruthie's favorite blouses. Violet had finally fallen asleep in the front room. It had taken a large glass of wine and at least half an hour of soothing words, but Inga had at last been able to sneak back into the kitchen. She hated just *sitting*—especially when she was as upset as she was right now. How could this have happened? Was Violet being willingly obtuse? Didn't she see what was going on? Calm down, Inga told herself. It won't do anyone any good if you have a stroke. Keep your wits about you. She patted her chest. Yes, that was better. Calm. Think.

Even though this was a disaster, someone had to pick up the pieces and make sure nothing worse happened. If Violet refused to deal with reality, Inga would have to do it herself. Violet had never been very good at facing bitter truths. She was too much of an optimist. Such a useless approach to life. Long ago Inga had realized one of the worst crosses she would ever have to bear was her sister's sloppy, sentimental optimism. There was no way to show an optimist the dark side. They just kept hoping for the best. Pure horse manure. Look at Elmer. A year from now he'd been going to retire. Live the good life. He'd saved his money for a comfortable old age. Look where it got him.

Inga flipped back the collar of Ruthie's blouse and noticed a small tear near the top button hole. She would have

91

to mend it before it got any larger. The utter simplicity of such an ordinary thought stopped her. Wasn't that always the answer? Take care of your own. Sitting down at the kitchen table, she looked out the gatehouse window, watching the fat snowflakes float silently onto the walk leading up to the inn. It wasn't hard to remember years ago when the big house across the way had been full of life and joy. She could still see her father in his bib overalls, standing at the workbench in the basement making some new toy for Ruthie. He loved to work with wood. Almost as much as he loved children. Silly old fool. He'd been an elementary school teacher all his life. An optimist just like Violet. Look where it got him! He trusted people. Trusted his own son. Daniel, Ruthie's no-good father, had been his worst and last mistake. Yet except for that flaw, Harlan Svenby had been an intelligent, decent man. After he'd retired from teaching, he hadn't had much of a chance to be around children anymore. Ruthie must have seemed like a gift from heaven. Inga could still hear Ruthie's voice echoing in the front hall. "Grandpa Harlan! Let's go outside. Let's play ball!" Every day he would take her somewhere. Swimming in the summer. Sliding in winter. Ruthie followed him around like a little puppy. They were inseparable. They even took their afternoon naps together. His death was the single worst thing ever to happen in Ruthie's life. The sadness had never left her eyes. Violet said she was exaggerating, but Inga knew what she saw.

She turned down the heat on the iron. These new synthetics were a pain in the you know what. Inga and Violet had moved to town several months before Daniel and Ruthie arrived back home. Inga could still hear Daniel's voice, pleading with their father to take them in. If only Daniel hadn't been so shiftless. If only he'd tried a little harder. He always thought of himself as life's great exception. Rules didn't apply to Daniel Svenby. It was a shame.

And such a good-looking boy. Dark, creamy skin. Well built. He could have been anything if he'd just put his mind to it. Look how he ended up. He wasn't the kind of example Ruthie needed. Inga had never admitted this to a single soul, but when her brother died, she wasn't sorry. Not the way a sister should be. No, it was a good thing Ruthie had her grandpa those first few years.

"Inga?" came a weak voice from the next room. "Could I have another sip of wine?"

"Of course, dear," called Inga. Her heart skipped a beat. Lifting down the bottle of Port from the top cupboard, she filled a small jelly jar with the ruby colored liquid and pulled the plug on the iron. One couldn't be too careful. Entire houses had burned down from leaving electric cords plugged in. Violet didn't believe her, but it was true.

"Here it is," she said, entering the living room. Violet's bony form was lying quietly on the couch. "Do you feel any better?"

Violet took a taste before speaking. "Yes, I think I do." She touched her hair. "I must look a sight."

"It was a terrible shock."

Violet nodded. "Have you heard anything more?"

Inga shook her head. "I've been ironing in the kitchen. I didn't want to leave you alone."

"That was sweet of you, dear. But maybe you should go back over there. See what they've found out."

"All right. Perhaps I should."

The back door opened.

"Must be Ruthie," said Violet.

"Must be," agreed Inga. "We're in here, dear."

Ruthie shuffled into the room looking exhausted.

"Is anything wrong?" asked Inga. "Why don't you come sit down? Talk to us for a minute."

"Nothing's wrong."

"You look awfully tired," said Violet.

"It's nothing. I think I'll lie down."

"You're sure you don't want to have a nice little chat first? I could make some fresh coffee." Inga's smile was strained. "Ruthie, this isn't like you. Please don't shut us out. You need us."

"I'm just tired! Really. Nothing to worry about. We can have dinner together later. Or something. Okay?"

"Did you hear about Elmer?" asked Violet, her voice very high and childlike.

Ruthie nodded. "I'm sorry. He was a nice man."

Violet sniffed.

"Yes he was, dear," said Inga.

"That's kind of you to say so," said Violet.

"Sure." Ruthie opened the door to her room and then shut it quickly behind her.

14

"How nice of you to join me," said Cordelia, a thermometer dangling casually from the corner of her mouth. In the dim afternoon light of the small sitting room, she sat draped over an arm chair, one hand pressed dramatically to her forehead. "I figured you'd be along any minute."

Jane plunked down in a chair opposite her. "Leigh's in her office talking to the police. I was just in the way." She kicked off her boots. "Do you have a fever?"

Cordelia pulled the thermometer out and eyed it suspiciously. "No. It's normal. I was just checking. You can't be too careful with winter colds."

Jane nodded. "God, wasn't that awful?"

"Which?" Cordelia's eyes traveled slowly across the rug to a large, dark stain just inside Jane's bedroom door.

Jane winced. She'd hoped the clean-up crew could erase it completely.

"This is not my idea of rest and relaxation," muttered Cordelia, lifting up a large tote bag and setting it in her lap. "So, what's the answer? Was Elmer's death an accident? What's going on around here!"

"I wish I knew. I can't help but think it goes a lot deeper than someone merely wanting Leigh to sell the inn."

Cordelia withdrew a can of cream soda and set it on the table between them. A second later several candy bars and a sack of cheese puffs appeared, followed by a package of chocolate cupcakes. "It helps me think."

Jane rolled her eyes.

"Well it does." She ripped open the cheese puffs and popped several into her mouth. "Now, you may begin your theorizing. Fortified with this abundance of brain food, I shall be able to instantly detect any wrong turns."

In spite of her mood, Jane began to laugh.

Cordelia leaned back more comfortably and attempted a look of thoughtful interest.

"I suppose I should take advantage of your willingness to listen."

"You should." Cordelia wiggled her eyebrows. "You have my complete attention."

"All right." She lifted her feet onto the coffee table and leaned back into her chair. "First of all, it seems to me that other than Leigh, there are six people staying here right now who have a past attachment to this house."

"Five," said Cordelia. "Leigh's two aunts, her cousin, and Per and Henry."

"You're forgetting Tess."

"Tess?"

"I'm almost positive she's been here before. Even Winifred mentioned that she was unusually familiar with the house."

"Interesting. Okay, six. But what's the point?"

"That's just it. Whoever is responsible for all the inn's problems has to be familiar with the house. That someone would have to have access day and night—or know how to *gain* access without calling attention to themselves."

"Or, maybe it's someone whose presence wouldn't be seen as anything out of the ordinary."

"Exactly. I don't care how much Leigh wants a comfortable answer, it's not some stranger from town. It's someone right here."

"But what's the motive?"

"Well, the most obvious is that someone simply wants to buy this place. Since Leigh is disinclined to sell, creating enough problems to force her hand financially would be a clever way to gain a certain leverage."

"You mean Henry." She chewed thoughtfully on a cheese puff.

"Yes. But I doubt it stops at simple ownership. Someone has gone to great lengths to drive Leigh out of here. There's a deeper reason, I'm sure of it."

"Like what?"

"That's just it. There's something—some piece of the puzzle—that's missing. Or perhaps it just hasn't become apparent yet."

"Oh goody." Cordelia opened the can of pop. "Something to look forward to."

Jane shook her head.

"So, who do you suspect?"

"Well, Henry of course. He could have a hidden reason

for wanting to buy the inn. And then there's Ruthie. She's a strange one. Closed off. I find her almost unreadable."

"It's anger."

"What do you mean?"

"I knew someone like her once. She worked at this crummy little bar where I used to hide after we were done rehearsing. It was the year I directed several Ibsen plays at The Blackstone Playhouse."

"I remember," nodded Jane.

"She was a waitress, and since it was usually pretty late when I got there, we always seemed to end up talking. Somewhere in her life she'd been hurt very badly. She never told me any of the details, but I assumed it had something to do with her childhood. At first I thought she was simply depressed. But as I got to know her better, I realized she was holding in all this rage. Rage at herself, at the world, and someone very specific. You know, even though I've only talked with Ruthie once, she reminds me a lot of this woman. Unless I miss my guess, she's repressing a great deal of anger."

"Anger at who?"

Cordelia shrugged. "I doubt even *you* will be able to drag that out of her."

Jane thought for a moment. "I know she's upset with Leigh for not spending more time with her."

Cordelia sat quietly and sipped her pop. The bag of cheese puffs in her lap was emptying rapidly. "How about Burton?"

"Burton! What makes you think he has anything to do with this?"

"I don't know. Maybe he doesn't. But if you're looking for motives, I can tell you that he's really frustrated with Leigh."

"He is? Why?"

"Well, I'm not sure exactly. When we were making

cookies yesterday, I could sense it. I don't remember any
specific comments, but it was definitely there."

Jane considered it for a moment. "You know, he was the
one who prevented Leigh from drinking that tea on Monday. But then he did something really stupid. He tossed the
box into the fire."

"Covering his tracks?"

Jane shook off the question. "Probably just bad judg-
ment."

"Okay. I'll accept that—for now. But what about Leigh's
aunts? You haven't mentioned them yet." She coughed into
a tissue.

"Yes. I've thought about that too. They have easy access
and plenty of opportunity, but once again, I don't have a
motive."

"I can think of someone with a very apparent motive.
Someone you've left out completely."

"You mean Stephen."

Cordelia nodded, raising an elegant eyebrow. "Didn't
Leigh say he wanted her to sell? He wants to use the
money to invest in some deal of his."

Jane looked down at her hands. "I think Leigh's terribly
threatened by that idea. It's the real reason she refuses to
see what's actually happening around here."

"She's making a mistake if she doesn't keep a sharp eye
on that guy."

"Why do you say that?"

Cordelia set the empty pop can down on the table with
a loud crack. "Janey, give me some credit. I've spent my
entire adult life in the theatre. I recognize acting when I see
it. Stephen is lying to Leigh. I know you're absolutely convinced the motive is something deep and dark, but wouldn't
it be interesting if it was as simple and grossly apparent as
greed? Think about it, dearheart. In the end, old Cordelia
might just be right."

15

Late in the afternoon, after the paramedics had gone, Burton found Jane sitting alone near a window in the parlor. The snow had finally stopped. The sky over the little town of Repentance River had turned a deep shade of peach.

"Would it be completely callous of me to ask you to take a look at that old summerhouse?" he asked. He leaned over to get a better view of the sunset. "I'd like to get my mind on something else for a while. I know it's probably a bad time, but you won't be here much longer, and I really need your input if I'm going to convince Leigh the renovation is possible."

Jane stretched and stood up, rubbing the back of her neck. "Sure. Why not? This whole day has been a disaster. I might as well do something useful."

Burton grinned. "Get your coat. I'll meet you in the kitchen."

Five minutes later they were standing in a large, run-down, screened building, walking off the distances between various points. The summerhouse was isolated from the main house by a thick patch of pine. It seemed an empty, alien shrine to another age.

"I think we could easily put fifty to sixty additional seats in here," said Burton. "Don't you think this is a great old

building? Look at that ceiling. All that beautiful tile. We'd
want to restore it. I see lots of windows and plants. Sort of
like a greenhouse. With the kind of interest I'm already
generating from the Twin Cities, we'd be filling this every
weekend. It won't be long before we'd be filling it every
night."

"It has a lot of possibilities," said Jane, silently admiring
the space. She knew Burton was aware of the inn's financial problems, but didn't want to dampen his spirits by telling him Leigh might be forced to sell. And anyway, the
restaurant was still making money. Leigh might still be able
to pull through. "The proportions are really quite lovely.
Whoever built it must have done a great deal of summer
entertaining. With that stone fireplace, you'd be warm
enough out here late into the fall."

Burton kicked a piece of broken pottery out of his way.
"Of course we'd have to enclose it completely. I don't
know what I'm going to do without Elmer. He always had
such good ideas. I suppose I'll have to get someone else
out here to finish the wine cellar. I've got a wine tasting
booked for the first part of February. We've got to get it
completed and stocked before that." He settled his bulk
down on a crate. "I don't mean to sound uncaring. I liked
the old guy. I talked to him a lot about my plans."

"Do you have a lot of plans?" asked Jane.

"I know what you're thinking." He leaned back against
a rusty screen and stroked his mustache. "You think I'm
overstepping my bounds. If I were you I'd think the same
thing. But you aren't working here. Take it from me, there's
big trouble coming. The place started out with such a bang.
This inn could make tons of money if it was handled properly. The only part that's really taken off is the restaurant,
and it's my goddamn ass that's on the line there, pardon my
French."

"You're paranoid," smiled Jane.

Burton looked at her carefully, narrowing one eye. "Come on, Jane. You and I both know I'm not. I quit a great job to take over as head chef here. I could see the potential right from the first. I mean, in some ways, the inn doesn't even have to make money. Given time, the food service will support everything. The inn part would just be gravy. This may sound strange, but in the past few weeks, it's almost like Leigh's lost interest. Every time I need her she's asleep upstairs. I know she's been under a lot of stress recently with all the crazy things happening around here. We all have. But she's got to get a grip! Or, and I know you probably won't approve of this either, she should sell." He glanced up defiantly. "Somebody would buy it in a minute."

Jane knocked an icicle down from the ceiling. "You're pretty entrenched here, aren't you?"

"Do you blame me? I've finally found a place where I can make my reputation as a chef. It's something I've been looking for ever since I graduated from that culinary institute out East. Chances like this don't fall in your lap every day, you know. And I'll be damned if I'll let Leigh's disorganization and lack of attention ruin my future. I don't want this just for myself, I want a safe, secure home for Dylan. It's better for him, growing up in the country. Ever since Nan died, I don't mind telling you it's been a struggle. But I finally feel like I'm making some progress. I can't just roll over and play dead because Leigh has a headache."

Jane could see his point. Still, she wondered how deep his frustration with Leigh went, and to what lengths he might go to make sure his position was permanent. "Well, I'll try to get her to take a look tomorrow. I think you're right. Your ideas will work. It's just going to take the right plan."

"I know," said Burton, pulling on his mustache. "And I've got the perfect plan." He stood, checking his watch.

"Thanks, Jane. I know I'm kind of on edge with everything
that's been happening. I appreciate your patience. I'm more
upset about Elmer than I'm showing. It's weird, isn't it? He
looked fine this morning when I went downstairs to check
on his progress."

"You saw him this morning?" said Jane. "What time was
that?"

"Let me think. Sometime after ten. I'd just finished with
lunch prep. He and Michael hadn't gotten much of a start
on the wall yet. Per and his father were down there milling
around. When Henry Gyldenskog gets going, you can't shut
him up."

Of course, thought Jane. That was it! That was what she
had missed earlier this afternoon down in the cellar. It was
the smell of pipe smoke. The only person she'd seen with
a pipe was Henry. But ten o'clock? Surely the smell would
have dissipated by the time they found Elmer's body. That
was nearly two in the afternoon. Unless? Had Henry gone
back downstairs later? Closer to the time Elmer died? "Do
you know why they were there?"

Burton shrugged. "When I walked in, Henry was trying
to convince Elmer that the best place for the wine cellar
was in another part of the basement. That guy thinks he
knows something about everything. He and Elmer had become pretty tight. When I came in on the conversation,
Elmer was saying he'd already had the same discussion
with someone else and he was sick of hearing about it.
What was the big deal, anyway? Since I was standing there,
I briefly explained my own reasons, and that ended it. What
could he say?"

"Do you know who else had tried to change Elmer's
mind?"

"No idea. He never said."

"Was Henry upset that you didn't take his suggestion?"

"Nah," said Burton, zipping up his jacket. "He could see he wasn't getting anywhere."

Jane walked over and examined the stonework around the hearth. "I don't suppose you saw anyone else down there?"

Burton shook his head. "Nope. Except for Ruthie. She was looking for something in one of the storerooms. Have you met her yet?"

"Just briefly," said Jane. "What do you know about her? I assume you've talked some."

"I'm not sure anybody knows Ruthie," said Burton. "I guess she lived here when she was a child. She and her father—I believe his name was Daniel—went to live with Violet and Inga when she was about five. That was after her grandfather died. From what I'm told, Violet, Inga, and Leigh's mother, Constance, were all years older than this Daniel. There's a lot of town gossip about him, too. He didn't work and he liked his liquor. If you ask me, the whole family is a little cracked. Except for Inga. She's such a great cook, I have to cut her a little slack. You understand."

"Of course," smiled Jane. "Completely."

"Well, if there's going to be any dinner tonight, I better get back to the kitchen. I've got some prime rib that needs checking."

"I'm going to stay out here for a few more minutes," said Jane, leaning against the fireplace. "Say, Burton, before you go, just one more thing. A thought just occurred to me. When did you first propose building the wine cellar?"

Burton lowered his head and thought for a moment. "Let's see. I guess it must have been late October, early November. I'd just put in my winter order with the wine distributor. He gave me the idea. Why?"

"Just curious."

"No problem," said Burton. "See you later, then." He pushed open the rusted screen door and steamed off toward the kitchen.

Jane stood in the growing darkness, listening to the sound of birds nestling into the tall pine trees for the night. So, a wine cellar was first proposed in early November. Could that be the event that precipitated all the inn's problems? What would someone have against a wine cellar? Still, other things had happened around that time too. Ruthie had moved into the gatehouse. Stephen began putting in lots of overtime. And what else had Leigh said? A new greengrocer had started making deliveries to the island. Jane had to agree. It was unlikely that meant much. But which events were significant? That was the big question.

In the distance, she could see the old house, its delicate gables gothic against the winter moon. Perhaps in the end, Stephen was right. Leigh should simply sell and cut her losses. Nothing was worth endangering people's lives.

Outside the summerhouse a branch snapped.

Intent on her own thoughts, Jane almost dismissed it. It was a small sound, yet something about it startled her. She couldn't help turning her head. Slowly, she moved from her spot next to the fireplace and crept over to a large hole in the screen. She listened for a moment. Everything was quiet. Even the birds in the trees had stopped their cacophony of bedtime chirping. Damn. Perhaps an animal had scared them. That was possible. But what if it was something else? Hastily, she took one last look around. She'd seen enough to know Burton's ideas would work. It was best to get inside now. Away from the dark. Before stepping through the hole, she arranged her keys between each finger, making a tight fist. Better to err on the side of caution.

Once outside, the night quickly closed in around her. High in the trees, a maze of black branches twitched and groaned in the wind. What had once seemed simply empty now was full of menace. She moved fast. The inn wasn't far away. She'd be safe once she got inside. This was silly, she told herself, sidestepping a patch of ice. Don't be such a baby.

"Excuse me," said a man stepping out from behind a tree. His hands were hidden deep in his jacket pockets.

Instantly Jane jumped back.

"Please," he said, reaching out to touch her. "I didn't mean to scare you."

"No!" she said, her eyes darting from side to side, figuring the best way of escape.

"Really. Don't be afraid." He withdrew his hand. "I just want to ask you a favor." Both arms shot up in the air like a man being arrested.

"A favor?" repeated Jane, still preparing to run.

"Right. Just a favor. Nothing else. I'm sorry I scared you. Really. Do you know a woman named Tess Ingman?"

That stopped her. She stared at him for a moment. He was very tall and lanky. At least six foot five. Even in the dim light she could see the scruffy beard he wore covered the scars from a bad case of adolescent acne.

The man waited, allowing her time to think. "I thought for a minute you were her," he said. "I mean, you look a little like her. I can see now that your hair is long. You've got it put up in that . . . thing." He twirled his finger.

"Who are you?" she asked, feeling the rigid keys between each finger.

"My name is Bo Dierdorf. I run a small grocery store in town. I've been making deliveries out here for a couple of months." He pulled off his cap and held out his hand.

Jane noticed now that he was going bald. "You're the new greengrocer?"

"I suppose I am. Are you a guest at the inn?"

Jane nodded, ignoring his outstretched hand.

"Great! So maybe you could do me this favor. I thought I saw someone I knew in town today. I haven't seen her for almost eighteen years. But I was sure it was her. The thing is, I don't know if her last name is still Ingman. But if there's a Tess staying in there," he nodded toward the house, "would you give her this message?"

Jane shrugged. "Why don't you go in and ask at the front desk yourself? I'm sure they have a list of guests."

His expression grew wary. "Well, see, it's like this. I'm not sure she'll want to talk to me. We didn't part . . . friends, let's say. Look, if you see her, will you just tell her Bo wants to talk to her. Just that. She'll know who I am. And give her this phone number." He pulled out a piece of paper and a pen, jotting it down. "Thanks a lot. See, this way, she can call or not. It's up to her."

Jane took the paper and stuffed it into the pocket of her jeans.

"What are you doing out here, anyway?" he asked, turning to look at the summerhouse.

"The inn is thinking of turning that into a second dining room. They need more seating space."

"Oh," said Bo. "I got it. But it's kind of a waste, isn't it? I mean, why wreck something as neat as that old place just for some restaurant."

"A lot of people think it's an eyesore."

Bo scratched his beard. "Crazy assholes. You don't just tear down other people's history. Sometimes it's better to leave old things alone. Build something new."

"That's an interesting philosophical point," said Jane. "And I think I probably agree with you. But I'm not so sure it applies to buildings."

"Even buildings," said Bo, looking at her very directly. "Sometimes it's not safe to tamper with the past."

16

"Fire away," said Henry, filling his pipe from a small pouch he'd lifted from his pocket. "I have no secrets from my son."

Jane had waited until after dinner to speak with Per and Henry. There were a couple of questions she hoped the senior Mr. Gyldenskog could clear up. A few minutes ago when she had knocked on their door, Henry had been only too delighted to talk to her. Per, on the other hand, seemed slightly annoyed that he'd been interrupted. He'd been working at the computer in his bedroom and only grudgingly agreed to turn it off and come into the sitting room.

"What did you want to speak to me about?" asked Henry.

"It's about this morning," Jane began.

Henry eased back into his chair; he lit his pipe and sucked deeply. "Yes?"

"I understand you and Per were downstairs talking to Elmer. You were trying to convince him to put the wine cellar in some other part of the basement."

Henry puffed for a few moments. "Right, I think we did talk about that. You understand of course, it was just conversation. I mean, what the hell would I care one way or the other?" He smiled, displaying a set of uneven, badly discolored teeth.

"I don't know," said Jane. "That's why I'm asking. There was no other reason?"

"A reason?" repeated Henry. "No. Not really. Jane, you don't know me very well. I'm a big conversationalist. Ask Per. Ask anyone around here. I love to talk. When you get old, all you have is time." He pulled the pipe out of his mouth and frowned. "That was terrible about Elmer. He was a good friend of mine."

"You talked to him a lot?"

"Sure. We had a great deal in common. He lost his wife years ago just like me. His death was such a rotten shame."

"Elmer said someone else was trying to change his mind about the location of the wine cellar. Do you know who that was?"

Henry hesitated a fraction of a second too long. "Why no," he said mildly. "No idea."

"You're sure? You don't remember anybody commenting on it?"

"No." His voice was firm.

"All right. Did you go back downstairs later?"

"Later? Why would you think that?"

"Just curious. If you did, you might have seen something you didn't realize was important."

"Why no. I don't remember going back down."

Jane was sure he was lying. She decided to try something. "I'm afraid someone saw you."

Henry bit down hard on his pipe. Slowly, his face broke into a smile. "I guess you caught me," he sighed. "You're right. I did go back down for just a minute."

Per stood. "Why did you lie, Dad?"

"Now Per, I wasn't lying."

"Of course you were!"

"Sit down. Don't get so excited. You're just like your mother. I merely thought it was best not to say anything.

After all, if he *was* . . . murdered . . . how would that look? Maybe I was the last person to see him alive."

"What time did you last talk to Elmer?" asked Jane.

"Oh, I don't know. I suppose about one-thirty. He seemed just fine to me. Oh, he often complained about his digestion. That was another thing we had in common. I think he did say something about needing an antacid. But that's all. He was fine, really." He showed Jane his most disarming smile.

"Why did you have to go back to the basement?" demanded Per. "What's going on?"

"Nothing is going on! You're acting like you think I had something to do with his death. I simply wanted to ask him a question."

"What?" demanded Per.

"Well, I wanted to know if he had any interest in inviting the girls—"

"The girls?" repeated Jane.

"You know. Inga and Violet."

Per groaned."They're women, Dad. Have you been living in a vault for the last twenty years?"

"Huh? Oh, of course. Sorry. Anyway, the four of us liked to take in a movie every now and then. There was a new one showing in town, and I wanted to know if Elmer was free tonight."

"That was all?" asked Per.

"Scout's honor." He raised his hand.

"And no one else came down while you were talking to him?" asked Jane.

"No. No one."

Per seemed about to speak but changed his mind. He paced in front of the TV set, deep in thought.

Jane wasn't completely convinced Henry was telling the truth, but she had no way of disputing his statement. Per seemed to be ill at ease about it, too. Yet if Henry did have something to hide, he certainly wasn't going to incriminate himself. Jane knew this was about all she was going to get.

"Thanks," she said, rising from her chair. "I hope you don't think I'm prying. I'm just trying to put Leigh's mind to rest about some of this. You understand. She's a very good friend. Hopefully we'll find Elmer's death was completely natural."

"Was there ever any doubt?" asked Henry, twisting out of his chair. He tucked the evening paper under one arm.

"I haven't heard anything more," said Jane.

"Well, let's hope we don't," smiled Henry. He put his arm around her and walked her to the door. "You come visit me anytime. Do you play checkers?"

Per went back to his room and turned on the stereo.

"Not very well," said Jane above the music.

"Good. I like someone I can beat. I often play with Ruthie in the mornings. We've gotten to be quite good friends. I like to think I'm the kind of person people can confide in. And then there's Stephen. He values a good game of chess. I even taught Leigh's two aunts how to play poker." He laughed. "I think I taught them too well. They've cleaned me out once too often. It's the damnedest thing. I've spent years trying to perfect a poker face, and those two ladies were born with theirs."

"Oh?" said Jane.

"Sure. You'd never know what those two are thinking unless they let you in on it. I'd be a richer man today if I had that talent."

"You're sure you don't?"

Henry's smile was indulgent. "Why Jane, I can't hide anything. It's impossible. Lies make my nose grow."

17

"And so the little red fox jumped out of his hole and ran all the way home. He never again looked for the shiny penny. He didn't need to." Winifred shut the book and put her arm around Dylan. "Did you like that story?" she asked, smoothing back his curly brown hair.

Dylan reached down and grabbed another book off the floor. "Now read this one," he said eagerly. "*Elroy the Elephant*. It's my favorite."

"I thought *The Little Red Fox* was your favorite," said Winifred.

"No," insisted Dylan. "That *was* my favorite. But *Elroy the Elephant* is my favorite now."

"I see." She took the book from his hand and opened it to the first page.

Jane stuck her head into the bedroom. "I thought I might find you two up here."

"Jane!" said Dylan, jumping off the couch and running to her.

She picked him up and gave him a hug.

"Wanna see what I made all by myself?"

"Sure."

Scrambling out of her arms, he raced over to his desk. "Look," he cried, holding up a white paper snowflake. "Winifred showed me how, but I did it all by myself." He beamed proudly.

111

"Bring a couple of them over here," said Jane, sitting down. She watched him pad across the floor in his over-sized night slippers. "Did you really make these?" she asked, looking at him seriously.

He nodded.

"They're absolutely wonderful. But what are you going to do with them?"

Dylan seemed puzzled.

"Maybe Aunt Violet or Aunt Inga would help you hang them up downstairs in the parlor," suggested Winifred. "That way everyone can see them."

Dylan was delighted by the idea. "Can I go down now?" he asked.

"Yes, you can," said Winifred, watching him run over and gather the remaining stack off his desk. "But be careful, you don't want to tear them."

"No," he shook his head.

"I think you'll find Aunt Inga at the front desk," said Jane.

Dylan held the snowflakes delicately out in front of him as he scooted out of the room.

"Remember," shouted Winifred, "bedtime is in half an hour."

Jane sat for a moment enjoying the feeling of being in a small child's bedroom. In the far corner was a large bean-bag chair, piled high with stuffed animals. Along another wall, a built-in shelf bulged with toys, games, and other childhood miscellany. The entire room was tucked snugly under one of the third floor eaves, creating a warm, inviting space for a little boy. An adult would have trouble with the low sloping ceiling, but Dylan was just the right size. Jane glanced at Winifred, noting that she, too, was admiring the space. "It's a great room, isn't it? Kind of reminds me of a house in England I lived in once."

Winifred fluffed the pillow behind her. "Yeah. Dylan

loves it. His window overlooks the barn. He can watch the horses out in the pasture from up here."

"You like children, don't you?" said Jane.

Her eyes softened. "Is it that obvious? You know, when I was in my early twenties, I thought I would never have children of my own. Unless I got married and either repressed my sexuality or fought some hideous court battle to adopt, children would never be a part of my life. I'm so glad things are changing. I mean, you and I both know there's a baby boom happening out there in the gay and lesbian community. Tess and I have many friends who either have kids, are thinking of having kids, or are pregnant."

"So what about you and Tess?" asked Jane. "Have you two thought about it?"

Winifred glanced sadly at the stuffed animals. "Tess won't even consider it. She says she's no good with children. And you know, by the way she interacts with them, I'd have to agree. On our drive up here, I thought I'd bring up the subject one last time. It's been on my mind a lot lately, and I thought since we had a couple of hours, we might talk things out. But all I could get her to say was that some people weren't cut out to be parents, and she was one of them. I suppose in theory, that's true. It certainly would be better to know something like that about yourself before you have the child. It's just that she's so adamant. And, at the same time, I can tell it makes her terribly sad. But what can I do? She says she knows herself better than I do and, for her, it would be a mistake. I have to honor that. I mean, I'd expect the same from her."

Jane pulled some crayons out from between the couch cushions. "I'm really sorry, Winney. I've never wanted children myself, but I enjoy them very much. I'm sure this is extremely hard for you. On the other hand, who knows? Maybe she'll change her mind."

"I'm not holding my breath. It's funny. Once Tess agreed

to come up here for the week, she just closed off. At first I thought it was because she felt I was pressuring her about having a child. Now I'm not so sure. The fact is, I don't have a clue to what's going on. I'm almost certain she's been here before, but when I question her about it she insists she hasn't."

Jane could see how upset Winifred was. She felt for the slip of paper inside her pocket. The one the man out by the summerhouse had given her. "Look, Winney, maybe I shouldn't be telling you this, but late this afternoon, when I was out looking at that summerhouse with Burton, I ran into a guy from town. His name is Bo. He wanted to know if someone named Tess Ingman was staying at the inn. I think he assumed from my reaction that I didn't know her. He asked if I'd find out for him. He gave me his phone number to give to her. According to what he said, he knew her eighteen years ago."

"I don't understand," said Winifred, clearly perplexed. "I've never heard her mention anyone named Bo. What made him think she was here?"

"He said he saw her in town this morning. From a distance. I don't think he was absolutely certain it was her. There are only a few motels around here. He's probably checking them all. The reason he didn't want to ask at the front desk himself was because, for some reason, they didn't part friends. Here's the number. Will you give it to her?"

Winifred took the slip. "What do you think this means?"

"I don't know," said Jane. "Maybe they knew each other in college. Didn't you tell me she went to the University of Minnesota?"

Winifred nodded.

"If you'd rather not pass it along, I will. I just thought . . ."

"No," said Winifred, slipping the note into her pocket.

"I'll make sure she gets it. It's just, I'm wondering if this isn't part of what she's been unwilling to talk about. I never thought we had any secrets. I don't understand what would cause her to keep something from me. Or worse, to lie." She thought for a moment. "You know, when Tess started coming to my new moon group about a month ago, I felt she was beginning to deal with something. Something pretty intense. At first, I was simply delighted she was showing an interest in such an important part of my life. Later, it struck me that she might be looking for something herself. Something quite specific. I figured she'd eventually tell me about it. She's not someone you can push."

"How long have you been a witch?" asked Jane.

"About seven years. It's hard for me to be absolutely accurate. I think I developed a certain spirituality in my life and only later found out it was witchcraft. Other women I've talked to have had the same experience. We seem to do it intuitively."

"What was that?" asked Jane, her ears picking up a noise right outside the door.

"What was what?"

Jane rose and moved quietly across the room. She motioned for Winifred to keep talking.

Winifred continued on the same subject, watching Jane tiptoe silently toward the closed door.

After listening a second longer, Jane pushed the door open and looked outside. The hallway was deserted, but at the far end of the hall she could hear the unmistakable sound of footsteps descending the stairs.

"Who is it?" whispered Winifred.

"I don't know. But it's not the first time I've felt someone was eavesdropping on a conversation." She walked back to the couch.

"Creepy."

Jane wanted to tell her about what had happened in her

room earlier in the day, but thought better of it. "They're
gone now. What were we talking about?"

Winifred seemed to have some difficulty regaining her
train of thought. "Oh yes, I remember now. I was saying
how upset I was about the way the solstice ritual ended the
other night. It was a disaster. But since I couldn't do anything about it, I just kept quiet. The problem is, we never
had a chance to deal with all the power we summoned."

"I don't understand," said Jane. She glanced toward the
door, still feeling a bit uneasy about who might have been
out in the hallway.

"Well, we raised a great deal of energy. You could feel
it, I'm sure. When you tap into something like that, you
need to perform what is called a grounding ritual before
you're done. That channels the excess energy safely back
into the earth. But everything ended before we had a
chance to complete the ceremony. Later, my coven got together to perform the ritual, but we had no opportunity to
do it as a group."

"What happens if you don't?" asked Jane. "Is there a
problem?"

"That's hard to say. Sometimes, when you don't ground
energy properly, people tend to have accidents. I don't entirely understand it myself. This is the dark part of the
year—the Goddess of the night reigns supreme. Under the
best of circumstances, it's often a difficult period. This inn
is a good example right now. Something is very wrong
here, don't you feel it? I'm not speaking about the inn's
current problems, but the essential karma. There's a gloom
pervading the very essence of this house. It's almost like
something is trapped. Blocked. I feel a frustration and a
very deep anger."

Jane listened closely, her skin beginning to prickle with
a strange sense of dread. "What can we do about it?"

"Bridge!" shouted Cordelia from the doorway.

Jane turned. "What did you say?"

Cordelia sneezed. "Excuse me. It's my incipient pneumonia. What I said was, a game of bridge is the solution." She bounced into the room nearly banging her head on the sloping ceiling. "I just caught your last sentence so I thought I'd offer my insights on the subject."

"And what was the subject?" asked Jane. "What's the game of bridge a solution to?"

"Well," said Cordelia, blowing her nose loudly into a tissue, "a dreary evening at The Fothergill Inn, of course. This house is like a mausoleum tonight. I don't mean to sound heartless, but can't we try to get our minds on something a little less heavy—just for a few hours. Tess is down in the parlor waiting for me to drag you two down there. Dylan has just finished installing his most recent kinetic art exhibit in the foyer, all of which—in true minimalist fashion—he merely refers to as 'Untitled Snowflake,' numbers one through one hundred and nineteen. And, at this very moment, he is being rounded up for bed. So. The fire is roaring. Burton has promised to provide beer and munchies. What more could simple folks like us ask on a wintery evening in the wilds of Minnesota?"

18

Thursday, December 24

"Will you repeat that again?" asked Burton, juggling the phone while trying to find a pencil. "An alkaloid, probably phytolaccine. Can you spell that?" He copied it down on a note pad. "And what else? Saponin? Okay," he said. "I've got it. That's all very interesting, but how did the coroner think he died?" He glanced up at Jane. "Paralysis of the respiratory organs. God, that sounds awful. I mean, you actually found those substances in that glass he was drinking from?" He waited. "I see. Do you have any idea what it was? Yes? A suicide? I really doubt that." Again, he looked up. "Okay. I'll pass the information on. Thanks." He hung up and threw down the pencil.

Jane leaned against the front desk, sliding the pad over in front of her. "Pretty fast work."

"That was the paramedic who was here yesterday. It seems they sent the body over to Cambridge last night. The coroner over there was leaving for Florida this morning. It's his Christmas holiday. I guess he must have worked late."

"What do they think Elmer drank?"

"Cranberry juice—mixed with poison. They're not absolutely sure, but it could be an herb."

"An herb?" repeated Jane. "Don't you remember? Leigh was sent that box of herbs just a couple days ago."

118

"Yeah, the tea. I remember. You sent it, didn't you?" He grinned.

"Right. That's my usual solstice gift."

A young man walked up to the desk and asked if he'd received any mail. Burton turned and looked in his box. "No," he said. "I'm sorry. Nothing."

The man picked up a morning paper, flipping some change onto the counter. "Thanks," he said, drifting off into the parlor.

After he was out of earshot, Burton continued a bit more quietly, "Well, someone sent it. All I can say is it's a good thing I studied herbs in culinary school or else somebody could have gotten hurt."

Jane had to agree. "Do they think it may be a suicide then?"

"They haven't come to any definite conclusion yet. The police will be over later in the day to talk to Leigh again and any others who knew him. It seems our sterling law-enforcement agency is a little shorthanded right now. Otherwise they'd be here this morning."

"Leigh's going to take this pretty hard," said Jane staring down at the note pad. "She hoped they'd find he died a natural death."

"Me too," said Burton. He looked up just as Winifred and Tess emerged from the dining room.

"Good morning," called Jane.

"It was delicious as usual," smiled Winifred. "We're getting so spoiled, we won't want to leave."

Burton tore the top sheet off the pad. "Thanks. We try to please."

Tess looked tired this morning. Jane wondered how late she and Winifred had been up after the bridge game last night. No doubt they had plenty to talk about.

After Burton excused himself, pleading a need to get back to the kitchen, Winifred laid her hand on Jane's arm.

"I was wondering. Tess and I thought we'd hike into town this morning. Would you like to join us? I thought perhaps we could find a store that sold herbs. I usually travel with some, but I don't have much with me this trip. Leigh seems so edgy. It would be nice to make her a soothing tea to calm her nerves."

"The Riverside Market," said a low voice.

Jane turned to find Ruthie standing just inside the archway to the parlor. She wondered how long she'd been standing there.

"Do you have an address?" asked Winifred.

"It's on Mill Street. By the river. I used to work there."

"Thanks," said Jane. She smiled somewhat wistfully. "I haven't been in that store since I was a kid. My family and I always shop at Hellstroms—on the other end of town."

"They don't stock herbs," said Ruthie. "Neither does Nordquists, Wallbergs, or The Piggily Wiggily out by the fairground. The Riverside is the only place. They have allspice, angelica, anise, asafetida, basil, bay leaf, borage, camomile, chervil, costmary, cumin . . ."

"Excuse me, Ruthie," said Cordelia, bustling into the foyer. She carried a bakery box filled with gingerbread men. "Before you start on the d's, I'd like to speak with Jane for a minute."

Ruthie stopped and stared at the cookies.

"We made way too many of these," said Cordelia. "Burton suggested Violet and I take the van and drive into Cambridge today. We're going to pass them out at a local hospital and also visit a couple of nursing homes. It will be good public relations for the inn. And besides, I need to get away from here for a while." She made a pathetic face as she looked up the stairs. "You understand. Burton insists he's got a Santa Claus outfit I can stuff myself into. Do you want to come along? I'm sure we'd be able to find you a suitable elf costume. Come to think of it, just wear your normal clothes, Janey. People will think you're trying to impersonate Paul Bunyan."

"No thanks," said Jane. She reached into the box for a cookie.

Cordelia slapped her hand. "Suit yourself. I shall return in time to accompany you over to your family's lodge for Christmas Eve. Cheerio." Pivoting on one heel, she marched back into the dining room.

". . . dill, dittany, fennel, fenugreek, hyssop, juniper berries, lavender . . ." continued Ruthie.

"Would you like to walk into town with us?" asked Jane, attempting to stem the tide of useless information. "We'd enjoy the company."

"I don't know," said Ruthie. She hesitated. "I'm kind of busy this morning. I might have to help Leigh do some work. Maybe some other time."

"Okay. Could we pick anything up for you while we're there?"

"No," replied Ruthie. "That's nice of you to ask, but I was just there last week. I've got everything I need." Her eyes held Jane's for a moment. "See you later." Slowly, she backed into the parlor and disappeared.

"Bye," said Jane, somewhat perplexed.

"We should get going," prompted Winifred, glancing at the clock. "I promised Leigh I'd have lunch with her today. I'd like to get back in plenty of time to brew the tea."

"I'll just get my coat," said Jane. "I'll meet you two back here in five minutes."

"This town is from another century," said Winifred, gazing up curiously at the wood sign over the post office door. Wood smoke belched from a blackened chimney in the back.

"The business district is on the east end of Repentance River," said Jane. "It consists of three main streets, each about four blocks long. Railroad tracks divide the town in half. On the west side is an insurance company, several churches, and the town hall with all the local government offices. The paper mill is up there too."

"What's the population of Repentance River?" asked Winifred.

"Just under two thousand. It's all because of the mill. It employees about three hundred people. The whole town has been built around it."

"How do you know so much about this place?" asked Tess. "Are you from around here?"

"My family has owned a lodge on Blackberry Lake since the early twenties. It's about four miles away."

"What's that?" asked Winifred. She pointed at a sign that said, *Norske Nook.*

Jane smiled. "It's a café. Cordelia would tell you they have great homemade pies. I prefer their meatball plate with mashed potatoes and homemade rolls." She shrugged. "What's that saying? When in Rome . . ."

"So where's this market?" asked Winifred, coming to the end of the block. She looked both directions.

"Follow me," said Jane. "If I'm correct, it's just a little ways."

A few minutes later they entered a long narrow building, warming their hands next to a cast iron stove by the door. Out from the back ambled an extremely tall man stuffing the last bit of a cookie into his mouth. Jane recognized him at once. It was Bo Dierdorf.

"Howdy ladies," he said, his eyes drawn like a magnet to Tess.

"Good morning," said Winifred. "We were told you stocked herbs. I'd like to look at them if I may. I was particularly hoping to find some skullcap."

"Sure," said Bo. "You're in luck. I'm the only place in town you'll find them." Without moving his eyes, he gestured toward an old bookcase along the side wall. "Over there. The skullcap is on the bottom shelf." Hesitating a moment, he swallowed hard. "I can't believe it's really you, Tess. I was sure I'd seen you yesterday when I was looking out the window. You went into the drugstore across the street. How are you? It's been a long time."

"I'm fine." The words came out tight and clipped. "Never better. I didn't expect to see you here either."

"Didn't you get my message?" he asked, looking puzzled. He glanced at Jane for an explanation.

"What message?" said Tess.

Jane raised an eyebrow at Winifred.

He shook his head. "It doesn't matter. What matters is that you're here. Listen, do you think we could talk for a minute? Privately, I mean?"

Tess blinked. "Talk? I don't know. I suppose." Slowly, she turned to Winifred. "I'll be back in a minute, Winney. Bo is . . . someone I used to know." Stiffly, she followed him into the back office.

Winifred waited until they were out of earshot before whispering, "I never gave her that note. It got so late last night after the bridge game, I thought we'd be up until dawn talking. I decided it was better to wait." She peeked around a shelf, noticing Bo close the office door part way. "I guess I'll just go look at those herbs. There's nothing I can do about it now. God, I'd sure like to know what they're talking about."

That makes two of us, thought Jane. It had never occurred to her Burton would order produce from such a small store. She waited until Winifred was ensconced over by the herb shelf and then began aimlessly wandering around the aisles, examining boxes of cereal and cans of lima beans. Standing at last behind a tall rack of paperback books, she was able to catch some of the conversation. Bo was speaking:

"I just want a chance to talk to you alone for a few minutes!"

Silence.

"Why don't you say what you want to say now," responded Tess. "Save us both the time. I can't see that we have anything to talk about anyway."

"Please," he said, his voice full of frustration. "You owe me that much."

"I owe you nothing! Less than nothing. Why did you stay here in the first place? Why didn't you get as far away from this godforsaken town as possible?"

"I couldn't do that," he said. "I needed to be close. To keep watch. I don't want anybody messing around out there."

"You're crazy," said Tess.

"I'm exactly the same guy I was eighteen years ago."

"Are any of the others left in town? I haven't run into anybody."

"No, just me. Shit, Tessy, meet me tonight at the log church. There's going to be a Christmas Eve service at midnight. You remember? After everyone's gone, we can talk undisturbed up in the balcony. I just want fifteen fucking minutes. Is that so much to ask?"

Jane waited, nonchalantly paging through a copy of *Staggerford.*

"Well?" he said after a minute.

"Okay. But I'm not staying. God, I don't know why I'm even doing this. How am I going to explain it to Winifred?"

"Who the hell is she, anyway?"

"You have no right to ask me anything about my life now, Bo. Is that clear? I never expected to see you again. This shouldn't be happening."

"Just come tonight and hear me out. You can leave any time you want."

Tess sighed. "All right. I must be crazy, but I'll come. The old log church at midnight."

19

About an hour before the lunch crowd was due to arrive, Burton found himself downstairs venting his growing frustration on the basement wall. It looked as if the wine cellar was never going to get finished unless he pitched in and did some of the work himself. The worst scenario he could think of was that the police would descend later in the day and rope the entire cellar off. If that happened, it might be weeks, even months before any more work could be done. The schedule for completion and stocking was already tight. Burton could see his plans crumbling before his very eyes. Wearing a ragged sweatshirt and heavily patched jeans, he slammed the sledge hammer next to the small hole Elmer had started.

"What are you doing, Daddy?" called Dylan. He jumped down the stairs step by step, watching his bowl of Jell-O jiggle.

"I want to open up this wall," said Burton. He hit it again, sending chips of brick flying. "Stand back, son. I don't want you to get hurt."

"Why would I get hurt?" asked Dylan, one hand on his hip.

"Go sit over in the corner," said Burton. He pulled a section of bricks onto the floor.

"Don't!" cried Dylan protecting his Jell-O from the dust. "That's not nice."

"Dylan, if you're going to stay down here, you're going to have to do as I ask. Now sit over there in that corner."

Dylan ran to the spot and twirled around, putting his face in the bowl.

Burton watched him for a moment. "What did I tell you about eating with your face? You should have a spoon."

Dylan shrugged.

"Agh," he said, shaking his head. He returned to the wall. As more of the bricks crumbled to the floor, he began to clean away some of the rubble. "You can help Daddy now," he said, pulling a wheelbarrow closer.

Dylan licked the bowl clean before setting it down. "Can I see inside?" he said, pointing to the hole.

"I suppose. It's pretty dark in there. Elmer threw some makeshift lighting up yesterday, but since Daddy couldn't figure out how he had it connected, he's having to tear this shit out—excuse me, Dylan—these bricks out almost in the dark. See if you can find a flashlight over on that work bench."

Dylan nodded, running to the table. "Here it is," he said, finding it almost immediately. Holding it tightly in both hands, he skipped over to his father.

"Okay. Let me take a quick look first. Then I'll lift you up and you can peek inside. I don't know why someone bricked this up in the first place. It was a stupid thing to do."

Dylan stood, holding on to his father's leg while Burton shined the light into the darkness. "Jesus Christ," he said, leaning further into the hole. "I don't believe it."

"I believe it, Dad," said Dylan, finding a marble in his pocket. "Wanna see my favorite marble?"

"Dylan, let's go upstairs."

"Okay, but can I see?"

"Not right now."

"But Daddy!" said Dylan. "You promised!"

"You can ride upstairs on my shoulders, how's that?"

"Okay," beamed the little boy, pulling on his dad's sleeve. "Lift me!"

Burton swept him into his arms. Quickly, he ran to the top of the stairs. Once in the foyer, he found Per talking local politics with Inga and Violet. The two women sat behind the front counter. Violet was laughing. Inga was frowning. "Call upstairs," he said, nearly out of breath. He put Dylan down. "Get Leigh down here right away."

"What's wrong?" asked Jane, coming through the front door followed closely by Winifred and Tess. Winifred carried a small brown paper sack.

"Downstairs," he said, catching his breath.

Two elderly women marched out of the dining room, arguing loudly about who was going to drive home. Burton waited until they had put on their coats and left before continuing.

"You know that old wall?" he said. "The one Elmer was working on yesterday? I decided to break through it myself. You're never going to believe what I found."

"What?" asked Per, folding his arms protectively over his chest. "Hidden treasure?"

"No," said Burton, clearly annoyed. "I don't need any of your humor right now, Gyldenskog."

"What did you find?" asked Jane.

He paused a moment, looking from face to face.

"Well?" demanded Per. "What?"

"A skeleton." Burton shook his head in amazement even as he said the words. "It's lying in a boat."

Jane knocked on Leigh's door.

"Come in," said a voice from inside. "It's not locked."

Jane pushed it open and found her friend lifting a ginger

jar filled with white chrysanthemums over to the coffee table.

"Hi," said Leigh brightly. "This is a nice surprise." She centered the vase on the table and then moved back, admiring her creation. "I suppose you thought you'd catch me napping. Well, no more. It seems all I need for this stupid fatigue is just a little pill." She giggled, adjusting one of the flowers. "It's helping, can't you tell? I know I've been a pain since you arrived. Only talking about the inn's problems. I mean, I can't tell you how sorry I am about yesterday. But I'm much more positive about everything today."

Jane stared. Leigh certainly had a point. She didn't seem a bit tired. She seemed like she was about to launch into orbit. "Where's Stephen?"

"He left. He had a few last-minute presents he needed to buy for his kids. He's going to spend Christmas Eve with them tonight. Then his wife gets them tomorrow for Christmas Day. He's got a room at the Embassy Towers in downtown St. Paul."

"His kids will stay there with him?"

"That's the plan," smiled Leigh. "He'll be back sometime tomorrow morning."

"Look," said Jane. "I've got something I need to tell you."

"If you mean about Elmer, I already know. Burton came upstairs earlier with the news. I wish the police could give us something definite. I hate this waiting."

"No," said Jane, moving into the center of the room. "It's something else. Burton was just down in the basement. He broke through that brick wall—the one Elmer was working on yesterday."

"And?" said Leigh.

"Well, he found something. A skeleton."

Slowly, Leigh turned to face Jane. "Is this a joke?"

Jane paced in front of the couch. "I don't know what it

means, but it must be important. My guess is that some-body buried a body down there and then bricked up the wall to hide what they'd done. It must have happened a long time ago."

Leigh's display of cheerfulness visibly dimmed. "Should we call the police?"

"I suppose. I thought maybe you'd want to go down and look at it first. Burton is waiting for us."

"Okay. You're right. I should go see it. God, no matter what I do, it starts all over again."

Jane looked away. "It makes me wonder if what hap-pened to Elmer yesterday wasn't someone's attempt to pre-vent that skeleton from being discovered."

Leigh's eyes widened.

"I think everything strange that's gone on around this house has been connected. And I doubt we've seen the end of it."

Leigh grabbed a bottle of pills off the coffee table.

"What's that stuff?" asked Jane.

"Stephen gave them to me. He said he uses them some-times when he has to work late. I think I'll take another." She popped the pill into her mouth and drank from her mug of cocoa. "There. That's better. So, come on. Let's get downstairs."

Burton stepped out of the basement doorway, a look of puzzlement on his face. "It's gone."

"What's gone?" demanded Jane as she entered the foyer. Leigh followed a few paces behind.

"The head. Someone's taken the head! I mean the skull. I just went back downstairs. Someone's already been down there."

"Think a minute," said Jane. "Are you sure the skull was actually there before?"

"Are you crazy? Of course I'm sure! I could have reached out and touched it."

"And no one's gone down these stairs?"

"No. Of course not. I've been standing here ever since you left." Burton nodded pleasantly to a party of four giving their names at the reception desk. "Nice to see you again." He smiled. "Let's keep it down," he said, moving closer to the stairway.

Jane glanced at Leigh. "Is there another way into the basement?"

"Sure. It's in back of the kitchen. By the delivery entrance. But we closed it off because it's unsafe. Nobody uses it any more."

"I wouldn't bet on that," said Jane.

"I should have thought," said Burton. "But who would even know it was there?"

"Anyone who has lived here before," replied Jane. "And I think that covers quite a few people. It's going to be nearly impossible to identify the body now."

"Why?" asked Leigh.

"Of course. The dental records," groaned Burton. "That's got to be it. Look, why don't you two go see for yourself. The flashlight is on the workbench. I've got to get back to the kitchen. Inga said she'd take over for me, but she can't handle lunch alone. This is really screwing up my day."

"You do what you have to," said Jane. "We'll call the police as soon as we're done."

"The police?" Burton stopped. "Why tell the police? Whatever happened down there happened a long time ago. How could it possibly affect us, other than to ruin my plans for the wine cellar. I mean, too bad. Somebody got buried behind a wall. Read the papers. People discover stuff like that in old houses all the time. Nobody ever figures these things out. It's the *here and now* I'm concerned with. If this gets out, we'll have curiosity seekers crawling all over the place for months. Do you want that kind of publicity? Think about it, Leigh. The police will be out here anyway this afternoon. Throw a blanket over the boat and pretend it isn't there. Drag it into another room. Do anything you want, but keep it to yourself." Angrily, he snatched his chef's hat off the front counter. "I'll be in the kitchen if anybody wants me."

Leigh led the way into the basement. "It's awfully cold down here. I hate cellars. When we're done, why don't we go back up to my room? I'll fix us both some cocoa."

Jane did feel the chill. "That's a deal." She found the flashlight and directed its dim light into the hole.

Leigh pressed in behind her. "God, what a grim sight." Inside, a small rowboat rested between two battered wooden sawhorses. A skeleton fell across and between the seats. A thick mat of dusty cobwebs covered every surface in the dark, airless chamber, giving the scene a sense of eerie timelessness. Shreds of grayish cloth stuck to some of the larger bones.

Jane pulled her head out and looked around the room. "Where's that other stairway?"

Leigh motioned for her to follow. Quietly, they moved into a long hallway.

"You need more light down here," said Jane, ducking under a low-hanging pipe.

"That's something Elmer was going to fix as soon as he was done with the wine cellar."

They rounded a corner and stopped. "There it is," whispered Leigh. "We closed it off because it's so narrow and steep. And, as you can see, there's no railing."

Jane pointed the flashlight at the top. "Look at that. The door's open a crack." She moved closer. "I thought we might find something like this. The dust is so thick it doesn't take a genius to tell someone's been here recently.

My guess is just a few minutes ago." Bending over, she shined the light on a small circle in the dust. "That's strange. What do you suppose made that mark?"

Leigh shrugged, batting down a cobweb hanging in front of her face. "God, I'd hate to meet the spider that made that one."

"And what's this?" said Jane, leaning down and picking up a small object near the bottom step.

"What is it?" asked Leigh.

Jane placed it carefully in her hand. "It's a bobby pin. And look. No dust."

"What do you think it means?"

Jane took a moment to organize her thoughts. "Well, I'd say it means whoever took the skull was a woman. Or," she added, bringing the light down on Leigh's face, "someone wants us to think it was a woman."

20

"Janey? Wake up!" Cordelia shook her by the shoulders. "It's after six. We've got to be over to your family's lodge in less than an hour."

Jane pushed Cordelia's hand away and rolled over onto her side.

"Listen here, sleeping beauty." Cordelia sat down on the couch next to her and slapped Jane's cheeks lightly. "None of your stubbornness, my dear. You have to get ready. *I* have to get ready." She could feel the sticky glue from the mustache she'd been wearing all afternoon still smeared to her upper lip. Playing Santa Claus had its drawbacks. "Janey? What's wrong?"

Jane covered her face with a pillow. "It's the middle of the night, Cordelia. Go away."

"It is"—Cordelia checked her watch—"exactly six-o-three in the evening. Do I need to get a glass of ice water and dribble some onto that handsome face of yours?" A sneeze tickled her nose.

Jane rubbed her eyes. "You're kidding!" She looked down at her fully clothed body. "I must have fallen asleep. I never take naps."

"Ah," said Cordelia, brushing a hair away from Jane's face. "Age comes to us all."

"No." Jane swung her legs off the couch. "That's not it. I almost feel like I've been drugged."

"Must be the country air. Don't worry. I won't tell John Calvin if you don't. Now, time to get ready for the festivities tonight." She sniffed.

"What's that on your upper lip?"

"Glue."

"Of course. Can I go back to sleep now?"

A few minutes later, Cordelia sat huddled in Jane's car. Pitifully, she clutched a box of Kleenex to her bosom. "Not only are we going to have a white Christmas, we're going to be buried alive."

Jane drove her aging Saab slowly through the winter storm. The winding back road they'd taken hadn't been plowed in several hours. Pine trees were weighed almost to the ground with snow. "You've got to get into the spirit of the evening. Snow is part of that special north country ambiance."

"How about a short rendition of 'Adeste Fideles.' It will

134 Ellen Hart

sound truly poignant sung by a woman with a plugged sinus."

Jane smiled, turning down the fan on the heater. "So any new thoughts on The Fothergill Inn?"

"I think they should relocate to Florida."

"Be serious."

"I am."

"Look, try to organize your gray cells for a moment. I could use some help. For instance, what do you think about finding that bobby pin?"

"I think it was very clever of you." She snuffled.

"But what do you think it means?"

"The thief was a hairdresser."

"Cordelia!"

"Yes?"

Jane swerved the car to avoid hitting a snow drift.

"You just use all your energies to drive the car, Jane dear. Remember, *prioritize*." She blew her nose delicately into a tissue. "All right. These are my thoughts about the bobby pin, such as they are. First, the logical assumption would be to figure the person who dropped it was a woman and she did so accidentally. The less-likely scenario would suggest that a man dropped it, and he did so on purpose. Now, the question is? Have I ever noticed a man with a bobby pin. I'm afraid the answer is yes."

"Yes?"

"Yes. I shall elaborate. Yesterday I was standing in the foyer explaining some of my vast knowledge of the theatre to Henry Gyldenskog. He was, needless to say, spellbound. I hate to say it, but Henry is an aficionado of the overstaged and underwritten. I attempted to shift his views—with some success, too, I might add. Anyway, as we were standing there, Burton flew at us, demanding a quarter."

"Is this a joke?"

"No joke. He needed it to pry open something in the

kitchen. Anyway, Henry dug into his pocket and pulled out quite an assortment of junk. There were at least three marbles, several paper clips, a dime, two quarters, and a bunch of bobby pins. Burton was delighted. After handing over the quarter, we were allowed to continue our conversation uninterrupted in the parlor over a cup of tea. And you'll be happy to hear this. I asked Henry about the contents of his pocket."

"And?"

"And he said it was second nature for him to pick up little things off the floor. They could so easily destroy a vacuum cleaner. I commended him for his diligence."

"I see," said Jane. "I'm not sure that gets us anywhere. Are those your only thoughts?"

"About the bobby pin, yes. I have a limited repertoire of bobby pin stories. But, if I may change the subject to something of more immediate interest, let me ask you this. Are you going to say anything to your father tonight about what Beryl is proposing? It might be the perfect opportunity."

Jane made an exasperated face. "Since I haven't really decided myself what I'm going to tell Beryl, it seems a bit premature."

"I thought you wanted Beryl to come."

"Yesterday I thought it was the greatest thing since buttered toast. Today, I'm not so sure. I guess you could say I'm having second thoughts."

"About what? Are you afraid she'll want to redecorate your house in chartreuse and raw umber?"

Jane smiled. "Something like that."

"You can handle it, Janey. I have faith."

"Seriously, Cordelia. There are some considerations I need to think about."

"Like what?"

Jane turned onto Highway 139. "You know. Like . . .

Beryl doesn't care for dogs. To be honest, she can't stand them."

"She'll cope. What else?"

"Well, what if I find someone . . . I really like . . . and I want to have them over to the house . . . and . . ."

"You're afraid Beryl will want to sit between you and your potential tootsie on the couch."

"No, not exactly. But it could be complicating."

"Nonsense. Just lock her in her room."

"Cordelia!"

"Well, you know what I mean. You can negotiate that. She's one of the least homophobic people I've ever met. She loved Christine. And she's not stupid. She knows you need your privacy. Who knows? Beryl may have a gentleman caller or two at some point. Rearrange that third floor. Or, how about the sun room you've got right off your bedroom. It's perfect for a little heavy duty *conversation*. Be creative. See? No problem. Next consideration."

"All right. What about money? I can't support another person on my income. What if she—"

Cordelia held up her hand. "Beryl would never think of staying with you without paying her way. She's not poor. Not rich either, but more than comfortable. Has she said anything about that?"

"Not a word."

"Well, don't worry. She will. Next point."

"There's my father to think of. If she stays, he may refuse to come over to my house. Or, more likely, he won't refuse, he'll just be too busy. Forever. He and Beryl genuinely dislike each other. I can't ignore that. What if it causes problems between us? I love him, Cordelia. I don't want to hurt him, and I think if Beryl comes to live with me, it will do just that."

"It might help if you got him to talk about why he and Beryl don't get along."

"I don't think I really want to know."

"It's probably something trivial. She used to beat him at croquet and he couldn't stand it."

"I don't think so."

"No. I suppose you're right. Well, all I can say is that you need to make your decision based on what you think is right for you. You can't let your father's inability to get along with someone you love dictate your actions."

"You sound like you're positive she should come."

Cordelia nodded.

"Why?"

"Well, a couple of reasons, I suppose. First, I think it would be nice for Beryl. Other than her son, you're her favorite relative. And I like to see families together."

"And?"

"And, the main reason is . . . I think it would be good for you."

"Me? Why?"

Cordelia took an extra second to dab at her sore nose. "Janey, in the last few years you've become . . . how do I put this . . . almost a recluse. Oh, I know you date occasionally. You put four hundred hours a week in at that restaurant of yours, and I know you've got friends there. But there's a difference. You've closed off from people. You never talk about yourself. Not really talk. Except to me. I've been your lifeline since Christine's death. And I'm not saying I minded. But it's time you thaw out, dearheart. You don't need a lifeline anymore. You need your life back. Oh, I know you'll always be that loveable, reticent, introspective introvert I've come to know so well. And that's fine. It's who you are. But you've got to stop feeling guilty."

"Guilty?" said Jane. "And what do you think I feel guilty about?"

Cordelia's voice grew gentle. "About being alive, dearheart."

Jane held on tightly to the steering wheel.

"Emotionally, I think living with your aunt would be great. I know you'll find another partner in time, if that's what you want. But you need someone in your life right now to love—other than your brother and me. Beryl is a good woman. She'll help you. You'll help her. I think she should come."

"Well," said Jane, turning up the defroster, "you've certainly got this all thought out."

"I do. And I'm right. Don't get pouty. You can tell your dad tonight or not tell him. It's up to you. But I don't think you should dismiss the whole idea of Beryl coming without giving it more time to rattle around in that brain of yours. Okay?"

Jane turned the car onto Kettle Creek Road. "Okay."

"So," said Cordelia, sneaking a peek at her friend out of the corner of her eye, "on to other family matters. Let's see. How does it feel to have Sigrid Munson as a potential sister-in-law?"

"I don't know," said Jane. "I haven't had a chance to give it much thought. Did I tell you she's in medical school now? She wants to go into psychiatry."

"Wonderful! You and your family will provide unending interest."

"Thanks." Jane cracked a small smile. "Look, there's the lodge. Can you see it?"

With her gloved hand, Cordelia wiped a circle in the steamed-up passenger window. "Oh gumdrops, we've actually made it!"

Jane drove off the paved road and skidded down the hill toward a clearing.

"This must be the place," said Cordelia. "There's Peter's Jeep and your dad's BMW. Welcome to Yuppieville."

"Is that a sneer I detect? Well then, you must be especially happy to arrive in my 1978 rust-colored Saab."

"*Happy* is not a word I have ever associated with lurching along in this vehicle. If my brake light hadn't come on just as we were pulling out of your driveway, we'd be riding in the palatial comfort of my beautiful black Buick LeSabre."

Jane snorted. "All you need on that thing to really make a statement are Miami license plates."

"I beg your pardon!"

Jane pulled to a stop. "Okay, you get the presents out of the backseat, and I'll get the food from the trunk."

"All I want for Christmas," said Cordelia, trying to unwedge herself from the seat, "is a new nose."

"Oh darn," said Jane, lifting open the trunk. "And I got you a hamster."

21

"Merry Christmas," shouted Peter as Jane and Cordelia entered through the front door. He set down his cup of coffee and ran over to give them both a kiss on the cheek. "Let me help you with all your bags. You're in luck. We haven't started to decorate the tree yet."

"Howdy sweetheart," called Jane's father as he emerged from the kitchen carrying a tray of Christmas cookies. "Your favorites, honey." He set the tray on the dining room table next to a thermal carafe of coffee. "I'm glad you guys finally made it. We were about to send out a search party."

Raymond Lawless was a large, square-faced man in his

early sixties. He possessed what people often referred to as a wonderfully theatrical voice. In his profession as defense attorney, he had learned to play it like an instrument. His silver hair was worn just a touch shaggy, softening the strong lines of his face. And, like Jane, he had a large nose and a broad infectious smile. "That car of yours doesn't exactly inspire confidence. I wish you'd consider something a bit more reliable."

"And something from this century," added Cordelia.

"If it's a loan you need, sweetheart, you can always count on your dad." He winked.

Jane bristled at the suggestion but caught herself and replied lightly, "You two should take your vaudeville act on the road. You don't recognize true quality when you see it." Why start out the evening with a sparring match, she thought. She was obviously glad her father was financially secure. Her own restaurant was doing fine as well. Still, things were tight. Her father had argued against opening it in the first place. He'd warned that all restaurants were black holes. Jane had listened politely and then done exactly what she'd planned to do all along. Yet she felt somehow undermined by his constant offering of money. Surely he must know that? Something about their relationship brought out all her stubbornness—a determination to move against the grain. But this was no time for analysis. She could smell the goose roasting in the oven. Several pies were cooling on the buffet. Tonight was for celebration.

"Where's the eggnog, Marilyn?" called Raymond. "Everyone's here, and we can't trim the tree without it."

"You know what, Ray?" said Marilyn poking her head out of the kitchen. "I think we forgot to buy any. Hi kiddos! Glad you made it."

"This is disaster," cried Peter. He got up from his kneeling position near the fireplace. "We can't decorate the tree without eggnog. We have to go get some. That superette is still open out on the highway."

Jane walked over and gave Marilyn a hug. Marilyn Washburn, a graphic designer for a small advertising agency in Bloomington, had been her father's housemate for almost twelve years. She was an energetic, articulate woman who kept her father constantly on his toes. Once, Jane had asked her dad why they never married. All she got was a wry look and the comment, "you're not the only one who gets to break the rules, sweetheart."

"Who wants to go with us to the superette?" asked Raymond, wagging his bushy eyebrows.

Marilyn raised her hand.

"Siggy, you want to drive with us?" called Peter.

Sigrid Munson stepped out of the kitchen, wiping her hands on a threadbare gingham apron she'd found in one of the kitchen drawers. Her long blond hair was pinned up in a braided bun. "Nope. I'll pass. I'd rather stay here with Jane and Cordelia and help get the fire going." She greeted them with an amused smile.

As Peter approached and gave her a lingering kiss, the phone began to ring.

"Why don't you answer that, Peter," said Ray. "I'll get our coats."

Peter flopped down in a big chair in the front room, picking up the receiver. "Hello," he said mischievously. "This is the butler speaking. May I help you?"

The line crackled. "Peter? Is that you?"

"Aunt Beryl," he cried, motioning Jane into the room. "How wonderful to hear your voice. How are you?"

Raymond emerged from one of the back rooms loaded with coats. His expression was stoic, but Jane could read the annoyance in his eyes.

"Merry Christmas," said Beryl. "I knew you would all be at the lodge for Christmas Eve. I calculated the time difference and determined when to call. Are you all well? Is Jane with you?"

"Everyone's fine," said Peter. "It's a shame you didn't wait and call a little later. I'm going to make an announcement tonight. Something pretty special."

"You can trust me, dear boy. I promise I won't tell a soul."

Peter could hear the twinkle in her voice. "I'll send you a note. Promise. Do you want to talk to Janey?"

"I'd love to. Congratulations on the forthcoming announcement, whatever it is. I shall drink a toast in absentia to it and your good health."

"Thanks," said Peter. "Here's Jane." He handed her the phone.

Ray sat down on the couch opposite them. He made no show of anything other than polite interest.

"Hello," said Jane. She could feel her stomach doing flip flops. "How are you feeling?"

"Much better. Very much better now that I hear your voice. You may put your mind to rest. I have not called to badger you about coming to visit. But my health is improving daily, thank you very much. A journey would definitely be a tonic. I don't suppose you've had much time to think about what we talked about last Sunday?"

So much for not badgering, thought Jane. "I have thought about it." She saw her father's eyebrows raise ever so slightly.

"I suppose Ray is sitting right there as we speak, glowering. Well, no matter. You take your time. I just wanted you to know about a decision I've made. I'm changing my will. I talked to Anthony yesterday. He assured me he has no interest in this cottage. He's doing well for himself, you know. Likes London. He'll never come back here. I'm leaving it to you, dear girl. It's your Christmas present. You've always loved it so. Jane? Are you there?"

"Yes," said Jane, trying to keep her voice calm. She looked up at her dad.

"You would want it, wouldn't you? I've always thought ..."

"Of course," said Jane. "You're sure Tony doesn't mind?"

"Mind? Child, you're like my own. He knows that. He would never question my decision. And as to my proposed little visit, I want you to know that I intend to pay my own way. You never say a word about money, but since Christine's death, I know you've had to take on that house mortgage all by yourself. I'm sure you could use a little added income."

This wasn't badgering, thought Jane. This was a sledge hammer. "I ..."

"I know you can't talk now," said Beryl. "Give Ray a big kiss from me. That should send him flying from the room. Ring me when you can. And give my best to Cordelia, too. Is she there tonight?"

"Yes," said Jane. "She is."

"Wonderful. The family is assembled. I look forward to seeing you all soon. Merry Christmas, Jane dear." She hung up.

Jane put down the phone.

Peter reached over and touched her. "What did she say? You look funny."

Jane swallowed. "She's leaving me her cottage."

"Damn," said Peter, squeezing her hand and smiling. "Good for you! That's great!"

Jane looked up at her father who sat unmoving on the couch.

"Bribery," he said softly.

"What?" said Jane.

"I said it's just some more of her silly bribery. That old

fool. Not even in her grave and she's handing out lollipops. Ask yourself why?"

"Why?" said Cordelia from the corner of the room.

"She wants something. That's why."

Jane took another hard swallow. "She wants to come for a visit."

Raymond stiffened. "God almighty. I'd hoped we'd seen the last of that woman. You told her no, didn't you?"

"I haven't given her an answer."

"Well then, give it! Call her right back and tell her to stay on her side of the Atlantic where she belongs."

"She's been sick, Dad. And very lonely since Uncle Jimmy's death."

"And? She didn't think *I* was lonely after your mother's death? Yet she took you. She took you and kept you from me for two years."

Jane could feel herself begin to tremble. "That's not true. It was my idea to go back to England."

"For two weeks. Not two years! I'll not stand for any more of her interference in this family! Do you hear me?" His face had turned a deep red.

"Calm down, Ray," said Cordelia, her voice firm.

Ray ran his hand roughly through his thick gray hair.

Cordelia continued. "Last I heard Beryl was not a member of the Nazi party. She doesn't eat small children. And she has a right to travel wherever she wants."

Jane was grateful. Cordelia had always been able to say things to her father he wouldn't take from anyone else. For some reason, he respected Cordelia. The rest of Jane's friends were simply lumped together as youngsters.

"Let's go get that eggnog," he said gruffly, pulling on his coat.

Reluctantly, Peter and Marilyn followed him out the door.

After they'd gone, Cordelia sat down on the couch. "Don't let his attitude spoil the evening. I can't believe

you're going to inherit that cottage right on the coast. You
deserve to be elated. *I* deserve to be elated, knowing as I do
how naturally generous you are. We will spend the autumn
of our years there sitting on the seashore, reading Bronte
and Austen to each other. Going for walks in the hills." She
sighed. And then sneezed.

A few minutes before Christmas dinner was to be served
at the inn, Dylan sat in the middle of the second floor hallway, examining his new toy truck. It was red and black,
with big wheels, and one door that opened and closed, and
a steering wheel that turned, and the back part lifted up to
dump things out, and it was just what he had asked for. He
was delighted.

"Vroom! Vroom-vroom!" he said, pushing it along the
floor. The darkened hallway was completely deserted. He
knew people got mad if he played too loudly in the parlor.
Up here was better.

"Turn the corner!" he ordered. He jumped up the steps
one by one until he reached the third floor. "Stop sign!" he
called, plunking down on the thick carpeting. He peeked
around to make sure he was still alone. Letting the truck
rev for a moment longer, he lifted it to the wide hand rail.
"Ready?" he asked. "Set?" he called, closing his eyes.
"Go!" He released his hand and sent it speeding toward the
floor below. At the sound of a loud crash, he scampered
down the steps. Lovingly, he picked it up and cradled it in
his arms, looking for signs of damage.

"Good truck," he said and patted it on its underside.
"You weren't scared, were you?" He dropped to the floor
and zoomed it past the closed doors, crawling straight for
the curtains at the end of the hall. The hairs on the back of
his neck prickled as he thought of the monster he had seen
once. It was in a dark hall just like this. And he was alone,

just like now. Daddy said he was dreaming, but Dylan knew better.

"Vroom!" he repeated. "You need gas. I got lots of pennies." He was almost to the end.

"Get ready," he told the truck. "It's not good to bump. It hurts!" He made a screeching sound. "Excellent!" he said, not saying the word quite right. "Good job." A second later, he noticed the feet.

"That's incredible," laughed Raymond. "What a story! You're going to make a welcome addition to this family." He smiled warmly at Sigrid, pouring her more wine. "How long have you been a psychiatric intern at that hospital?"

Sigrid wiped her mouth with a napkin. "Two months. It feels like two years. The psychiatrist I work with should be in lock up, if you ask me. He's got more problems than the patients."

Jane leaned back in her chair, watching Sigrid and her father talk. After Peter had made the grand announcement, the tone of the evening had become decidedly more upbeat. The call from Beryl seemed to be forgotten.

"Tell everyone about that guy who thought his wife was a nymphomaniac," prodded Peter.

Cordelia groaned.

Sigrid held up her hand for silence. "Several weeks ago, this strange little man walked into the office. He announced that his wife was a nymphomaniac. Dr. Rumford asked how he knew that for sure, to which the man responded that his wife was sleeping with the next door neighbor, the paperboy, the mailman, the meter reader, the garbage haulers and any other male who happened to come within shouting distance of their house. He was sure she was frolicking wildly every afternoon. She apparently worked in the mornings. He admitted he'd never actually *seen* her with another man, but . . . you get the picture."

"Classic male paranoia," interjected Cordelia, using her best Viennese accent. "We must immediately reprogram his brain with old episodes of *I Love Lucy*."

"Shhh," said Peter.

Sigrid continued. "Have you confronted your wife about it? asked Dr. Rumford. No, said the man, his face registering a strange little smile. It didn't really matter though. He'd come up with the perfect solution. Even though it was working just dandy, he wanted to know if Dr. Rumford would consider seeing his wife to help her with her *problem*. Rumford asked what this temporary solution was. Well, he said, you see, the wife has this insatiable sweet tooth. So, every noon, he'd bring home a big, fancy dessert. It seems a number of sleeping powders are almost undetectable when combined with something sweet. She would blithely eat her chocolate mousse and spend the rest of the afternoon conked out on the couch. Brilliant, he thought. He didn't have to worry about her sexual appetite if she was in dreamland."

"Isn't that incredibly bizarre?" said Peter.

"It's terrible!" said Marilyn. "That guy should be put away! I hope someone thought to call his wife and tell her what he was doing."

"Something sweet," repeated Jane under her breath. She stared down at her plate.

"What's up, Janey?" asked Ray. He watched his daughter carefully for a moment. "You know honey, for someone who has been on vacation all week, you look awfully tired."

Cordelia snorted.

Jane shot her a look that said—*zip it!*

"I visited that old Fothergill house once," he said. "Beautiful old place. Not in very good shape though. Of course, that was many years ago."

"Why were you there?" asked Jane.

"It was kind of silly, really. I'd met Harlan Svenby at a

town fair years before. I don't know why he remembered
me, but he dropped by the lodge one summer afternoon. I
just happened to be here. It seems his son—I don't recall
the name . . ."

"Daniel," said Jane.

"Right. Danny. Seems he'd gotten into a fight. He'd been
drinking and hit some guy pretty hard. Broke the man's
nose. Anyway, the guy decided to press charges. Harlan
wanted me to represent his son if it came to that."

"What happened?" asked Cordelia.

"Well, I drove over to the island to talk to this Daniel.
He was properly contrite. An odd kid. Seems to me he had
a little child. I have no idea where the mother was. Anyway, the upshot of it was that I talked to the guy he hit. We
were able to settle out of court. It cost old man Svenby a
pretty penny, I remember that much. He was a nice old guy.
I was sorry when I heard he'd died. What ever happened to
the son?"

"He died about a year after his father," replied Jane.

"Really? I don't remember that. Oh well, it was all such
a long time ago. My memory is disintegrating rapidly."

"I didn't realize you knew the family," said Jane, pushing her potatoes around the plate with her fork. "You said
Daniel was an odd kid. Why?"

Raymond picked up his wineglass and thought for a moment. "Oh, you know. I suppose it was the way he talked
or something. Maybe it had to do with that wolf business."

"Wolf business?" repeated Marilyn.

Raymond folded his hand over hers. "As long as I can
remember, people from this area have talked about wolf
sightings. It's crazy because everyone knows wolves don't
come this far south. I don't think anybody's ever really
seen one. I know the hardware store in town sells a fair
amount of traps every year. That Svenby kid probably said

something about it when we were talking. I remember
something like that."

"That's all?" said Jane.

Raymond smiled. "You cross-examine like a lawyer,
darlin'. Too many years around your old man. Really, it
was just an impression. I thought he was kind of slippery.
Good looking, but, how do I say this? Cold. And the fact
that he was willing to let his dad pay that guy off without
even offering to pay part of it himself, well, it suggested to
me that he was pretty spoiled."

"Or broke," offered Cordelia.

Once again, the phone began to ring.

"I'll get it," said Jane, taking a sip of water before excus-
ing herself. "It might be for me."

Dylan's eyes traveled up the curtain as a hand appeared
and slipped between the heavy folds.

Gulping back his fright, he picked up his truck and held
it to his chest.

The figure stepped out into the hallway.

"Who . . . who are you?" he asked, his eyes fixed on the
strange face.

"I'm your friend," whispered the figure. "You're a good
boy, Dylan. Don't be afraid." The figure started to back up
the stairs.

With a hushed voice, Dylan asked, "You're the monster,
aren't you?" His eyes grew wide.

"No! I'm not a monster. Don't say that!" Turning
quickly, it hurried up the stairs.

Scrambling to his feet, Dylan hitched up his pants and
tore down the hallway.

"Whoa," said a deep male voice. "Where are you headed
at that speed?" Burton laughed as he caught Dylan in his
arms.

"Daddy!" he cried, letting his truck drop to the floor. "I saw it! I saw it!"

"Saw what?" asked Burton, ruffling his son's hair.

"The monster!"

Burton picked up the truck and hoisted his son into his arms. "You're eating way too much sugar, young man."

"But Daddy!"

"Not another word. I expect you to eat some vegetables tonight."

Dylan wrinkled up his face. "I did see it," he said, lowering his eyes in a pout.

"No excuses, okay?" Burton stood for a minute, trying to decide something. "Dylan?"

"What?"

"What did the monster look like?"

Dylan leaned his head against his father's shoulder. "Like the mask Jimmy DeGidio's mom made him for Halloween."

Burton squinted into the dim hallway. "It won't hurt you, son. Daddy would never let anything hurt you."

"I know," said Dylan. He patted his dad's hair.

Jane picked up the phone. "Merry Christmas!" she said cheerfully.

"Jane, is that you?"

"Yes it is." She didn't recognize the voice.

"This is Violet. Violet Svenby."

"Hi! What's up."

"Jane, Leigh has had a bad spell."

"What do you mean?"

"We were having dinner together, and she started to feel funny. It's awful! We can't get her to stop crying. I tried to contact Stephen, but his room doesn't answer. I didn't know what else to do. Is there any way you could get back here? I know you and Cordelia were going to spend Christmas Eve with your family."

"Where is Leigh now?"

"Inga took her over to the gatehouse. We've got her in Ruthie's room. She was shaking so hard, we didn't know what else to do. I wonder if I should call a doctor?"

"Absolutely," said Jane. "If we have to take her over to the clinic in Cambridge, it's going to be a long drive. The roads are pretty bad. I'll see if I can borrow my brother's Jeep."

"Oh Jane, you're a lifesaver. I know Leigh would be so upset if she knew I'd interrupted your family Christmas."

"That's not a problem," said Jane. "Tell her to hold on. I was planning to come back tonight anyway. There was a midnight Christmas Eve service in Repentance River I wanted to attend."

"Oh, you mean the one at the Swedish log church? That's so lovely. Inga and I went together last year."

"Violet," said Jane, hesitating a moment, "will you do me a big favor? Please don't tell anyone I'm going into town tonight. I sort of want to do this alone. Without any company."

"I understand," said Violet. "Inga is the same way. She likes to do things by herself. Don't worry. We'll see you soon then?"

"It should take me about half an hour. I'll have to make some excuses to my family, but Cordelia can stay and do her famous impressions of me. That should save the day."

"I'll tell Leigh you're coming," said Violet. "I'm sure that will make her feel better. She thinks the world of you, you know."

Jane stared absently at the congealing grease in the enamel roasting pan. "See you in a few minutes." She hung up. Thankfully, it would take at least half an hour to get back to the inn. An idea had been forming in her mind all

evening. The drive back would allow her some critical time
to think. Right now, a little clarity would go a long way.

22

"Where is she?" demanded Jane, running up the steps
into the gatehouse.

Violet held open the door. "She's in Ruthie's bedroom.
Inga is sitting with her. Winifred brought over some more
of that tea she made earlier. We all thought it might be
soothing." She led the way through the bright yellow
kitchen into a long, dark hallway. The house had the familiar smell of stale cooking and Lysol.

"Did you get hold of a doctor?" asked Jane.

"We have a call in to our clinic in town. It usually takes
them a while. I would suspect on Christmas Eve, it may
take even longer."

Jane unzipped her jacket as she entered the small, dimly
lit room. Against the far wall Leigh was sitting on the bed
wrapped in a patchwork quilt. Her legs were pulled up
tightly to her body. Under the covers she was shivering. As
Jane sat down next to her, she couldn't help but notice
Leigh's eyes. They looked hollow and deeply frightened. "I
hear you aren't feeling so hot," she said gently.

Leigh shook her head. "God, that was awful. I've never
felt like that before in my entire life. Maybe I should see
a doctor. All this tiredness I've been having—and now tonight. What if something is really wrong with me?"

"Can you tell me what happened?" asked Jane.

Leigh pulled one arm out from under the quilt and ran a shaky hand over her face. "We were sitting at dinner. I don't know, I've been thinking. Could it be those pills I took? The ones Stephen uses to stay awake? I suppose I overdid it. But Jane, it was the first time in weeks I've felt like I've had any energy. Whatever it was, I just started to feel so strange. Almost like I was drunk. I could tell people were staring at me. Both my aunts said my speech sounded slurred. And then, when I stood up, the room started to spin. That's when I fell. All I remember is I couldn't stop crying. I knew I was making a scene, but I couldn't control myself." She let her head fall forward onto her knees.

Inga touched Jane lightly on her shoulder. "We're going to leave you two alone," she said softly. "If you need either of us, we'll be in the kitchen."

Jane smiled her thanks. "Do you want to hear what I think?" she asked, knowing that Leigh would probably resist what she was about to say.

Leigh lifted her head. "Sure."

"All right, but this is going to sound pretty bizarre." She heard the door click shut. "Before you say anything, just listen for a minute. I think it's possible someone has been slipping you something. Something to make you feel tired. Probably some kind of sleeping powder."

Leigh's expression was blank. "How? Why?"

"That cocoa up in your room. Remember? You fixed me a cup this afternoon. Cordelia could hardly wake me when she got home at six."

"But I had some too. To be accurate, I've had at least four cups. And today was the first day in a long time I haven't felt the need to sleep all afternoon."

"Sure, but that was because you were loading up all day on Stephen's pills. I'm sure the interaction between those two drugs could make you feel pretty crazy, especially as much as you were taking. That's why you felt so awful this evening."

Leigh listened quietly.

"If my theory's true, it's no doubt connected to everything else that's been happening around here. It goes much deeper than someone merely wanting to take the inn away from you. Unfortunately, I have no idea what the underlying motive is. I think we can be pretty sure it has something to do with the skeleton found in the basement. Someone killed Elmer to keep him from knocking through that wall. I've never trusted coincidences. I don't believe his death was an accident."

"I can't believe any of my friends or family could do something like that."

Jane shook her head. "Maybe not. You're right, I can't prove it."

Both women were silent for a moment.

"Look, Leigh, I don't think anything's really wrong with you. But I'd like you to be careful what you eat for a few days. Fix the food yourself. I'm sure your aunts would let you use their kitchen. And don't drink any more of that cocoa. I'll give it to Peter tomorrow. He can take it back to Minneapolis and have it analyzed. In the meantime, you need to get some rest tonight. I think it's best if you stay here. Ruthie won't mind being tossed out of her bedroom for one night. She can sleep over at the inn. There are several vacant rooms right now."

"More than several," said Leigh. "Except for the members of Winifred's coven, dead bodies and old skeletons have pretty much decimated our guest list." She let her head sink back against the pillow. "Maybe I should call a real estate agent. This is getting too bizarre."

"It's up to you," said Jane.

Leigh closed her eyes. "Let me sleep on it. Stephen will be back in the morning. Maybe he'll have a brilliant idea."

Jane looked at her watch. It was approaching midnight. If she didn't get to that church soon, she'd miss her chance to eavesdrop on Tess and Bo's conversation. "I'm going to go out and talk to your aunts for a minute. Then I'll come back in, but I can't stay. You'll be fine now. Really. I'll bring you some warm milk before I go, and I want you to drink it. Are you hungry?"

Leigh shook her head.

"Okay. I'll be back in a minute. You just rest." She rose, feeling inside her pocket for the address of the church.

Inga looked up from a huge mug of steaming tea as Jane entered the kitchen. "How is she?" Violet was standing at the stove heating soup in a small pan.

"Better, I think. Listen, I need to talk to both of you."

"Of course," said Violet, turning down the flame. She sat down at the table next to Inga, her expression eager and serious. "What can we do?"

Jane began a bit tentatively. "This may sound kind of crazy, but . . . look, I think someone may have been drugging Leigh."

Neither Violet nor Inga moved.

"I'm going to need your help. Leigh may want to use your kitchen to cook some of her food."

"What do you mean?" asked Inga, gripping her mug so tightly her knuckles turned white.

"It's a long story. I don't have time right now to go into all of it. We can talk more later if you'd like. The thing is, I don't know who's responsible. I suppose it could even be you two."

Violet stood up, emitting a short, angry gasp, rather like a bark. "That's ridiculous. How could you think such a thing."

"Sit down," said Inga. "Jane's just using her head. After all, she doesn't really know us. If something funny's going

on around here, she should suspect everyone. You may not
believe this Jane, but Leigh means the world to us. She and
Ruthie are all we've got left."

"I'm not accusing you," said Jane, choosing her words
carefully. "But I think my theory is correct."

"It hurts me to think you would suspect Inga or I of
something like that," said Violet. She returned to stir her
now bubbling soup. "Do you think we had something to do
with Elmer's death too?"

"Calm down, Violet. Jane's only doing what she thinks
best. I'd be proud to have a friend like that." She sipped her
tea.

"Maybe." Violet conceded the point grudgingly. She
lifted the pan to the sink and poured its contents down the
drain. "Burned. Completely ruined."

"Canned tomato soup is hardly a tragic loss," smiled
Inga.

"It is to the person who was going to eat it." Violet
leaned over the sink and peered out the window. "What on
earth was that?"

"What was what?" asked Inga.

"I thought I saw something move past the kitchen window."

"Maybe it was Big Foot." Inga looked up at Jane. "She
has a vivid imagination."

From the bedroom came a frightened shout. "Jane!"

Bolting into the hallway, Jane ran to the bedroom door.
The water pitcher next to the bed had shattered in pieces on
the hardwood floor.

Leigh pointed to the window. "Something was out there.
It was watching me! The face was . . . I'm not hallucinating, Jane. I'm not!"

Jane stepped over to the window and looked out. She
didn't see anything. "You stay with her," she said to Inga.
"I'll be right back."

"Of course. You do what you have to."

Jane rushed down the hall and burst out of the kitchen door. The cold night air hit her face like a slap. Outside, the porch lights from the inn cast a faint yellow glow over the gatehouse and the woods beyond. Everything was quiet. The new fallen snow covered the distant countryside in a soft blanket of white. It was an idyllic winter scene. Peaceful and silent.

Zipping up her coat, she walked briskly around to the side of the house. Underneath Ruthie's bedroom window she could clearly make out one set of footprints. She traced them with her eyes until they ended about fifty feet away, behind a large oak. Suddenly, out from behind the tree a strange face appeared. What the hell, she thought to herself. What on earth is that? She squinted into the darkness until her eyes adjusted to the light. The face looked like a dog or a bear. No, that wasn't it. It was a wolf! "Who are you?" she called, her heart thumping inside her chest. "Do you hear me? What are you doing out here?"

The face retreated behind the tree.

"I know you're there. This isn't funny. I'm not leaving until you answer me." She felt her fear quickly turn to anger.

Again, the head darted out.

"Who are you?" she demanded, this time getting a better look. She began running toward the tree.

Abruptly, the dark figure turned and sprinted off into the woods.

Jane knew there was no way she could chase it down in the darkness. Who on earth would be wearing a mask and peeking in windows on Christmas Eve? Could it be the same person responsible for everything else happening at the inn? But what was going on now? Was this an attempt to frighten, or merely to watch? Disgusted at her inability to make sense of anything, she headed back toward the house. No use freezing to death in the cold.

Once safely inside the bright, warm kitchen, she decided to start heating the milk she'd promised Leigh.

"Did you see what it was?" asked Inga, coming into the room carrying a dustpan and a broom. She leaned both against the side of the refrigerator and walked over to the cupboard, getting down a mug.

Jane shook her head. "It was too dark. I couldn't really tell. If it was Halloween instead of Christmas Eve I'd have a logical explanation." She looked toward the bedroom. "How is she?"

"Better. I'm glad you're here." Inga handed her the mug. "She wants to see you before you leave."

Jane poured the milk. "I think I'll come back and sleep here later, if it's all right with you."

"Be my guest," said Inga. "We've got an old cot we can put in Leigh's room, if you'd like. Or you can sleep out on the couch. It's tolerably comfortable."

"Thanks. I'll see if Leigh has an opinion on the subject."

As she entered the bedroom again, Leigh looked a bit more comfortable. The TV was on and the window shade had been pulled. "How are you doing?" asked Jane, sitting down and handing her the mug.

"Okay. I think. But what was that at the window? I wasn't hallucinating, was I?"

"No," smiled Jane. "Someone was out there wearing a mask. I saw it too. I don't know what's going on, but you're safe in here." She took hold of Leigh's hand. "You're going to get better now. You'll see. No more cocoa or pills, okay?"

"That *would* be crazy." She looked up, her eyes still a bit frightened. "I don't suppose I could convince you to stay here and watch an old movie with me?"

Jane squeezed her hand. "I'm going to come back later.

I can sleep on a cot in here, or out on the couch. Do you have a preference?"

"Not really. But thanks. Where are you headed at this time of night, anyway? Kind of late for a social call."

"Oh, well, you know what a staunch churchgoer I am. I thought I'd catch a midnight service in town."

Leigh scrunched up her face in disbelief. "Huh?"

23

Jane shook the snow off of her boots in the vestibule of St. Jude's Lutheran Church. Inside, she could hear the congregation singing the last verse of "Silent Night." Even though the attendance was small, a pipe organ made up for the lack of voices, filling the sanctuary with thunder. Stepping briefly into the back, she gazed up at the exposed log rafters. Her eyes traveled along the arched beams to a single, round, stained-glass window high above the altar. A lighted Christmas tree dominated the right side of the room. Tiny blue and red bulbs twinkled in the semidarkness. As the minister stood to pronounce the benediction, Jane slipped back into the vestibule and began her search for the stairs leading up to the balcony. Halfway down a deserted hallway she found them.

The elegant strains of a Bach toccata signaled the end of the service. People began filtering down, talking softly and nodding to her as they moved past. She waited for the stairway to clear and then quietly tiptoed up to the top. After a quick perusal, she located Tess and Bo sitting in one of the front pews.

"Excuse me," said a young woman, brushing past her. "Merry Christmas."

Jane returned the greeting. Inching into the room behind a large palm, she was glad to see the balcony had almost completely emptied. Her luck was holding. Tess and Bo were so intent on their own conversation they hadn't noticed her entrance. She crouched down and moved carefully up the aisle, ducking at last into one of the side pews. From there, she could clearly hear their hushed voices. Tess was speaking.

"If you believe that," she said, her voice angry, "you never knew me at all. I've spent years trying to piece together the case against us. Sometimes I feel like Hester Prynne. Did you ever read *The Scarlet Letter?* I have this strange sense that the truth has been branded somewhere on my body. Anybody who looks hard enough can find it."

"But you left so suddenly," said Bo. "We never really talked."

"What was there to talk about? God knows, we both would have changed things if we could. It wasn't possible."

"It just seemed like afterward, I was never able to break through your silence. That was the worst. I mean, as long as we had each other . . ." He laid his arm along the back of the pew behind her.

"It wasn't the worst," said Tess coldly. "And we didn't have each other."

"No! It wasn't like that. We could have worked things out if only you'd stayed. I mean, we loved each other!"

Tess shrugged. "I suppose. At first maybe. But I was so young. So were you. I was what, nineteen? And you were twenty. I didn't know what I wanted back then. I didn't even know who I was. Our whole group seemed to be floating. Everyone who came up to that old house had dropped out in one way or another. I mean, what arrogance! We thought we'd escaped. None of society's mindless conformity for us. Forget our parent's stupid expectations. But what did we escape to? Look at the mess we made, Bo. Look at what we did!"

"You think it was all my fault, don't you? But you can't blame me for everything."

"Believe me," Tess assured him, "I don't. I've spent the last eighteen years blaming myself. I've lied about it to everyone. And now those lies are becoming as intolerable as the truth."

"I know," said Bo. "I know." He began to cry.

"Why do you stay here?" she asked, her voice full of frustration. "How could you live so close? My God, you're reminded every day."

"I had to keep watch. It's a kind of a graveside vigil. I owe him that. And since November, I've made myself indispensable to the head chef at the inn. He orders a lot of special things from me. I'm out there all the time making deliveries so no one pays any attention when they see me hanging around."

"God," said Tess, "I can hardly stand being there. Every room holds a memory."

"But some of them were good, weren't they?" His eyes quietly pleaded.

"Bo, that's over. I don't know what you were expecting tonight . . ."

"Nothing. Really. Not a thing. It would be stupid to assume you don't have someone else. I mean, you do, don't you?"

Tess nodded.

"It figures. A good-looking woman like you. I don't suppose it's anyone from the old days?"

"No," said Tess. "It's someone I'm terribly lucky to have found. It's the only part of my life that has ever made any

sense. We've been living together for the last six years."
She hesitated a moment. "You don't know her."

Bo looked up. "Her?"

"Yeah. The woman you saw me with this morning. The
one with the long red hair."

Bo stared openly. "Does that mean what I think it
means?"

Tess stared back.

"Forgive me, but it's going to take a minute for that to
sink in. I mean, I never thought you were . . ."

"Would you like me to say the word, Bo? It won't bite."

This time it was Bo's turn to be silent. "Look," he said
scratching his beard, "I'm not a bigot. I won't have you
thinking that. It's just, I mean, we had such a good relationship. You know what I'm saying."

Tess sighed. "Our relationship may have felt right to you,
but it never did to me. And anyway, that's all in the past.
I've finally found something that makes me happy. I would
hope you'd be glad."

Bo laughed. "Glad? That's not the first word that comes
to mind." He looked down at the altar. "I guess maybe I
did think we still had a chance. I've been alone so long."

"I'm sorry."

"Don't be. It's what I wanted." He removed his arm
from behind her. "Are you going to say anything?"

"You mean to Winifred? I don't know. Maybe."

"You're probably not very interested in my opinion, but
I hope you don't."

"Look," said Tess, her voice low and angry, "what I say
to her is my business. You have no right to issue orders.
Not anymore."

Out from a side door stepped a small, heavy-set man
wearing a janitor's uniform. He began picking up discarded
Christmas programs from the empty pews. "I'm afraid I'm
going to have to ask you good people to leave," he said

cheerfully. "We lock the doors in ten minutes." He moved on up the center aisle. One more row and Jane knew she would be discovered. Without stopping to think, she jumped to her feet, nearly knocking him over as she ran past.

"Who was that?" called Tess, turning to look.

Jane didn't wait to hear if the answer was accurate.

Once outside, she raced down the street to where Peter's Jeep was parked. Thank God she didn't have her own car. Half the time it didn't start even on summer nights. She got in and fumbled with the keys, finally finding the right one. She slipped it into the ignition, pumped the gas pedal several times, and gave it a try. The engine coughed but wouldn't start. Damn. She looked behind her. So far, no one had come out of the church. She tried again. The motor turned over but still wouldn't catch. Was it the temperature? It must be close to zero. Or maybe Peter had simply forgotten to explain his cutesy little trick for starting the damn thing. Whatever it was, the battery had one good crank left. After that, she could get out and run. She pumped the gas pedal several more times, waited a second, and then gave it one last try. Miraculously, the engine caught. She slipped it into gear and skidded off toward the center of town. Before turning the corner, she looked over her shoulder. There, in the center of the deserted street, stood a man silently watching the Jeep drive away. It was Bo.

PART TWO

Sitting on a Pin

We all live in the past, because there is nothing else to live in. To live in the present is like proposing to sit on a pin. It is too minute, it is too slight a support, it is too uncomfortable a posture.

Viking Aphorisms
G.K. Chesterton

24

Friday Morning, December 25, Christmas Day

"You want me to *what?*" demanded Cordelia as she stood smack in the center of the inn's parlor. Her voice echoed off the walls.

"Calm down," said Jane, pulling her over to a chair. "And lower your voice."

Cordelia sat down. "What makes you think I want to have any part in this little scheme? I am not a second-story woman. Breaking and entering is not my forte."

"You never know unless you try." Jane smiled.

"Very cute."

"All right, but just listen for a minute. First, the gatehouse isn't locked, so you won't have to break in. Second, no one will be there. Inga is helping Burton in the kitchen this morning. Violet is at the desk. Leigh promised she'd keep Ruthie upstairs wrapping presents until we let her know we're out. Come on, Cordelia. I've searched this house from top to bottom. We've got to at least try to find that skull. And I've been thinking. If Inga or Violet, or even Ruthie is behind all this, the gatehouse would be a perfect place to hide it. All you have to do is head over there while I do one last brief search of the cellar. Then I'll join you. Just look everywhere. Think of yourself as Arthur in search of the Grail."

167

Cordelia narrowed one eye. "All right. But just remember. You owe me."

"I'll remember." She stood, dragging Cordelia out of her chair. "Now get going. I'll join you as soon as I can."

After finishing up in the basement, Jane climbed the steep back steps to a narrow hallway that ran behind the kitchen. The first door on her right was a dry-storage room. The second appeared to be a large walk-in freezer. A thought struck her as she stopped directly in front of it. The freezer would be another great hiding place. A sign on the outside said:

INSIDE HANDLE BROKEN
PLEASE PROP DOOR OPEN WITH BOX

On the floor next to her foot rested a small pear crate. She opened the heavy door and pushed it in place. Automatically, a light went on inside. Steam swirled around her head as she entered and found the usual metal shelves on either side of the long room, stocked to the ceiling with frozen food. She looked up at a thermometer that hung from the top rack. The temperature registered five below zero.

Pulling her sweater tightly around her body, she began her search. First she moved a stack of boxes and peered between the end of the shelves and the wall. Nothing. Next she dragged out a small step ladder and climbed to the top. Again, nothing looked out of order. None of the boxes seemed large enough to contain a skull. Everything was neatly stacked and labeled, suggesting that Burton ran a tight ship. As she was about to climb down, she heard a noise in the hall. It was the sound of something heavy being dragged across the floor. Before she could react, the crate was pulled away, plunging the room into silent blackness.

* * *

Cordelia entered the gatehouse and stopped. Displayed on top of a small piano near the front door was a grouping of framed pictures. So this must be the famous Harlan Svenby and his recalcitrant son, Daniel. They looked just about the way she had pictured them. Harlan was a large man with intelligent, kind eyes set off by a deep, massive brow. He looked a bit like the Hollywood stereotype of a sea captain. Hardy and weathered. Daniel, on the other hand, even though he was handsome, had a certain weakness about the mouth. A slightly receding chin. He resembled a corporate banker Cordelia had once known. Somewhat weaselish under a pretty exterior.

Detecting the aroma of coffee, she followed the scent into the kitchen. There, on the counter next to the coffee machine, was a plate filled with fresh danish. Be still my heart, she said to herself as she sidled up to it. Carefully she eyed the offerings, choosing the largest one she could find. Reverently she lifted it to her lips. Ah, she said out loud, sinking her teeth into the tender edge. Her eyes rolled. *Ambrosia.* Perhaps this little excursion wasn't going to be as bad as she'd first thought. In two more bites, the pastry was gone. The plate beckoned to her once more. Studying the remainder, she picked a cherry-filled and set off happily in the direction of the bedrooms.

As she sauntered down the hall, she noticed one of the doors standing open. Peeking inside, she called, "Plumber. I'm here to fix your pipes, lady." No response. This was too ridiculous. Spending Christmas morning sneaking around corners, looking for some ancient skull, was totally beyond the pale. Lethargically she pulled open a drawer. Nothing. She opened a closet. A box of shoes fell onto her head. Disgusted, she left the room and walked back into the hall.

Now what? She opened another door. This room was more interesting. Posters of famous people filled the walls. Hart Crane. Judy Garland. Arthur Koestler. Marilyn Monroe. Sylvia Plath. This must be Ruthie's room. She made a mental note to send her an autographed publicity photo. It was the least she could do. Ruthie was quite obviously a slob. Cordelia immediately felt a certain kinship. The bed was unmade, and the floor littered here and there with books and assorted junk. She tried one of the desk drawers and found it locked. How intriguing. Locked drawers usually meant secrets. But the space was too small for a skull. She tugged harder. No luck. Selecting a letter opener from a glass filled with pens and pencils, she slipped it carefully into the slim opening over the lock. Something inside the mechanism sprung upward. Cordelia felt a certain devious thrill as she slid the drawer all the way out. There, in front of her eyes rested a small gun. She picked it up and examined it briefly. Why would Ruthie need something like this? Protection from the odd rabid squirrel? And look here. It was loaded.

Out in the front room a door opened and then shut. For an instant Cordelia froze. Steady old girl, she told herself. It's only Jane. She returned the gun to its hiding place and picked up what was left of her danish. Before she reached the living room archway, she heard someone turn on the radio. That was odd? Why would Jane do that?

Ten feet in front her, Ruthie floated through the passage, headed for the kitchen. Realizing she had only an instant to react, Cordelia edged her way into the living room and dove behind the first large object she could find. An old comfy chair. Now what? So much for Jane's great ideas. This was the last straw. Definitely the very last straw.

Out in the kitchen the phone began to ring. Ruthie picked it up.

"Hello," she said.

Silence while she listened.

"I didn't think you needed me any longer, Leigh. I'm

sorry. You seemed like you wanted to talk to Stephen. I felt like I was in the way."

More silence.

"Well I said I was sorry. But I can't come back now."

Cordelia could hear Ruthie pouring herself a cup of coffee.

"No, I can't. What? No, no one else is here. Why do you ask?"

Cordelia thought of the roast goose she had eaten for dinner last night. A few more minutes and she would know exactly how the poor thing felt.

Jane sat huddled on the step stool, conserving what little body heat she had left. Every few minutes she would feel her way over to the door and pound on it. At least it brought some sensation back into her hands and feet. She had no idea how long she'd been trapped. And worst of all, there was no longer any doubt in her mind that Elmer had been murdered and that she was the next victim.

A few more minutes passed. Cordelia was probably wondering what had happened. Maybe she would come looking for her. Yes, that was it! Cordelia would come to the rescue! But what if she was too late? Freezing to death was a terribly painful way to go. And how would she know where to look? Jane could already feel her feet beginning to ache. What was one more dead body in the scheme of things? She should have been more careful. But hindsight couldn't help her now.

She climbed stiffly off the stool and dragged herself over to the door again. This time she kicked at it, yelling, "Help! Help me!" Feeling a slight shudder inside the room, she looked up as the condenser clicked off. Instantly, the fan stopped. The room became deathly silent. Fighting down her panic, she felt her way back to the step stool and pulled it over to the door. She grabbed it firmly and began whacking it against the heavy metal. Surely someone could hear that! Her lungs ached from breathing the icy air. The tips of her fingers had gone numb.

Still no response. No one had heard. Inside her head the sound of her own heartbeat grew louder until she felt it would swallow her if she couldn't get away and run. Her body heaved violently as she doubled over, her eyes filling with tears. This can't be happening! She pulled her sleeve roughly across her eyes. No! Get a grip! Desperately, she struggled to control her terrible trembling.

And then a miracle happened. The door handle slowly turned. Jane held her breath as a flood of warmth and light engulfed her. She fell out of the doorway and landed on her knees in the hallway.

"Jane!" said Stephen. "What's going on?" He leaned down to help her.

Jane could feel her cheeks burn. She cupped her hands over her ears.

"How did you get in there?" Stephen took one of her hands in his and began rubbing. "You're like a block of ice. You've been crying! Jane, are you all right? Can you talk? How did this happen?"

Jane's mouth felt tight. Her skin was on fire. "I was . . . just . . . looking around. I thought it might be interesting to see how Burton . . . organizes his freezer. I'm a restaurant owner, you know, so things like that interest me." She knew she was babbling.

Stephen frowned. "Didn't you see the sign?"

With Stephen's help, Jane got to her feet. "Sure. I used the crate, but someone pulled it out."

Stephen's frown deepened. "I see. I don't know what to say. No one was back here when I arrived. I suppose it could have been an accident." He looked genuinely upset.

"What are you doing here?" asked Jane, shielding her eyes from the brightness of the bare ceiling bulb.

"I got home a little while ago. Ruthie was helping Leigh wrap some Christmas presents upstairs, so she shooed me out. When I came down for breakfast, I saw that the guy from the Riverside Market had just made a delivery. He usually leaves everything in the hall. I thought I'd help Burton do a little of the stocking. Since it's Christmas Day, he's shorthanded."

"Bo Dierdorf was here?" asked Jane.

"Yeah. Why? Do you know him?"

"We've met." Her body shivered involuntarily.

"What you need is to soak in a hot bath," said Stephen.

Jane thought of Cordelia. "You say Ruthie is still upstairs with Leigh?"

"Well, I'm not really positive about that. Ruthie slipped out when Leigh came into the bedroom to talk to me for a minute. She probably came back though. I left just as Leigh was going to look for her."

Again, Jane felt a sense of fear grip her body. She had to get over to the gatehouse fast. "Thanks Stephen. You may have saved my life."

"Where are you off to in such a hurry?" He stepped in front of her.

"It's kind of a long story. I'll tell you about it some other time." Sidestepping him, she headed straight for the delivery entrance. It was the quickest way. "Catch you later," she called over her shoulder.

Cordelia sucked in her stomach and attempted to think small.

Ruthie reentered the living room; slicing an apple in half with a small paring knife, she stopped in front of the piano and gazed down quietly at the pictures.

Cordelia watched from her vantage behind the chair. An entire plate full of danish in the kitchen and this scrawny woman chooses an apple. Life was not fair. Ruthie seemed to be transfixed by something in front of her. One of the pictures had caught her eye. Cordelia noticed Ruthie's hand squeezing the knife again and again. Very strange behavior indeed.

The front doorbell sounded. Ruthie set the apple halves down on a table and went to answer it. Behind her back she still held the knife.

"Hello there, Ruthie," said Henry Gyldenskog. He took off his hat and stepped inside. "I thought I might find you here. Listen, kiddo, I won't be able to make our morning game of checkers today. I'm sure you understand what with it being Christmas and all. I've got to deliver some presents to several friends in town. You understand."

Ruthie nodded. "You don't have any time. It's okay."

"Now, now, don't look so glum. Maybe we can get a game in this afternoon."

"Sure," said Ruthie. "Maybe." She glanced over at the piano and then back at Henry. "You've tried to be a good friend to me."

All the way across the room Cordelia could hear the blankness and finality in Ruthie's voice. It chilled her to the bone.

Henry looked puzzled. "You sound like you think I'm on my death bed. I assure you I'm very healthy. I've got lots of years left to play checkers." He grinned.

"Of course," said Ruthie. Behind her back she tightened the grip on her knife. "I have a present for you. I'll bring it up later."

"That's sweet of you," smiled Henry. "And I have one for you too. I'll see you this afternoon then?"

"Yes. You'll see me."

"Great. Give my best to your aunts." He tipped his hat and left.

After he'd gone, Ruthie turned around and brought the knife out from behind her back. She touched the tip with the index finger of her left hand, pressing down until her expression showed a flicker of pain.

From the kitchen came the sound of a knock on the back door.

"Damn," she muttered, dropping the knife on the table next to the apple. Quickly she exited the room. After a few seconds, Cordelia could hear Jane's calm voice. Well, rudy-toot-toot. The Marines have finally landed. It was about time.

Cordelia jumped up from her kneeling position and raced to the front door. She opened it softly and then closed it behind her. She stood in the cold for approximately one minute and then knocked. Without waiting for a response, she opened it again and shouted, "Anybody home?"

Ruthie and Jane entered the living room together.

"Ah," said Cordelia, leveling a disgusted gaze at Jane. "I thought I might find you here."

Jane looked relieved. "Cordelia, how nice—"

"Hello," said Ruthie.

Cordelia kept her eyes on Jane. "I need your help. Could you come with me? *Now.*"

"Of course," said Jane. "I came to talk to Violet, but she's not around."

"How sad. Let's go."

Jane wished Ruthie a Merry Christmas and then followed Cordelia out the front door.

The snow scrunched under their feet as they walked quickly back to the inn.

"Where were you!!!" snarled Cordelia. "Do you know what it's like to try and pack my bulk behind a tiny chair?"

Jane started to laugh.

"You think this is funny?"

"No," said Jane, grabbing Cordelia's arm. "I'm just so glad to see you."

"What?"

"I'm sorry. I'll explain everything. I have a good excuse for not joining you sooner."

"You damn well better."

"So, did you find anything?"

"I found out Cousin Ruthie is a psychopath. She likes to play with knives, and she owns a gun."

Jane stopped. "A gun? You found a gun?"

"I will say no more until I am comfortably ensconced in the dining room with my breakfast laid out before me." She turned and headed up the steps.

25

"You don't really want to make a snowman, do you?" Cordelia scowled. "Why Dylan, you surprise me. This is Christmas Day! You don't want to do something so boring. So prosaic. So totally lacking in . . . in . . . *umph*."

"What's *umph?*" asked Dylan, sitting on the bench watching Jane unlace his new ice skates.

"Right, Cordelia. Define *umph* for us."

Cordelia smoothed out her scarf. "Why, everyone knows what that means." She glowered at Jane.

"I don't," said Dylan, eying her expectantly.

"Well . . . all right. But I don't have my handy-dandy pocket dictionary with me this afternoon. Nevertheless, I suppose I could take a stab. *Umph*," she said, putting her hand over her heart. "A noun. Webster defines it as the quality of being *umphy*, as in, Ms. Toffelmeyer was looking unusually *umphy* today in her new red-flannel shirt. Derived from the Latin, *umphium*, meaning that which has attained *umph*. There. I believe that approximates one of those wonderfully helpful dictionary definitions."

Dylan pulled on Jane's sleeve. "Huh?"

"Okay, I'll try again." She sat down next to him and pulled a tissue out of her coat pocket. "When something doesn't have *umph*, Dylan, it isn't fun. Like a snowman isn't fun compared to say, a snow turtle. Or a snow rabbit. Or even a snow dragon!"

The little boy thought for a moment. "I want to make a snow monster!"

"Ah," said Cordelia, her momentary triumph sinking into despair. "A monster? But Dylan, that's so . . . so nonspecific."

"What?"

Jane took hold of his hand. "A snow monster it is. Where shall we build it?"

"Over there by the porch," he said, pointing. "Come on Cor-deel."

"That's Cordelia. *Cordelia*, you silly person." She hissed through clenched teeth. Remaining seated, she watched Jane and Dylan rough out a spot near the steps. "Is this a male or female monster?" she shouted, feeling the question particularly pertinent.

Jane listened to Dylan for a moment and then shouted back, "neither."

Great, thought Cordelia. Just what the world needs. A monster with sexual identity problems. Nothing good will come of this. She dabbed lightly at her sore nose.

"That's a great toe!" said Jane, helping Dylan form the feet. "What do you think? Are they too big?"

"No!" he cried, his eyes wide. "Now let's roll the snow."

Jane hollered to Cordelia, "You want to help us make the body? The snow is perfect this afternoon. Nice and sticky."

"I'll watch, thank you very much. I need a long rest after this morning's insanity." Cordelia swept over in her long red cape and sat down on the steps. "By the way, I assume Leigh must be feeling better."

"She is. You know, I forgot to tell you something. Last night, when she was staying over at the gatehouse, someone wearing a mask tried to peek in her bedroom window. I didn't get a very good look because it was so dark, but it really scared her. What do you make of that?"

Cordelia shrugged. "I don't know. Did anyone order a pizza?"

"I can tell you're in one of your helpful moods."

"I beg your pardon?"

"All right, let's change the subject. Did you have a good time at the lodge after I left?"

"So so."

Jane helped Dylan lift the ball on top of the roughly formed feet.

"Let's roll another one," he shouted, running back into the center of the yard.

Jane followed.

"Unlike me, sometimes your dad lacks subtlety."

"Right," said Jane. "Fine comparison."

"Humph. I suppose that was another one of your veiled slurs." She kicked an icicle off the railing. "The wedding is going to be next May."

"I know. I was there, remember?"

"True," said Cordelia, "but since you had to leave so abruptly, you aren't invited."

"Very funny." Jane rolled a huge snowball over to the steps. "Help me with this, will you?"

Cordelia stood. "Step aside," she said, leaning down and hoisting it up, placing it carefully on top of the other. "I may be a general all-around lump, but I'm not weak."

Jane bowed. "Now, how shall we do the head, Dylan?

VITAL LIES

179

Maybe we can roll a smaller ball and make the hair out of sticks."

"That's not scary!" A slight pout grew around the corners of his mouth.

"I could go in and get some ketchup from your father," offered Cordelia. "Would you like it to dribble out of its mouth in true Stephen King fashion?"

Dylan put his hands on his hips and glared.

"Sorry. It was just a suggestion. You needn't get huffy."

"What do *you* think we should do?" asked Jane bending down. "You know Dylan, a monster doesn't have to be scary. We could make it a nice, funny monster."

"Sure," said Cordelia. "Sort of like a Republican."

Dylan continued to glare. "It's no fun if it's not scary." He stuck his hands inside his pockets and looked glum.

"Of course," said Cordelia. "I quite agree. Think of something, Jane! Chop chop."

"Well," she said, standing up and brushing the packed snow off her knees, "let me see."

"I know!" cried Dylan. "I got something real scary. You wait." He raced off toward the back of the house.

"What do you suppose he's up to?" asked Cordelia. She sighed. "All that energy in one little person makes me tired. Are we getting old, Janey?"

"He's probably got something hidden in the barn. At least, that's the direction he was headed."

"In the barn, you say? How charming. I think that's my cue to make a swift but graceful departure." She stood.

"You mean you aren't going to stay and see the final result?"

"Oh, deary me, look at the time. I'm going to miss my favorite TV evangelist if I don't get crackin'. A daily dose of tears and terror is essential to my moral development."

"Come on," said Jane, "you can't miss the grand finale."

"I can't? I thought I could."

"I got it," cried Dylan, running toward them.

Jane could tell he had something hidden under his jacket. "What do you have in there?" she asked, watching him skid to a stop in front of the steps. "Can I see?"

Dylan clutched the lump in his coat tightly. "Okay. But this is real scary." He pulled out a skull.

"Dylan!"

"Are you mad at me?" he asked, looking as if he expected the worst.

"No no. I'm not mad. I'm just a little . . . surprised. You're right. This is a scary head."

"Damn straight," said Cordelia, tapping Jane on the arm. "Especially with that little hole right through the temple. I don't think that skull died of old age."

"Do skulls die?" asked Dylan, closing one eye and squinting up at her.

"Listen, Dylan. A skull is the bone that lives inside our head. That's all. Cordelia was just trying to amuse us."

"She was what?"

"Trying to be funny."

"She was?" He didn't smile.

"Everyone's a critic," snarled Cordelia.

Jane crouched down next to the little boy. "Listen, Dylan, I need you to tell me where you found this."

Dylan's feet played with the snow.

"It's not wrong for you to tell me. It would be very good if I knew."

Dylan gave the snow a good kick. "By the barn."

"By the barn," said Jane, looking up at Cordelia. "How did you know it was there?"

He played with the fringe on his scarf. "I saw 'em."

"You mean you saw someone put it there?"

Dylan nodded.

"This is very important," said Jane. "Can you tell me who it was?"

The little boy shook his head. "No."

"You can't or you won't?" asked Cordelia, picking up the interrogation.

Dylan looked up at her defiantly. "Daddy says I'm not supposed to be a tattletale."

"Oh Dylan," said Jane, giving him a big hug, "you aren't being a tattletale."

"Certainly not," Cordelia assured him. "And besides, this is important! There's a lunatic around here—"

Jane shook her head for Cordelia to stop. "Will you listen to me for a second, Dylan? You don't have to tell me who you saw put it in the barn, okay? I understand. You want to do what your daddy says. But it would be okay if you helped me with one small thing. You'd like to help me, wouldn't you?"

"Yes," he said softly.

"All right. Then just answer one question. All you have to do is say yes or no. You don't have to say a name."

"Okay."

"Great, Dylan. Now listen carefully. Was the person you saw hiding the skull a woman?"

Dylan looked from Jane to Cordelia and then back again. "Yes," he whispered.

"I thought so! Thank you, Dylan." She gave him another hug. "Cordelia," she said, standing up. "That confirms it. I know who did it. Here." She handed Cordelia the skull. "You take this and wrap it in something. A towel or a jacket. Then take it to my car."

"I will do no such thing!"

"Yes, you will," said Jane firmly. "And then, why don't you go sit in the parlor? Have a sherry and sit in front of the fire if you like. I may have something very interesting to tell you in a few minutes."

"Can I come too?" asked Dylan, pulling on Cordelia's cape.

"Why not? I feel like I'm in the army. I might as well act the part." She straightened up and looked down at him, shouting, "March!"

Dylan took off running toward the parking lot.

26

"I need to talk to you alone," said Jane, pulling off her ski cap and shaking out her long brown hair. She leaned up against the front desk in the foyer of the inn. "It's important. Maybe we could use one of the empty guest rooms."

Inga looked up from her book, her wafer-thin lips fixed in a sweet smile. "Of course. I can give you a few minutes. I hope it's not about Leigh. She was feeling so much better today."

"No," said Jane. "It's not about Leigh."

"I see. Well then," she mumbled as she dialed the kitchen, calling a young woman out to take over for her while she was gone. After getting her organized behind the switchboard, Inga led the way upstairs. "Two-o-seven is one of my favorite rooms." She opened the door and switched on a small table lamp. "Violet and I helped Leigh pick out some of the furnishings from one of those antique stores over in Hammerville."

"It's very nice," said Jane, too preoccupied to really notice anything. She slid out a chair and sat down.

Inga perched hesitantly on the edge of the bed. Her ve-

neer of calm was beginning to fray. "So, what was it you
wanted to talk to me about?"

Jane took a deep breath. "Look Inga, I know you took
the skull. Let's not pretend, okay?"

Inga's hands fluttered about her hair. "Well, I'll say this
much for you. You come right to the point."

Jane remained silent.

Inga's quiet brown eyes examined her for a moment.
"All right. I knew it was only a matter of time before
someone put two and two together. Leigh told me about the
bobby pin. But how did you know it was me?"

"Burton said you were in the kitchen taking over for him
during all the commotion after the skeleton was found.
From past association with the house, you would have
known about the old stairs, and since the kitchen is close to
the back hallway, you had easy access to it. No one would
think anything if you were gone for a few minutes. Your
hair was pinned up under the chef's hat Burton insisted everyone wear. You took it off and set it on the steps because
you knew it was going to get in your way. That's what created the circle we found in the dust. I imagine that's also
when the bobby pin must have fallen to the floor. If it
hadn't been for those two things, I might never have come
to the correct conclusion."

Inga smiled. "You're quite clever. Where is the skull
now?"

"I have it locked in my car. When we're done talking, I
intend to take it over to the police station."

"I understand," said Inga. "I suppose I should have done
that myself."

Jane was even more puzzled. "If that's true, why did you
take it in the first place?"

"It's a long story." She looked away.

"I need to hear it, Inga. Too much has happened that

needs explaining. We're not leaving this room until I know what's going on."

For a fleeting second, Inga fixed her gaze on something just above Jane's head. Closing her eyes, she sighed. "All right. But some of what you want to hear is very painful for me." Her hands lay passively in her lap, as dry and brittle as withered leaves. "The fact is, my original plan was to take the entire skeleton. I got scared when I heard someone coming down the stairs, so I just grabbed the skull and left. It never occurred to me the police would remove it all. If I'd known, I'd never have gone to the trouble in the first place."

"But who was the man buried in the boat?"

Inga shook her head. "I'm afraid I can't help you there. I needed to get rid of it because of Ruthie."

"Ruthie? What does she have to do with any of this?"

Inga's voice dropped to a whisper. "I didn't know what else to do. And I was right to worry. Last night I found her down in the cellar sitting in that old boat. She was playing with the little bell attached to the front end. And she was humming."

"Humming?"

"Yes! Of all the crazy things. This house is making her sick. I can feel it. It all started when we moved here last spring. Back then, Ruthie was living in town and had a good job. Everything was just fine. She was working at the Riverside Market. It's a nice little grocery store. The inn buys a lot of its fresh produce there. Anyway, until she quit, Ruthie worked there for years." Inga paused for a moment. "You know Jane, I don't feel comfortable talking about this. But since you're so adamant, perhaps I should tell you something that might help you understand a little better. First, you have to promise you won't tell Violet. I'd never hear the end of it if she thought I'd told you any of this."

"I promise," said Jane. "Don't worry."

"All right. I do trust you. The truth is, Ruthie spent a short time in a mental hospital when she was in her late twenties. She'd been terribly depressed. It got to the point where she wouldn't even come out of her room. We finally had to call a doctor because we were afraid she might hurt herself. Later, after she was discharged, the doctors made her promise to find a job and move out of our house. I don't mind telling you, I was pretty upset by that. They obviously didn't think we were competent to care for her. But what did they know? Ruthie has always been an unusual child. She needs special understanding. I, for one, didn't think living on her own was a good idea, but the doctors insisted. They said she needed to be more self-sufficient. She depended on us too much. Well, of course the child depended on us. What are families for?"

Jane was more than surprised Inga still referred to Ruthie as a child.

"Ruthie's father, our brother Daniel, died in a tragic accident when she was only six. He'd been up on our roof doing some minor repairs when he fell. He was killed instantly. At the time, he and Ruthie were living with us."

"I thought Ruthie lived here on the island when she was a child."

"Well, that's true. She did. For a while. You see, my brother Daniel was many years younger than Violet, Constance, and myself. Constance is Leigh's mother. We all sort of raised Danny. Our mother died shortly after he was born. By the time he went off to college, Violet and I had been living and working in Repentance River for many years. But Dad continued to rent this house even though Danny had left. He loved it here. The whole family was so proud of Daniel going off to college like he did. You can imagine what a surprise it was when one night he appeared on Dad's doorstep holding a baby. Ruthie was two months old at the time. Danny explained that he'd gotten someone pregnant and she'd given birth, but her parents insisted they put it up for adoption. I guess he couldn't stand the idea, so one morning, he just walked in and took the baby and left. Then he hopped a bus and came home. Since Dad didn't know what else to do with them, they simply moved in. Danny and Ruthie lived here until he died, then they came to live with us in town."

"How did your father die?" asked Jane.

"Dad? He had a heart attack. He'd been warned by his doctors to take it easy, but would he listen?" She shook her head. "He was a hopelessly stubborn man. I suppose I learned my stubbornness from him. Ruthie took his death pretty hard. After she and Danny moved to town with us, we encouraged our brother to find a job. He was never much interested in working. He did take a special interest in his daughter though, and he made us promise that we'd take care of her if anything ever happened to him. I know both Violet and I took that promise seriously. We've raised her like our own."

Jane found the digression interesting but wanted to get back to the point. "You said you thought this house was making Ruthie sick. What do you mean?"

"I guess you could say it all began last summer. Occasionally, she would come to visit. She'd stay a night or two in our guest room. It was like pulling teeth to get her to leave. Finally one day, here she comes walking up the back steps carrying a suitcase. She said she'd quit her job and given notice at her rooming house. No reason offered, just that she'd done it. That was early August. Even then I could see how being back here affected her. She lived with us nearly a month. It took some doing, but we eventually convinced her to leave. Violet talked Mr. Dierdorf into giving her another chance, and I found a room to rent. Everything went along all right until November. One evening she just walked in and informed us she'd quit again. She was determined to live with us here on the island. Somehow it seemed inevitable."

"I still don't understand," said Jane, trying not to sound impatient. Inga seemed to need to talk. She wanted to explain things in a certain way.

"Yes, I'm getting to that. You see, ever since she'd begun spending time on the island again, we've watched her mental health deteriorate. Oh, she tries to act like nothing's wrong. But sometimes she overdoes it. At first she followed Leigh around like an adoring child—she wanted so badly for them to be close. But now, it's almost like she's given up. At the same time, she refuses to talk about what's bothering her. That's God's honest truth, Jane. She sits in that boat downstairs and hums, or recites poetry. It's not healthy. She's becoming preoccupied with death. I've seen some of what she's written lately. That's why I wanted to get rid of the skeleton. There's no telling what crazy idea she might get into her head."

In the dim light of the table lamp, Jane could see Inga struggling with her emotions. It was apparent the woman cared deeply about her niece. Ruthie was more troubled than Jane had imagined. "Inga," she said, hating herself for having to ask the next question. "Please don't be angry, but I've got to ask you this. Do you think it's possible Ruthie might be responsible for everything that's been happening around here?"

"What do you mean?" asked Inga, her expression wary.

"Well, you know, like the ruined copper pots or the bomb threat? You're the one who took the call that night. Could it have been Ruthie's voice?"

Inga's face grew rigid. "Never! I won't hear of it. You can't believe Ruthie would do that?"

"I don't know what to believe," said Jane, "but if she's really that mentally unstable, she might—"

"Impossible! Get that idea out of your head right now. I

know you're Leigh's friend, but that doesn't give you the right to go accusing her relatives of such things. It's bunk. Do you hear me? Bunk!"

"I'm sure you believe that, Inga. I haven't discussed this with Leigh yet. I know she doesn't think any of you would intentionally hurt her or this inn, but I'll be honest with you. I'm not convinced."

Anger flared in Inga's eyes. "Have you ever been a parent, Jane?"

"What? No, I haven't."

"No. I didn't think so. Let me tell you something. There are times, as a parent, you are called on to make a decision. It has to be done, so you do it. In hindsight you may realize you made the wrong one, but you live with it. Families are supposed to be based on mutual love and trust. I firmly believe that. But perfect parenting never exists. What you do can affect people for the rest of their life. Your only guide is your love. You never know until later if your decisions were the right ones. We made some mistakes with Ruthie, I admit that. But I know her. You don't. You think she had something to do with Elmer's death. That's where you're headed with all your questions, isn't it? But Ruthie could never hurt anyone. *Trust* is what it's all about, Jane, and you have to trust that she wasn't responsible."

Jane followed her words, if not her logic. Yet she was strangely touched by Inga's fierce defense of her niece. "I'll have to think about what you've said."

Inga looked away. "You do that."

The strain of the last few days was beginning to take its toll. A burning sensation behind Jane's eyes told her how tired she was. "I appreciate how candid you've been with me."

Inga rose stiffly and walked to the door. Without turning, she said more softly, "I'm sorry I got so agitated, Jane. I didn't mean to lecture you. Violet and I will take care of

Ruthie. We always have. I know you've still got a lot of questions. To be honest, so do I. But if you're looking for answers from me, you're going to be disappointed. I'm fresh out."

As expected, Jane found Cordelia sitting in the parlor in front of the fire sipping a tiny glass of sherry. "Let's get going. I want to take that skull over to the police station right away."

"Aren't you going to fill me in on the big news? I've been waiting on pins and needles for your return."

"You do look positively ridden with anxiety," said Jane. "Come on. I'll tell you in the car."

"Miss Lawless?" said a voice from the archway. "You had a phone call a few minutes ago. You weren't in your room so I took a message."

"Who was it?" asked Jane turning around.

"Someone from your restaurant. They didn't give a name. But they want you to call back right away."

Cordelia pulled on Jane's hand. "You take your time, dearheart. I'm satisfied to sit here the rest of the afternoon. Leigh said a group was going to gather 'round the baby grand later and sing Christmas songs. I thought I'd add my golden voice to the throng."

Jane wondered who would call from her restaurant. It wasn't even open on Christmas Day. "Fine," she said, following the woman out into the foyer. Inga had resumed her seat behind the counter. "May I use your phone here at the desk?"

"Of course," said the young woman. She turned to Inga. "I'm going back to fold some linen."

Jane dialed the number. On the fourth ring she got a recorded message that said the restaurant would reopen tomorrow with normal hours. "Hum," she said, hanging up the phone.

"Problems?" asked Inga.

"I don't know. Maybe." She picked up the phone and dialed her private line.

"Hello," said a male voice.

"Felix!" said Jane. "What are you doing there today?"

Felix Mulroy was the night manager. "Jane. Hi. I thought I'd get a little work done on the price list from that new dairy vendor. It's so quiet around here today. Perfect for concentrating. And you know me. I'm not much for all this Christmas hoopla."

"You didn't call me here a little while ago, did you?"

"Me? No."

"Is anyone else around?"

"Not a soul. Why?"

Suddenly, it clicked in Jane's mind what was happening. "Thanks, Felix. I'll talk to you later." She hung up.

Shouting into the parlor for Cordelia to follow, she raced out through the front porch and around to the side of the house. Her car was parked at the far end of the lot.

"What's this all about," said Cordelia, puffing up behind her.

Jane caught her breath for a moment and then continued running toward the car. "Where did you put the skull?" she shouted over her shoulder.

"In the backseat. Under an old quilt."

Jane skidded to a stop next to the rear door. Just as she expected, both the skull and the blanket were gone. "Damn," she shouted, looking up at the back of the house. The blinds were pulled in Henry and Per's suite, but she thought she could see someone peeking through the sitting room shade.

Cordelia ambled slowly up the shoveled walk. "Don't tell me. We've been robbed."

Jane leaned against the car with one hand and shook her head. "You got it."

27

The little rusted bell on the boat's bow tinkled in the dank loneliness of the cellar. Again and again, Ruthie reached out and tapped it lightly. Why did it call to her so fiercely, as if, when it rang, something inside her pulled and twisted, struggling to get out? Was she crazy? Certainly, no sane person would be sitting in an old boat in a dreary cellar on Christmas Day. If she wanted proof, there it was.

Again, she poked the bell with her finger, the sound echoing in the small chamber. Why had she closed her eyes every night since childhood and seen such images? Darkness. Blood. A wolf so close she could hear it breathing. And a light. Not an ordinary light, but one so bright it made her eyes water. Made her want to cry out. She had tried to make sense of her feelings. Nothing was more important. She had examined the house and the island as if they were part of some ancient forgotten poem. But too many of the verses were missing. Nothing was complete.

One question led simply to another. One fragment of memory led only to another imperfect, uncertain insight. Nothing fit. On the other hand, that probably did make *some* sense because there was nothing to fit. Nothing to figure out. She was crazy, that was all. Depressed. Fixated. The anger she felt at others was nothing compared to the anger she felt for herself. Ruthie was wrong. Ruthie was

unlovable. Worthless. That elemental truth was the answer
to all her sadness. She'd always known it.

Yet not everything was simple, was it? All her life she
had felt like a woman born in darkness, living in a deep
cave that no light could penetrate. But wasn't the chaos inside her belly her own fault?

No!

Often in dreams she would wake, knowing she had
glimpsed the answer. It was right there. So close she could
almost touch it. The truth of her life beckoned to her. Yet
hadn't she always possessed the truth? Even though she'd
been surrounded by lies since childhood, she had always
recognized them for what they were. Ugly. Pathetic. The
frightening thing was, people believed their own lies. And
unless she knuckled under and embraced them, too, *she* became the outsider. Lies were so much simpler. So much
more comfortable. And yet, finally, so pitifully empty.

28

Jane paused on the bridge; she chipped a piece of packed
snow off the railing and let it drop into the swiftly flowing
Repentance River. The walk into town had been a tonic.
The crisp afternoon air seemed to refresh like nothing else
could. During the past hour she had finally been able to
calm down. Allowing the skull to get away from her the
way it had was incredibly stupid. She should have never let
it out of her sight. Yet nothing could change it now. It was

probably useless to attempt another search. This time, the skull would be hidden beyond anyone's reach.

"Good afternoon," called a voice from halfway down the bridge. "Are you out for a stroll? Or are you considering the pros and cons of jumping into the deep?" Per strode toward her, his wheat blond hair catching the last rays of the afternoon sun.

"Nothing quite so drastic." Jane smiled.

"Kind of a long way down, isn't it?" He stopped beside her and peered over the railing. "I've never liked heights."

"We have something in common," she said. "Under the best of circumstances, taking a swim in the Repentance River wouldn't be much fun. How's the book coming?"

Per got out a pack of cigarettes and offered her one.

She shook her head.

"Kind of slow. I've had too many things on my mind lately." He lit the cigarette and flipped the match over the side.

Jane dropped another chunk of snow into the turgid, root beer-colored water, giving herself a moment to gather her courage. She hated the question she knew she had to ask. "Per, I don't mean to upset you, but there's something I've been wondering about ever since Burton found that skeleton in the cellar."

Per shifted uncomfortably away from her. "What's that?"

"Well, remember you spoke about your friend, Randy? You said you felt his disappearance was kind of strange. You've never seen or heard from him again."

"You think he was buried behind that wall?"

"It did occur to me."

Per sighed deeply, his eyes fixed on the horizon. "To be honest, I'm worried, too. I called Randy's mother yesterday. I suppose I shouldn't have, but I did. With very little ceremony, she informed me he was dead. Oh, she doesn't know that for a fact, but apparently they haven't heard from him in over twenty years."

"I know this is an awful thing to suggest, but if it is Randy, could your father have had anything to do with it?"

Per shook his head, an angry frown drawing deeply at the wrinkles around his eyes. "I don't know. But I'm sure of one thing. My father won't talk about that time in our lives. It makes me wonder if he doesn't have something to hide. I know he's not supposed to be stressed, but I can't let him hide behind that forever. The real truth is, I think I've been afraid to press him on it because of what I might find out."

They both leaned against the railing while Per finished his cigarette. After taking one last puff, he tossed it over the side. "I better get going. I need to have it out with him before I lose my nerve."

Jane turned to face him. "I wish you luck."

Per nodded his thanks. "Are you going to be at the new moon ritual Winifred is guiding tomorrow night?"

"I am. It's the last planned event before the week is over. Cordelia and I are driving back to Minneapolis on Sunday. But if things aren't resolved around here, I may stay on a bit longer."

"I guess I'll see you tomorrow then. I can't help but remember what happened at the last ritual. I hope we don't have a repeat of anything like that. Well, Merry Christmas." His voice was sad. "It's kind of an empty saying right now, isn't it?" He swung his wool scarf around his neck and waved as he headed back toward the inn.

Jane watched until he rounded the end of the bridge. Turning to the river once again, she allowed her mind to drift to the sounds of the flowing water. A huge chunk of ice had broken loose from the shore and was caught in the current. It floated silently under her as she watched the sun begin to set over the island. It was a lovely sight, yet something about it seemed touched with a faint sense of menace. Deep in thought, she was abruptly jolted back to reality by the sound of a truck pulling onto the bridge. By the time she turned to look, it was too late. The truck careened wildly from side to side, heading straight for her. With no time left to think, she leapt up on the narrow railing, frantically fumbling for a grip. The truck sped past, missing her by inches.

"Damn asshole!" she shouted as she jumped back down. She squinted into the distance trying to see who was driving. It was no use. The truck was already too far down the bridge. Dipping her head into the wind, she began running toward the island. Whoever was driving that heap of junk had some explaining to do.

Even in the fading twilight, Jane had no trouble making out the truck parked askew on the rounded drive in front of the inn. In the distance, she could hear the sound of shouting. Bo and Tess were standing by the barn, arguing loudly.

"Look there," said Bo, his tone mocking. He pointed toward Jane. "It's one of your special friends."

"Get a grip," said Tess. "You're making a fool of yourself."

Unable to control her anger any longer, Jane shouted, "You nearly killed me on that bridge!"

Bo regarded her with a certain bleary-eyed curiosity. He staggered a step backwards as Tess grabbed hold of him, spinning him around. "Is that true?"

"No, of course not." He yanked his arm away. "No one was on the bridge."

"Wrong, Rambo. *I* was on the bridge." From ten feet away Jane could smell the alcohol.

"Well if you *were*," he said, wiping his mouth roughly, "so what? It's a free country. As far as I'm concerned you can stand on that fucking bridge for the next century. I don't give a damn."

"He's been drinking," said Tess, trying to offer some explanation.

"Don't make any excuses for me. I don't need them. I don't need your help," he snarled. "Come to think of it, I don't need *you!*"

"Stop it," cried Tess. "Do you think I came back here to listen to this crap?"

"Me!" said Bo indignantly. "What did I do? I just wanted to talk to you. Talk some sense into you. Nobody belongs out here anyway. This inn," he shouted into the wind, "it should be shut down. Condemned. Burned to the ground."

"And I suppose you're just the guy to do it?" said Jane.

He backed up a step, pulling a bottle of vodka out of his coat. "I know what I need. I need to finish this." He got out his car keys. Before he realized what was happening, Jane had knocked them out of his hand. "Hey," he said angrily. "What are you doing?"

She reached down and picked them up. "You can get them in the morning. They'll be at the front desk."

"You can't do that," he insisted, dropping his bottle.

"If you come any closer, I guarantee you'll regret it. Maybe we should call the police. Would you like that, Bo? We could discuss why you're so interested in this island. I'm sure everyone would like to know why you're out here all the time."

"You think you're so tough."

"In case you're too impaired to recognize it, this is called anger! If you weren't so out of it, I've got a couple questions of my own I'd like you to answer." She kicked the bottle against the side of the barn. "I suppose I have to trust that you know how to drive when you're not drunk. Otherwise, I'd have you arrested! Got it? You can find your keys at the front desk in the morning."

"God, a do-gooder!" he shrieked. "Just what the world

over his middle. A football game blared from the TV set in
the corner. Per watched him snore for a moment before entering his own bedroom. He took off his coat and hung it
on the back of a chair. The old man might as well rest for
a few more minutes. Briskly, he walked over to the closet
and lifted down the Christmas present he had bought for
Henry several weeks ago. It was a new rifle scope. Something Per knew his father had been wanting. He set it carefully on the bed and moved to the mirror, examining
himself for signs of age. At forty-one, Per was no longer a
young man. His hair was starting to thin, and his skin had
lost some of its youthful elasticity. The face that stared
back at him was so like his father's it made him turn away.
He opened the top dresser drawer and felt around for his
metal comb. Damn. His dad must have borrowed it again.
It would be nice if, just *once*, he'd remember to put it back.

Per slipped out of his room and opened the door to his
father's bedroom. Immediately he spied the missing item
resting on the night stand. Sitting down on the bed, he realized he'd never before come into his father's room uninvited. Privacy had been a major issue between them. Well
damn, if old Henry was going into *his* room to borrow *his*
things, screw it.

Next to his foot he noticed the tip of a quilt peeking out
from under the spread. Wasn't that just like Henry? Why
spend time folding something when you could just as easily
stuff it somewhere out of the way. Leaning down, he pulled
it free of the bed. As he stood to shake it out, a round object rolled onto the carpeting. For a moment, Per ignored it
as he finished smoothing the blanket. As he was about to
take it over to the closet, his eyes briefly focused on the
ball at his foot. My God, he said out loud, leaning down to
pick up the skull. His eyes blinked again and again as he
fit his little finger into a hole in the temple. Dropping it like

a hot coal onto the bed, he stood motionless, unable to think.

Several minutes later, Per reentered the sitting room. He switched off the TV set and took a chair across from his father. Crossing his arms over his chest, he cleared his throat.

Henry opened one eye. "Son, is that you?"

Per waited.

"Did you have a nice walk?" He sat up and ran a hand over his white hair, patting it back into place. "What time is it?"

"Almost five."

"Five? You were gone a long time. Switch that game back on, will you? I want to catch the score."

Per didn't move.

"What's wrong? You look kind of funny?"

"I don't feel very funny. We have to talk."

"Sure," said Henry, standing up and stretching. "But later, okay? I promised I'd have dinner with Violet and Inga. I need to get ready."

"No," said Per. "Sit down. We have to talk *now*." The look in his eyes must have frightened his father, because the older man resumed his position on the couch.

"What's up?" asked Henry, scratching his stomach.

"I need to know the truth. Don't give me any more of your fucking pain. I'm not going to be put off anymore. I want to know what happened to Randy."

Henry looked surprised. "I thought we made a deal never to talk about that again."

"No more deals, Dad. It's time for a little truth telling."

Henry rubbed the back of his neck. "There's nothing more to tell. And besides, it's so long ago, I hardly remember."

"Is that skeleton in the basement him?"

"What?"

"You heard me. Did you kill him, Henry?"

"Per!"

"Don't you think I know when you're stalling? Tell me the truth!"

"No! Of course not. How could you think something like that?"

"Then why do you have a skull in your bedroom? The man down in the cellar was murdered! There's a bullet hole in the temple, Dad. Did you put it there?"

"Per!"

"Stop it! Should I call the police? Is that the only way I'm going to get the truth?"

"No!"

"Then why?"

Henry twisted his hands together. "Don't press me on this, son. Please! It's not what you think. You've got to trust me."

"Trust you? How can I?"

"I'm your father!"

"Then tell me the truth! You saw Randy again after that night you found us together, didn't you?"

"Per, it's all water under the bridge. Why bring it up now?"

"Why? For chrissake, Dad. You've got a skull hidden in your bedroom!" He gripped the arms of his chair. "Tell me the truth!"

Henry picked up the newspaper and folded it neatly, giving himself a moment to think. "All right. But you're not going to like it."

Per stared straight ahead.

"I had to do it, son. I had to go to his parents' home. The next afternoon."

"You what?"

"You needed to be protected from someone like him. I told his parents what he'd done. He came in when we were talking, and there was an ugly scene. His father hit him pretty hard—but not any harder than I would have. He ran upstairs. Before I left, I told them I never wanted to see their son again. If he came around my boy, there was no telling what I'd do. His father assured me they'd take care of it."

Per gritted his teeth. "How could you do that? You think Randy caused me to be gay?"

"Of course he did! What else could it be? That's the way it is. Those people proselytize. They take decent young boys and turn them into . . . into—" He looked away.

"Dad, that's garbage. It doesn't happen like that. I knew I was gay long before I met Randy."

Henry squared his chin. "Are you saying I wasn't a good father?"

"Oh, Christ, that has nothing to do with it. But now that you bring it up, you weren't."

"That's right." Henry stood, clenching and unclenching his fists. "That's right. It's all my fault. Do you know why I spent so little time with you when you were a kid? Well I'll tell you. It's because I knew you thought I was a failure. I could see it in your eyes every time you looked at me. Always judging. Always making me feel like two cents. Well maybe I wasn't such a great provider. Maybe I did drink too much. But I couldn't stand my life. My wife had died—the only woman I ever loved—and all I had left was you. A snot-nosed kid who saw me as nothing. Less than a man."

Per didn't move.

Henry wiped his mouth. "Sure I thought what you were doing was my fault. It was just one more way you could spit on me. I even talked to this psychologist once. He said you were looking for male approval, male companionship. In other words, I had failed as a father."

"I *was* looking for those things," said Per. "But that's not why I'm gay. I've known it ever since I was a little boy.

Maybe I've always known it. It had nothing to do with how you treated me."

"I don't accept that. That's why when I saw that Randy again in town . . ."

"When was that?"

"God, Per, it was so long ago. I don't know. Maybe a week later. I think it was just before we packed up and left. He was walking with some other guy. My blood just boiled when I saw them together. I pulled the car to a stop and got out. I could tell he didn't want to see me, but what the hell did I care. I told him to leave you alone. He said not to worry. I could keep my precious son. He wanted nothing more to do with you."

"No!" cried Per, nearly jumping out of his chair. "He wouldn't say that!"

Henry stopped, putting his hand on his heart. "Can't we put this to rest, once and for all? I told you, son. I can't accept what you do, but I love you. Isn't that enough? Isn't anything ever enough? You know how much I wanted to be here with you. Maybe I haven't said that very often—"

"Try never," said Per.

"Well, all right. Okay. That's my fault." He sat down heavily. "We should have talked more. But it never seemed to be the right time. I didn't want this all to end in another argument with you walking out. I'm an old man. I'd like to think my son and I can be friends. But how can we if you never let anything drop? Christ, that all happened over twenty years ago. I didn't hurt your friend. I don't know what happened to him after we left." He paused, fidgeting with a button on his sweater. "I never saw him again."

Per sat rigidly in his chair. "I want to believe that."

"Then believe it. Just put it out of your mind."

"I can't."

"For the love of God, Per, how can we go on if you don't?"

Per was silent.

"Call his brother."

"What?"

"He's got a brother here in town. I saw the ad for his insurance agency in the paper today. Evan Willard. Call him. Maybe he knows something."

Per's eyes darted around the room. "Evan. Why didn't I think of that? All right. Sure. Tomorrow morning I'll call. I won't bother him on Christmas Day. He's probably over at his parents' home anyway."

"Good. You'll see. Who knows, he might be able to help you." He picked up his pipe off the coffee table. "And . . . about that skull. Do me a kindness, son. For my sake, don't tell anyone about it right now, okay?" His frown turned to a smile. "Let's make a deal, what do you say? Let's bury the past. It's dead anyway." He stood and walked over to Per's chair, sticking out his hand. "Let's shake on it."

Per got up, angrily brushing past him. "I can't," he said, stopping at the door. He turned. "You don't get it, do you? You never have. So listen closely, Dad. I'm going to say this once more—very slowly—in *English*. For me the past isn't dead. It isn't even past."

30

Jane closed the double doors separating the main parlor from the smaller, more intimate rear sun porch. One of the

staff had already started a fire in the stone fireplace, filling
the room with the pungent, resinous aroma of burning pine.

Wearily, Tess removed her coat and sank into a wing
chair. Jane shut off the overhead light and then joined her.

"Excuse me," said a young woman popping her head inside the door. "I have those two brandies you ordered." She
entered and set the glasses on a small table between the two
chairs. "Cordelia Thorn was looking for you earlier, Ms.
Lawless. You, too, Ms. Ingman. I believe she wants to organize a game of charades for after dinner."

"Is that right?" said Jane. "Well, I'll find her when we're
done. Will you be sure to close the door tightly on your
way out?"

The woman nodded and left.

"Charades," repeated Jane, smiling in spite of herself.
"Leave it to Cordelia. The problem is, I think that's already
the game of choice around here."

Tess shifted uncomfortably in her chair.

Jane continued. "I owe you an apology for last night. I
don't usually eavesdrop on personal conversations. Bo had
a right to be upset with me, but not to run me off the side
of the bridge."

"I'm sure he didn't do that on purpose," said Tess. "I've
never known him to be vindictive."

"Well, be that as it may, I'm sorry for spying on you. My
only defense is that Leigh asked me to help her find out
what's behind all the awful things happening at the inn.
Since you weren't particularly forthcoming about the obvious fact that you've been here before, I had to wonder what
else you might be lying about."

Tess held her glass up to the firelight. "I see."

"There are still a lot of unanswered questions. Like
Elmer's death. And the skeleton found behind that basement wall."

"I'm afraid I don't know anything about either," said

Tess. She bit nervously at her lower lip. "I've had enough problems of my own to deal with lately. I wish I could give you the answers. I know how strung out Leigh's been."

"All right," said Jane. "But if that's true, why lie about being here before? And what's got you and Bo so tied up in knots? Who is he keeping watch over out here?"

"You *did* get an earful last night, didn't you? Given what you must have heard, I don't understand why you didn't come banging on my door at the crack of dawn."

"Don't think it didn't occur to me."

Tess sighed and lifted the brandy glass to her lips, taking a small sip. "Yeah, I suppose. Well, I guess I should thank you then. I know you're trying to handle this discreetly, and I appreciate it. Coming back here after so many years has been pretty traumatic. I expected it to be bad, but not quite this bad. I mean, under normal circumstances, I would never have set foot on this island again."

"But you did. Why?"

"Yes, I did. Part of it is pure happenstance. Who would have thought one of Winney's old friends would buy this place. When she came home with the news, I was speechless. I tried for years to bury this part of my life, but when Winney started coming here so often—"

"Three times, I believe," said Jane.

"Was it only three times? It seems like more than that. Anyway, she kept insisting that I come with her. I couldn't tell her the truth, so I kept making up excuses. I finally ran out of anything that seemed plausible." She took a large swallow of the brandy. "You see, when I was eighteen, I went away to college at the University of Minnesota. I'm from Madison, so I knew very few people in the Twin Cities. I've always had a hard time meeting people. It was worse when I was younger. That was 1969. Do you remember what college campuses were like back then?"

Jane nodded. "Vividly."

"Well, after a few months I met this girl who introduced me around to some of her friends. Most of them weren't politically active—just scared and young, like me. It was in this group that I met Bo. He was funny and gentle, and loved to read. And he was terribly shy. I think we were drawn to each other almost immediately. He fell in love, and because I desperately wanted someone in my life, I let him move in. We were so frightened by the huge impersonality of the university; I think we both craved the safety of a relationship. At least that's how it felt to me. But Bo was right when he accused me of never loving him. I never did. Not the way he wanted.

"Winter quarter, several people in our group began talking about quitting school. Finding something more relevant. You remember the litany, don't you? Communes were the hot topic. One day, a guy we liked a lot—his name was Wiz—came into the coffee house over on West Bank where we were all sitting and talking. He was so excited. He'd found this really neat old house on an island about fifty miles north of Minneapolis. He was sure it was the perfect place for us to start our commune, since it was completely deserted. The funny thing was, before that moment, it never occurred to me anybody was actually serious about it. I don't really think we *were* serious. But here was this guy throwing down a challenge. Did we mean it or didn't we? Spring was just around the corner. We could plant a garden. Live off the land. It sounded scary, but it also sounded exciting, and I think we all craved excitement, even though what we said we wanted was peace. God, we were so naive. Needless to say, quite a few of us dropped our plans for spring quarter classes. We packed our bags and left with him.

"And then reality hit. You have no idea what this inn looked like back then. It was a nightmare. Nothing worked. We were all middle-class kids who had never been without electricity or functioning plumbing a day in our lives. If it hadn't been for peer pressure, most of us would have left the first day. Initially, we all bunked in this room because it was the smallest space with a working fireplace. When spring came, we moved off into different parts of the house, depending on who was sleeping with whom at the time."

"How many of you were there?"

"Seven. But later, in the summer, people started drifting in and out. Some used the place to crash for a day or two. Some stayed longer. It was in April that Bo and Wiz went into town to talk to the people who managed the house. Bo was pretty handy at fixing things. He wanted to strike a deal with the rental company. If they would pay for the materials, he would do repairs for free, that is, *if* they'd let us live out here without paying rent. I suppose since they didn't have anything to lose, they agreed. Occasionally, a representative from the company would come out to check on things, but most of the time they left us alone. The only thing was, some people in town weren't very happy to have a bunch of hippies living out on the island. Three of our core group were black. Repentance River is about as white as you can get—physically and psychologically. As you might expect, we weren't invited to many lutefisk dinners in church basements. Bo especially hated the guys down at the hardware store. They made fun of his hair and his beard. One guy called him a faggot—asked him if he had a *boy* friend. Things like that. But for the most part, we tried to ignore what was happening in town, and they ignored us.

"About that same time in April, I noticed I hadn't gotten my period. Bo and I always used contraception back in college, but since we'd all pooled our money, and since condoms weren't high on the list of priorities, our use became sporadic and eventually nonexistent. Doctors weren't very high on that list either, so I simply waited to see what would happen. After another month, it became clear I was pregnant. Bo was delighted. I'll admit I was pretty happy too. I'd always wanted children. And Bo had such dreams of fixing up the place, living here with our friends and family. We were both swept away by it all.

"The only thing that made me feel uncomfortable was not seeing a doctor. To calm me down, Bo kept reassuring me that I was healthy. To him that meant I didn't need a doctor. After all, a baby wasn't a *disease*, he would say. He even went into town and ordered books on natural childbirth from the library. He really got into it. He started reading things on herbs and natural medicines. By mid-summer he said even if we could afford a doctor, he wouldn't let one touch me. So, that was that.

"Sometime late in the fall, Bo finally got the furnace working. When the baby was born, we named him Martin, after Martin Luther King. We wanted him to have a good namesake. At the time, it was one of the few things we could give him. It wasn't an easy birth. I was in labor for almost thirteen hours. But he was such a beautiful boy—so tiny and perfect. He cried a lot at first but after a couple of months he seemed to mellow.

"Bo and I were closer than we had ever been. I know neither of us thought it was possible to love something as much as we loved Martin." She lowered her eyes. "And then one day, Martin got a fever. Bo said babies got fevers all the time. It was nothing to worry about. I begged him to reconsider his stand on doctors, but he said no, he was the head of the family and he knew what Martin needed. It's hard to believe now that I put up with such crap, but at the time, it seemed natural. Bo prepared some kind of herbal concoction. He'd been studying that stuff for months. So I waited. As the days passed, Martin just got weaker. One night, he fell asleep in my arms. He never woke up."

Jane could see Tess's body begin to tremble.

"The thing is, I didn't expect it. I had actually convinced myself he was getting better." She leaned toward the fire, wiping her eyes with a shaky hand. "I'm sorry Jane. I thought I'd dealt with this years ago. You see, I'm responsible for his death."

"Please, Tess—"

She held up her hand. "It's okay. You can't possibly hate me any more than I already hate myself. The truth of the matter is, I should have insisted that we see a doctor. When Bo didn't agree right away, I should have bundled him up and walked into town. Surely somebody would have looked at him. Even if I didn't have any money, somebody would have taken pity on a tiny baby!" Her voice began to shake. "But what did I do? I just sat in that chair holding him. Singing to him. Later, I tried to figure out what had happened. The only firm conclusion I ever came to was that I had killed my child. Bo was too wrapped up in his own ego to see the danger, but I saw it and still I did nothing. I felt so wrong I never thought I could *be* right again. So often in life, we get a second chance. But this was absolute. I would never lay my head on a pillow at night again and not remember how he smelled, how his little body fit to mine when I held him. Everything was gone. And I could never get it back." She covered her face and turned her head away.

"Tess, we don't have to—"

"No," she said, wiping her arm roughly across her eyes. "I want to finish this. At last I'm going to tell someone the truth." She cleared her throat and took another sip of brandy. "I left shortly after he died. I knew Bo and I weren't going to make it. I'd never really loved him. I didn't know what was wrong until years later when I met Winifred. I just thought I was cold. Men never really interested me. I went back to the university and finished my degree in English. I felt like a zombie. After I graduated, I took a job at a bookstore in Milwaukee. As the years went by, I buried the truth deeper and deeper under a thick covering of lies. I even started to believe some of them myself. The funny thing was, all this time I was training myself to feel rejected by children. You see, it wasn't that I rejected them, but the other way around. Deep inside, I knew I couldn't be trusted with a child. They sensed that about me. I was dangerous. After many years it was just easier to say I didn't care for children. And then came Winifred.

"I knew how much she liked kids right away. She never hid it. I suppose I should have realized it might become a problem some day. Still, I couldn't stand the thought of living without her. She was the only thing in my life that had ever made any real sense—she made me feel I might be worth something after all. So I just put it out of my mind. The subject never came up until a couple of months ago. Even though by then I trusted her love, I couldn't tell her what I'd done. Especially not her, knowing how she felt about children. I knew she'd try to understand, but it wouldn't be long before she'd hate me. How could I blame her? I hated myself."

"I think you underestimate Winifred," said Jane softly. "You did make a terrible mistake. No one's denying that. But you didn't intentionally injure the child. It wasn't a willful act, it was done out of ignorance. Surely you can see the difference and have some pity on yourself."

"No," said Tess, shaking her head, "there's no excuse for what I did. None. Don't you think I've used all those rationalizations at one time or another? They aren't real. What's real is that I allowed my baby to die. I thought this morning maybe I should just get on a bus. Leave. I don't think I can deal with that new moon ritual Winney is guiding tomorrow night. I've been to one before. It's all about births and beginnings. The solstice celebration was bad enough." She leaned her head back against the chair. "But here I am, still here. Am I a coward to stay or a coward to go? I don't know anymore."

"Does that mean you're going to tell Winifred?"

Tess closed her eyes and whispered, "I have to. I owe her an explanation. She knows something's been wrong—she knew from the first night. Remember Michael Paget? He said he was seventeen years old. Did you catch the significance? Martin would have been seventeen this year, if he'd lived. Michael even looks a bit like the way I imagined Martin would look. Oh, I've seen lots of boys over the years who made me think of my son and how he would have been, but meeting Michael here made him special. At first I was fascinated. Almost mesmerized. Then I was appalled by my fascination. Here was the living image of what could have been; what I killed through my own passivity. God, how can I tell Winney?" She closed her eyes and leaned her head back wearily against the chair.

"So that's why Bo stayed in town all these years," said Jane softly. "He's been watching over his son's grave."

"Oh, I don't think that's the only reason," said Tess, wiping her eyes. "He likes it up here. It's quiet. Peaceful. And he has that small business. But then again, yes, he said he wants to stay close. Martin is buried out in the woods near the summerhouse. That's where we had the funeral. Wiz said a few words. I don't remember any of it."

Jane finished her drink. "I still think he's being a bit overeager about protecting this island. What happened to this guy, Wiz? Was he a good friend of Bo's?"

"Yeah. They were pretty tight. I have no idea what became of any of the people living up here. I just packed my bag and left one day while Bo and Wiz were out hunting in the woods."

"You don't think there's any other reason he wants to keep watch out here?"

"Not that I'm aware of. He'll sober up eventually, and I suppose I could ask him."

"I don't expect you'll get an answer."

Tess took her last sip of brandy and then stood, setting her empty glass on the mantel. "I think I better go find Winifred."

"Good luck." Jane reached up and took hold of her hand. "If you need to talk later, you know where to find me."

The inn's foyer was already beginning to fill with guests waiting to be seated in the dining room. As Jane walked past the reception desk on her way upstairs, Violet stopped her.

"Jane," she called, "you have a message in your box. Just a second and I'll get it for you." She turned her back, retrieving a thin white envelope from the narrow slots along the back wall. "Here you are," she said, handing it to her. "I just came on duty a few minutes ago and noticed it was there."

"Thanks." Jane paused briefly to tear it open.

"Something unusual?" asked Violet, watching her curiously. "Jane? Are you all right?"

Slowly, she dumped the contents onto the counter.

"What is all this?" asked Violet.

"They're family pictures—from my wallet." She picked up a torn fragment that had once been her favorite photo of Christine. It was taken at the state fair eight years ago.

"I don't understand," said Violet, her look puzzled.

"I don't either."

"Someone has ripped them to pieces. Why?"

Jane felt a chill settle around her like a mist. "I don't know." At the sight of her brother's head severed from its body, tears began to well behind her eyes.

"I'm sorry," said Violet, laying her hand on Jane's arm. "Do you want me to call Leigh?"

Jane shook her head. "No. There's nothing she can do." Brushing the pieces back into the envelope, she headed quickly up the stairs.

31

Saturday Morning, December 26

"Have you considered varying your wheats?"

Cordelia glanced sideways at a woman seated at the next table. "I beg your pardon," she said, looking up from the script she was reading.

Patiently, the woman repeated her question. "I said, have you tried varying your wheats?"

Cordelia stared at the wall, then at the ceiling, and finally at the woman. "Is this a cryptic message of some kind? I mean, should I respond by saying something like, 'The columbine are blooming in Albania'?"

It was the woman's turn to appear confused. "What?"

"Then you tell me what my mission is, should I choose to accept it."

"I'm sure I don't know what you're talking about."

"That makes two of us, sweetie." Cordelia wiggled her eyebrows. She returned to her script.

The woman silently sipped her juice. She continued, "All I meant to suggest was that since you seem to be sneezing and blowing your nose all the time, you might be having an allergic reaction. Varying your grains might help."

Cordelia closed her eyes for a moment and then turned to the woman. "But I vary them all the time. Sometimes I have toast and jam. Sometimes french bread with a little sweet butter. Once in a while I have cereal or a caramel roll. I've even been known to have a muffin or two in my day. Then, there are pancakes, waffles—"

"No no," said the woman. "You misunderstand. What I've noticed is that you only eat *white* bread."

Cordelia stiffened. "But I *like* white bread."

"That's the whole problem. Why don't you try some of the whole grain products here. They're very good."

Cordelia's smile became distinctly smarmy. "What an interesting idea. I shall have to give it some thought." Out of the corner of her eye she noticed Stephen enter the dining room followed by a weedy looking middle-aged man in an expensive business suit. Behind him trotted Henry Gyldenskog.

"If that doesn't do the trick," continued the woman, "you can always eliminate bread products altogether."

Cordelia glared. "But my dear lady, life wouldn't be worth living without a Twinkie now and then."

"A what?" said the woman.

"A Twinkie," repeated Cordelia. "I have some up in my room. Would you care to join me later?"

"Join you for a Twinkie?"

"It's my last package but I *am* willing to share."

The woman wiped her mouth, delicately laying down the napkin. "I . . . I don't know. I don't think so. I'd have to see."

"Well, suit yourself." Cordelia smiled warmly. "I'm in suite three-o-two if you change your mind. I usually have my Twinkies and milk around three."

The woman nodded and stood, making a swift exit. Cordelia now turned her full attention on Stephen and his guest.

"Are you going to be well enough to join us for the new moon celebration by the river this evening?" asked Jane, pulling out a chair and sitting down.

Cordelia waved her fork in greeting and stabbed the last sausage on her plate. "Yes, I was planning on it. I'll dress warmly. Everybody around here seems terribly into it all. Of course I suppose that's because most of the people left are members of Winifred's coven. By the way, I hear Burton is making a hot wassail bowl for the occasion. He's going to serve it out in the woods. Isn't that atmospheric?"

"Delightful." Jane grabbed an apple slice off Cordelia's plate. "Who's that with Stephen?"

"I haven't the slightest." She chewed her sausage thoughtfully. "Oh goody! Look. Here comes Henry Gyldenskog to breathe life back into our waning conversation."

"Be nice," said Jane.

"I'm always nice," snarled Cordelia.

"Good morning, ladies. May I join you?" Without waiting for a response, Henry settled himself into a chair, waving for a waiter.

"Yes sir?" said the young man.

"I'd like a cup of coffee. Black. And my usual."

"Of course," said the waiter. He weaved off through the tables and returned a moment later with the coffee pot.

"What's your *usual?*" asked Jane.

"Creamed herring on toast. Ever since I was a kid, it's been my favorite breakfast. I've been here long enough that Burton has agreed to accommodate some of my dietary idiosyncrasies."

Cordelia pulled her head into her shoulders like a turtle. Covering her mouth, she wheezed into a tissue.

"Bless you, my dear," said Henry.

"Who's the man with Stephen this morning?" asked Jane.

"His name is Nelson Meyers. He's a real estate appraiser for Saxhaug Developers."

"An appraiser," repeated Jane softly. "I see."

"I think Stephen wanted to get a jump on things. See what the old place is worth after all the renovations."

"Are you still interested in buying?" asked Jane.

"I don't know. Depends on the price. I think I might have some new competition. I saw Winifred Vinson talking with Mr. Meyers earlier. He was explaining how real estate is rather soft right now. The market is overloaded."

"Winney?" said Jane, glancing momentarily at Cordelia. "What makes you think she's interested in buying the inn?"

"I don't know. Nothing really. She was probably just making small talk. Like me most of the time." He winked.

"I don't suppose you know if Leigh is aware Mr. Meyers is here?"

"I doubt it. Stephen seemed quite eager to get him in and out quickly. As soon as he saw him talking with Winifred, he whisked him away. I don't think he wants to upset Leigh."

"How kind of him," smiled Cordelia.

Henry sipped his coffee. "Do I detect a note a disapproval?"

Cordelia stifled a small burp. "Me? Disapprove of the greatest financial wiz since Ivan Boesky?"

Jane kicked her under the table.

"Stephen's under a lot of pressure right now. But he's not a crook."

"*I am not a crook,*" repeated Cordelia. "Seems to me I've heard that somewhere before." She shook her jowls and made a victory sign with both hands.

Henry scowled. "He'd never do anything to hurt Leigh."

"May we quote you for *Business Week?*" asked Cordelia.

The waiter arrived with Henry's herring.

"Ah," he smiled, flapping his napkin in the air. "Would anyone care for a taste?"

Cordelia sniffed the aroma like a prairie dog. "Thanks, no. If you two will excuse me, I need to . . . how shall I put this nicely? Stand in front of an open window and breathe deeply. *Bon appétit.*"

32

"I wish you'd asked me first," said Leigh, pulling the saddle off Dudley. She lifted it over to a low rack and grabbed a rag off the bottom rung. After the brightness of the midday sun, the interior of the barn seemed dim.

"I should have," admitted Stephen. "I just thought getting an appraisal might help you make a more informed decision." He leaned up against one of the sleighs, running a hand along the smooth leather seat. The cold December air had finally put some color back into his face, so pale since his return from St. Paul yesterday morning.

"I see."

"No you don't. You think I'm pushing you." His eyes darted nervously to the barn door.

"Are you expecting someone?"

Stephen shrugged. "No."

Leigh stopped wiping down the saddle. This was ridiculous. If he didn't stop acting so jumpy, he was going to spook the horses. "What's wrong, then? Ever since you got

back yesterday you've been acting ... I don't know ...
like a caged animal."

Stephen turned his back to her, pretending to examine a
scrape on the side of the sleigh.

"Well?"

"Well what?"

"I don't have time for this. Are we going to play a game
or have a conversation?"

"I'm not sure I'm up for either."

She watched him turn around. "What's that supposed to
mean?"

"If you're sure you want to know, I'll tell you."

Leigh waited.

"All right. I suppose you have a right to hear this.
It's ... Marjie. We ..." His eyes dropped to the floor.

"Just say it!"

"All right! Give me a minute, okay?" He took a deep
breath. "The truth is, we've been talking a lot lately. After
we split two years ago, we were both so angry, we never
talked anything out. We couldn't. Every time we tried, it
ended up in a fight."

Leigh stared straight ahead.

"Things ... have kind of changed recently. We've even
broached the subject of ..." His voice trailed off.

"A reconciliation."

Stephen nodded.

"Is this your idea or hers?" She steadied herself on the
saddle.

"It's mutual. Oh Leigh, I didn't mean for this to happen.
I do love you, you must know that."

"I thought I did."

"It's just, there are a lot of things to consider. I have my
kids to think about."

"Right. I understand. And your finances."

Stephen looked up. "What's that supposed to mean?"

"If you stayed with me you'd have all that child support and alimony to think about. This way, no more legal hassles. You can buy your way into that partnership and sail off into financial heaven."

Stephen gripped the side of the sleigh. "Not exactly. Leigh, I still . . ."

Leigh's eyes grew wide. "You're kidding! You're not going to ask me for money now?"

"Don't make this any harder than it already is." He ran a hand through his slick, black hair. "You're right. I don't have enough capital to buy into the firm. Not without . . ."

Leigh was almost too stunned to speak. "Not without the money from the sale of this inn."

He nodded.

"God, I can't believe my ears! Have you left the planet, Stephen? Do you really think I'd give you a penny?"

"I thought . . . we love each other, don't we? I hoped we could still be friends. Could still help each other out. I mean, as long as it's mutually beneficial?"

"And to show my *friendship*, I should buy you the partnership."

"It's not like that, and you know it."

"I don't know anything of the kind!" She could feel her anger rising. "You know what your problem is, Stephen? You have no passion. No dreams of your own. You're like everyone's stereotypic yuppie. First—and perhaps last—you feed off society's grand dream. Money. You're not inventive enough to figure out something of your own. Along the way you acquire your two-point-three kids, your house in the suburbs, and your wife. Except you got bored with that, didn't you? You started looking around for something new. That's when you found me! Lucky me. You bought *my* dream this time. I mistakenly thought it was our dream. But you got bored again, didn't you? I should have seen it coming. You're good at what you do, Stephen. You know all

the right buttons to push. The right words to use. And even
now, you know what? I still believe you were sincere. You
want to know why? Do you?"

Stephen glared.

"Because, upstairs—in your mind—*nobody's home!*"

"I'm not going to stand here and listen to this."

"Good! Leave! Go back to your wife and kids. You
won't need to be circus daddy anymore. That's what I used
to call my own father. After the divorce, unless he was
flush—unless he could buy me things—I never saw him.
Just spending time together wasn't enough. When I was little he let me play with his wallet. Count the money,
sweetie, he'd always say. You're even beginning to sound
like him! If you're really so sick of all the financial
hassles—sick of being everyone's success object, then stop
whining and get off the merry-go-round!"

"You think it's that simple?" snapped Stephen. "You're
such a *new woman*. Tough. Independent. And smug! All
right, Marjie, I'll say. You put me through school and I'm
grateful. But you'll have to fend for yourself now, because
I'm checking out. I'm off to sell Birkenstocks on the beach
in Florida. Give my best to the kids."

"I'm not saying that!"

"It sure sounded that way. I asked for your help. A business deal based on our friendship. What do you do? You attack me! I know you have a right to be angry. But can't
you see I'm trying to give you a choice? Shit, Leigh.
You're going to have to sell this place if your profits continue to decline. Somebody around here's got it in for you,
and they're going to push and push until you cry uncle. Sell
now and invest with me, and I'll make sure you come out
of this a rich woman. You can buy yourself another inn
somewhere else. Keep your dream, Leigh. I hope you do."
His eyes softened. "I do still love you. This was not an

easy choice, no matter what you think. I'd hoped we could still be friends. Talk things out rationally."

Leigh could feel an ugly flush climbing her cheeks. "*Rationally?* Stephen, I don't even know you. And you know what? I don't want to."

Stephen moved stiffly across the hay-strewn floor, coming to stand right in front of her. "I'm not the evil person you'd like to make me."

"No? Whose baby is your wife carrying? How long have you been sleeping with her?"

His face drained of color. "Once. That's all. And for your information, it was a disaster. I never thought she'd speak to me again after it happened. But I got lucky. She did. It's what started us talking again. And you're right. The baby could be mine. Most likely it isn't, but I did lie to you because I didn't want to lose you. I know that was wrong. I guess I wanted everything, Leigh."

"Get out!" She pushed him away. "I want you out of my house!"

"Does that mean—"

"You and your partnership can rot in hell for all I care!"

"You're making a mistake."

"Is that a threat?"

Stephen reached out and gripped her arm. "It's a mistake, Leigh. Trust me."

33

"Over here!" shouted Cordelia, waving her hands madly at Jane. She stood next to the bonfire, a blanket pulled tightly across her shoulders.

Jane tramped through the snow carrying a stack of firewood. She deposited the logs in a heap next to Cordelia's feet.

"Did you ride out on the hay wagon?" asked Cordelia.

"No," said Jane. She moved in closer to the fire. "I helped Burton with the wassail bowl. He brought everything out in one of the sleighs. Dylan and I followed behind on a snowmobile."

"Ah," said Cordelia, watching a group of women sway to the sound of a solitary flute. It was an eerie, haunting melody. "I wondered where you were."

"Who's that playing?" asked Jane. "I don't think I've met her yet."

Cordelia bent her head down and whispered, "Her name is Carrie Tweed. She varied her wheats with me earlier this afternoon."

"She what?"

Cordelia held a finger to her lips. "Shhh! This isn't public knowledge." She glanced about furtively, putting her arm around Jane's shoulder and drawing her close. "Carrie and I shared a package of Twinkies in my room this afternoon. It was her first time. I'm glad I could be there to

222

share it. Shhh!" she said again, her eyes roving apprehen-
sively. "Nobody is supposed to know. See, Carrie runs a
health food store in River Falls. She's part of Winifred's
coven." She squeezed Jane's shoulder. "You understand the
problem, Janey. May I count on your discretion?"

Jane stifled a laugh. "Is that all you shared?"

Cordelia released her grip. "And who do you think you
are? The moral squad?"

Jane rolled her eyes.

"Well, suffice it to say, our friendship is *in process* at this
very moment." She gave a little wave to the flautist.

The woman waved back.

"See?" said Cordelia.

"I do. Well. This is certainly an interesting turn of
events."

"I dare say," smirked Cordelia.

"She runs a health food store?"

"Yup."

"A marriage made in heaven," whispered Jane.

"What?"

"Nothing. Not a thing." Jane turned her attention to the
circle of faces vividly etched in the light from the bonfire.
Some were lost in thought while others stood together in
small groups talking. Winifred began tapping her tambou-
rine in time to the music. Another woman pulled out a
drum. Jane noticed Violet over by the trees helping Burton
set up a small table. "Have you seen Tess this evening?"
she asked.

"Yeah," said Cordelia, pulling the blanket more tightly
around her shoulders. "She was over there." She nodded to
an empty spot near a clump of evergreens. "I guess she
must have left. Why do you ask?"

Jane wondered how Tess's talk with Winifred had gone.
"Oh nothing. I was just wondering how she was."

"She seemed kind of preoccupied. You know. Spacy."

"Is that right?" Jane watched Leigh toss several more logs onto the fire. Across the circle, Per was standing next to Henry, listening intently to the flute. They both appeared to be in good spirits.

Per waved for her to come over.

"See you in a bit," said Jane. "I want to talk to Per for a minute."

Cordelia nodded, swaying to the sound of the drum.

Jane walked around the back of the circle until she was directly behind Henry.

"Hi," said Per, turning to greet her. "I was hoping I'd see you tonight."

"How did everything go?" asked Jane.

They moved away from the group.

"Randy is alive!"

"How do you know?"

"It was right under my nose all the time. Until two days ago I had completely forgotten he had a brother. I called him today. He said he hears from Randy all the time. He's living in St. Louis. Apparently, his brother doesn't have any problem with him being gay. He just never tells his parents anything. But Randy's okay! He has his own business, and I don't think he's living with anyone. I'm leaving Monday morning. I have to see him. We both deserve to resolve an unfinished past. And then, who knows? If nothing else, at least I'll have had a vacation. I could use one right now." He glanced back at his father.

Jane was delighted. "I'm glad for you, Per. Really. How are you and your dad doing?"

"All right. He's going to stay at the inn while I'm gone. He's happy here. And he's got some unfinished business he says he needs to take care of." Per peered over Jane's shoulder. "What on earth is that? Look over there." He pointed to a figure emerging from the woods. "What is it?"

Jane recognized the mask at once. It was the same frightening wolf face she had seen two nights ago outside the gatehouse. Without stopping to explain, she made a wide arc around the back of the circle and ran almost smack into the masked figure. "Who are you?" she demanded. "What are you doing here?"

A gloved hand reached out to touch her.

She took a step back.

The hand reached up and pulled off the mask.

"Michael!" she gasped. "What are you doing? You nearly gave me a heart attack."

Michael tried to straighten his mussed up hair. "I did? Gee, I'm sorry. Really. I asked Winifred if I could wear this. She said it was fine. She said people often wear masks to rituals. You can ask her if you don't believe me. I'm not doing anything wrong, really!" He looked down at the mask in his hand. "I think it's kind of neat. Sort of primitive. When Ruthie offered it to me this morning, I couldn't refuse. She gave me some other great stuff too. Some tapes and her favorite book of poetry."

Jane was nonplussed. "You mean to say this mask belonged to Ruthie?"

"Sure. She made it years ago. It was some kind of therapy exercise. She said when she wore it, it made her feel invisible. Isn't that great! I mean, things like that do happen. I've got a book at home that tells all about stuff people can't explain. I wondered if it would make me feel invisible, too. Maybe I'd even *be* invisible!"

"A *therapy exercise?*" repeated Jane.

"Yeah. She said she didn't need it anymore. It's okay if I wear it, isn't it?"

Jane glanced at Leigh. So Ruthie was the one wearing the mask outside the gatehouse window. In a sense, she *was* invisible since no one could see her face. Convoluted logic at best, but then, Ruthie was a convoluted person. "Listen, Michael, will you do me a big favor? Will you not wear that mask tonight? It's important. I'll explain everything to you later."

"Okay," he shrugged, a bit disappointed. "If you say so."

"Thanks. Have you seen Ruthie this evening?"

He shook his head. "Not since earlier this afternoon. She was burning some old diaries back behind the gatehouse. I smelled the fire while I was taking out the kitchen garbage, so I went to check just to make sure everything was all right. She wasn't in a very talkative mood. All she said was that it was time to clean house. Oh, before I left, she did ask what time the ritual was tonight. I told her seven."

"Did she say she was planning to come?"

"Nope. She only asked the time. I could tell she wanted to be alone, so I didn't stick around."

Jane searched carefully through the faces assembled around the fire. Ruthie was missing. "Thanks again," she said.

"No problem." Michael smiled. "I guess I better go give Burton a hand. I promised I would help with the refreshments."

Jane nodded and watched him walk away. This was too strange. Why hadn't Ruthie answered the other evening when Jane had called to her? Could she be the mastermind behind everything? And why had she given the mask to Michael?

Jane stuffed her hands into the pockets of her hunting jacket, trying to concentrate. In her right pocket she felt a piece of paper. Drawing it out, she realized it was the crumpled note Ruthie had tossed into the ravine several days ago. She hadn't worn this particular coat since that day.

"Cordelia?" she called, running back over to the bonfire. "Can you make any sense of this?"

Cordelia had managed to borrow a small drum and was emoting heavily in a rather jazzy rhythm.

"Cordelia?"

"What?"

"Look at this."

"I can't. I'm busy. The muse is upon me."

"Cordelia!"

"What!!" She stopped and glared.

"I need you to look at this."

Cordelia grabbed the paper. "What is it?"

"Can you tell me if it's anything you recognize?"

"It's smeared."

"I am aware of that. Some water got on it. But a few of the words are still legible."

Cordelia leaned toward the fire light. "Sure. *Hamlet.* Act I, Scene II."

"*Hamlet.* Really. Can you repeat the words?"

"Of course." She waved flirtatiously at Carrie Tweed.

"Well?"

"Well what?"

"Repeat the verses!"

"All right, all right. You needn't shout." She cleared her throat. "I shall begin: 'O, that this too too solid flesh would melt, thaw, and resolve itself into a dew! Or that the Everlasting had not fixt His cannon 'gainst self-slaughter!' "

"What?"

Cordelia repeated rapidly, " 'Or that the Everlasting had not fixt His cannon 'gainst self-slaughter.' Now hush." She continued in a low voice, " 'O God! God! How weary, stale, flat, and unprofitable seem to me all the uses of this world! Fie on't! O, fie! 'Tis an unweeded garden ...' "

"An unweeded garden," repeated Jane softly.

"Don't interrupt. 'An unweeded garden that grows to seed; things rank and gross in nature possess it merely. That it should come to this!' "

"That's enough."

"I beg your pardon? I was just getting started."

Winifred's voice rang out over the assembled crowd.

"Will everyone gather round. We're going to cast the circle and begin." She lit several large sticks of sandalwood incense and walked behind the group, calling on the Goddess for a blessing. Jane was just about to join in when a thought struck her with the intensity of a thunderbolt. Of course! That had to be it. There wasn't a moment to lose. Reaching inside her pants pocket, she got out the keys to the snowmobile. That was the quickest way. And this time, she knew for sure it was a matter of life and death.

34

Jane pulled the snowmobile up in front of the barn. From outside, the inn appeared quiet. Many of the lights were on downstairs, but on the second and third floors, most of the rooms were dark. She crossed the yard and entered through the front door. "Hello," she called. "Anybody here?" The silence in the house was enormous.

Quickly, she grabbed the flashlight from under the front desk and headed toward the basement. If Ruthie was in the house, she might very well be down there. From what Inga had said, she was spending more and more of her time sitting in that old boat. Jane switched on a light and crept quietly down the stairs. At the bottom of the steps, she noticed a flickering light coming from the area of the wine cellar. Carefully, she crept closer. As she rounded the corner, she was stopped cold by the sight of the small rowboat entirely surrounded by small votive candles. It almost looked like a shrine. Inside, sat Ruthie, her back very straight, eyes closed. In her right hand, Jane could make out the form of a gun.

Sensing someone in the room, Ruthie opened her eyes. Instantly, she shielded the gun from Jane's view. "What do you want?" she asked angrily. "This is private. Please leave."

Jane moved a few inches closer. "I can't do that."

Ruthie's mouth set in a grim line. "Why not? I don't want any company right now, can't you see that? Go away."

"Listen to me for a minute. I know you've had a lot of problems, but they can be solved. I suppose that doesn't help much right now, but this isn't the way to solve *anything*."

Ruthie seemed surprised. She took a few moments before speaking again. "Leave me alone. Just go away. I don't want to talk."

"But you might ... hurt yourself."

"And what if I do? What's it to you?"

"Will you at least tell me what's bothering you? I know you're in pain. I don't want to minimize that." She paused. "Look, you don't have anything to lose by talking to me. I can't prevent you from using that gun, if that's what you want. Just give me a couple of minutes. Tell me what's so wrong."

Ruthie looked away. "My whole life is wrong."

"Your whole life?" said Jane. "How? What is it about this house that upsets you so much?"

"If I knew that, I wouldn't be *crazy Ruthie*." She laughed bitterly. "Maybe they're right. Maybe I am crazy!" She pulled out the gun and leveled it at Jane.

For a split second, Jane's eyes froze on the barrel. "You haven't answered my question. What's got you so upset?"

"I don't know," shouted Ruthie. "It's just me. I'm wrong.

I have all these feelings ... these, sensations. Bits and pieces. Nothing makes any sense. My whole existence is one big mistake. And what do you care anyway? Are you going to be my good friend now? Are you going to save me? Forget it. I've heard all of it before. There's nothing left for me but more antidepressants. More hospitals. More of those wonderful doctors with their blithe condescension. My God, I'm not stupid. I'm not a child. I know my future's just going to be a repeat of my past. I don't want it! I just want everything to stop. Just leave, okay? Don't pretend you care what happens to me."

"But *I* care," said a familiar voice from behind them.

Ruthie looked up.

Inga walked into the room and stood next to Jane.

The sight of her aunt seemed to make Ruthie even more upset. "I don't want an audience! Go away, both of you. I need to be alone."

Inga stepped closer, reaching out her hand. "Ruthie, you have to listen to me for a minute. Maybe I can help."

"You!" said Ruthie, her voice indignant. "Are you kidding? All you've ever done is lie to me!"

Inga took the words like a blow. "That's not true, child! Violet and I love you!"

"Love? Why? What's to love? My own father never loved me, why should you?"

"Of course he did!"

"More lies," shouted Ruthie. "If he loved me so much—like you always say—then why did he kill himself?"

"Ruthie! Whoever told you that? He fell. It was an accident."

Ruthie covered her ears with her hands. "I can't stand it anymore. Don't you think I know the truth? I've always known. I overheard you and Violet talking about it right after it happened. Poor Ruthie, you said. Poor Ruthie! It's always been poor, sad, pathetic Ruthie! Why? Because you

knew. Everyone knew. Her own father didn't love her
enough to stick around. I probably drove him to it."

"How can you even think such a thing? He loved you!
His death had nothing to do with you!"

"I don't believe that! You were always telling me what
a good man he was. How special. He was a loser, Inga! A
misfit, just like me. Didn't you think I'd hear stories? It
makes me wonder what else you lied to me about."

Inga's hands twisted nervously in front of her.

"You're kidding! There's more?" She pointed the gun at
her aunt. "What else should I know, dear Auntie? Tell me!"

"Stop it! I can't stand it when you talk like that." She
took out a handkerchief and wiped her eyes.

"No? Won't talk? Still afraid *poor Ruthie* can't take the
truth? Well, maybe you're right. What's the difference, anyway? It all ends right here." She turned the gun on herself,
sticking the barrel into her mouth.

"No!" Inga moved towards her. "Ruthie don't!" She
stopped, holding her breath. "Please!"

Ruthie withdrew the gun.

"Good. That's good." She wiped the back of her neck,
taking a moment to organize her thoughts. "All right. Maybe
there are a few other things we haven't told you. But you
must understand why Violet and I kept it from you. It wasn't
to hurt you, though I can see now we've hurt you terribly.
Before this moment I never understood why you were so depressed. I always thought the sadness inside you would go
away in time. We tried to love you as much as we could.
You felt loved, didn't you?"

"Yes," said Ruthie, her voice wooden. "I felt loved."

"Good. That's good. And what we've done—what we've
kept from you—was out of love. I mean, you don't just
give a child that kind of information."

"What are you talking about? I can't stand riddles! Get
to the point."

"Well, you see ... it has to do with your father, Daniel. You were so young when he ... died. Do you remember living here with him and your grandfather?"

"Yes," said Ruthie. "But not very well."

"No, of course not. You were just five when you came to live with us in town. I'm sure you don't remember much of anything before that. You see, that's why we never told you. What purpose would it serve? I know we did the right thing. Your father made us promise never to tell you what really happened. He pleaded with us. But maybe now, it's time you knew. If you see what kind of hurt a person can cause their loved ones by a reckless action, you'll reconsider ... this." She pointed hesitantly at the gun in Ruthie's hand. "Think about that, okay? This all has to do with the night your grandfather died. You and your father were living here then. You said you remembered."

"I do. Get on with it."

"Well, it was Christmas Eve. We were all supposed to drive to Minneapolis to spend the night with your Aunt Constance. You and your dad were invited, too, but Daniel didn't want to go. Grandpa felt terrible leaving the two of you here. The only way we could persuade him to come was by agreeing to let him take his truck. He would follow Violet and me in our car. That way, he could drive back to Repentance River later in the evening. He wouldn't have to stay overnight in Minneapolis. We started out about four in the afternoon. As we got closer to The Cities, it started to snow. But we kept on driving. Coming through Anoka we realized your grandpa wasn't following us any longer. Before we left, he'd said that if the roads got bad he was going to turn back. Violet and I pulled over and waited. But he never came. Eventually, we started to get worried. What if something had happened? That old truck of his wasn't reliable. What if he had car trouble? Well, that did it. We turned around and headed home. We got all the way across the bridge and up into the yard before we saw the truck. By then, the snow was really coming down. Thankfully, the truck was safely parked by the barn. We were so relieved. Violet got out and started running toward the front porch when she tripped over something in the snow. I ran to help her."

Inga bit her lower lip and looked away. "Ruthie, it was your grandfather. I tried to get him to talk to me, but he wouldn't respond. Then we saw the blood. I ran to the house for help. Your father was sitting on the couch with a rifle in his hand, and an empty bottle of whiskey next to him on the floor. I asked what was going on, and he said he'd finally shot the wolf. I couldn't believe my ears. I knew he'd been talking about wolves for months. But nobody paid any attention to him. Why should we? He was drinking all the time. And besides, everyone knew there weren't any wolves around here. It was only later we found out he was right. He had seen a wolf. Somebody on a farm near town had been keeping one as a pet. They had it locked up in a cage. Somehow, it got out, and your dad must have seen it in the woods. It terrified him. When I came into the parlor that Christmas Eve, he was absolutely elated that he'd finally found it and killed it. His family was safe."

"I remember him talking about the wolf," said Ruthie, her voice like a little child's.

"Ruthie, listen to me. Your dad wasn't well. Maybe in more ways than we ever realized. He had a drinking problem. It got so bad that some nights he wouldn't even come home. Finally, your grandpa made him promise to quit. Told him he'd have to leave if he didn't. We all thought he had. He hadn't had a drink in weeks. But that night, he must have gotten very drunk. I suppose he waited for us to leave and then dug out his bottle. When I found him, he had no idea he'd killed his father—your grandfather. Later, when he realized what he'd done, he went to pieces. He became terrified he'd go to jail. He was weak, Ruthie, and I despised him for that. But we couldn't let anything happen to him, could we? He was our brother! No matter what he'd done, we loved him. We had to protect him. Besides, he hadn't shot your grandfather on purpose. It was an accident. So, we made him promise never to talk about it ever again. And he gave us his word he'd never touch another drop of alcohol. Violet and I took Papa, your grandpa, down into the cellar. We laid him in that small boat he'd built and gave him a decent Christian burial—just the three of us. We didn't know what else to do. The ground outside was frozen. The next day, your father bricked up the wall so no one would ever find him. Then the two of you moved in with us. Your father was never the same after that. He was broken." Inga's mouth twisted in pain.

"I saw him."

"What?" said Inga.

"I saw him kill Grandpa."

Inga gasped. "You what? That's impossible. You were asleep in your bed when we got home."

"But that's it, don't you see? I couldn't have been asleep. No!" Haltingly at first, and then faster, her words came tumbling out. "I remember now. I saw you come into the room, so I closed my eyes and pretended. You shined that horrible light in my eyes and told me to get up. Then you must have helped me dress. But I'd never really been asleep. I watched it all from my window. It overlooked the barn, right? And this boat, this is Grandpa's boat! He put that little bell on the front just for me." She started to cry. "I remember now! I remember."

"I don't believe this," cried Inga fiercely. "It's impossible. You were only four."

"But that's it," said Ruthie. "Nothing made sense to me and that's why! All this time, deep down, I knew. Don't

you see? Daddy sent me to bed early. He said Santa would
be coming soon, but I needed to be asleep first or else he
wouldn't come. Tomorrow was Christmas. He promised
we'd have lots of presents. But I couldn't sleep. I sat at the
window looking up at the sky, waiting for Santa's sleigh. I
sat there a long time. I saw Grandpa park his truck.
Then . . ." She began to cry.

"My God, how could this have happened!" Fitfully, Inga
kept explaining. "Ruthie, don't you see? That's why I did
what I did here at the inn. I could see this house was de-
pressing you in some horrible way. I thought it was because
you were so sensitive. Your grandfather's death was so hard
on you. I wanted you to get away from here. Remember?
I've tried everything to get you to leave. But you wouldn't.
I tried to get Leigh to sell, but she wouldn't. What alterna-
tive did I have? I had to *make* her sell to get you out of
here once and for all. But it wasn't happening fast enough.
I did things, Ruthie . . . bad things. But I had to protect
you. Nothing means more to me than you do! You must see
that. We didn't make a mistake not telling you. We promised your father. We had to take care of you. You're too
fragile!"

"I'm not fragile!" screamed Ruthie.

"It was you?" said Jane, her voice amazed.

For a moment, Inga seemed suspended in time. Slowly,
she turned.

"You locked me in that freezer?"

"Oh, Jane, you must see!" Her voice implored. "I would
never have let anything happen to you. I was coming to let
you out when I saw Stephen. Don't you understand? I had
to scare you off. You were getting too close! You could
have ruined everything. I thought if I could convince you of
the danger, you'd get Leigh to sell. I was desperate!"

"You tore up my family pictures?" Jane was surprised by
the depth of her own anger.

Inga looked away.

"You dumped that vile thing in my bedroom?"

Inga's entire body sagged. "I found the deer on the side of the road near town. A car must have hit it in the night."

"Do you realize what you've done?" Out of the corner of her eye, Jane noticed a small movement. She turned to find Ruthie holding the gun directly in front of her face, her eyes fixed on the trigger.

"Careful," said Jane, stepping closer. "Will you give me that?"

Ruthie seemed startled by the suggestion.

"Please," said Jane. "This isn't the way. You must know that." She held out her hand.

Silently, Ruthie looked around the small room. "No. I suppose you're right." Her voice was full of weariness. "All these years. All these lies." She glanced up at her aunt. "What a waste."

Climbing out of the boat, she stood next to it for a moment, reaching out her hand to ring the bell one last time. "Merry Christmas," she whispered.

35

Sunday Morning, December 27

Cordelia flopped backward onto the antique brass bed, violently shaking the four knobs on each end. "You're kidding! Inga?"

Jane nodded, pulling on her favorite rag wool sweater.
"She was behind everything. The ruined copper pots, the
bomb threat—even the burning snowmobile. She had some
help on that one. Elmer showed her how to do it. She apparently appealed to his disgust over the solstice celebration. He thought we were all a bunch of heathens. But he
didn't have any idea she was going to set it on fire. I don't
think he would have jeopardized his job over something
like that."

"I hate to speak ill of the dead," said Cordelia, "but every time I saw that man he looked like he needed a good
burp."

Jane stopped and stared. "Cordelia, you never cease to
amaze me."

"I know," she grinned, propping a pillow behind her
head. "But why did Inga do it?"

"Mainly, it was because of Ruthie. It seems she was convinced very early on that Ruthie's presence at the inn was
affecting her in some extremely negative way. And because
of Ruthie's past, she got scared. Within a few days after she
moved in with them last November, it was clear to Inga
that something had to be done. First, she worked on Leigh.
She suggested perhaps it might be wise for her to listen to
Stephen. Perhaps selling the inn was the right thing to do.
When that fell on deaf ears, she got the idea to start creating problems here and there. She was hoping to prove
that running the place was simply too much trouble. She
got hold of the tin of cocoa Henry Gyldenskog had given
to Leigh and laced it with a sleeping powder. It was enough
to keep Leigh tired all the time. It made it harder and
harder for her to handle her responsibilities."

"That's pretty nasty. Didn't she feel terrible doing it?"

"I'm sure she did. But she knew it wouldn't cause any
permanent damage. She also knew Leigh would make
money if she sold. In the long run, it wouldn't hurt

anyone—it might even be a blessing in disguise. One way or another, she was going to get Ruthie out of here. That was her first priority. When we arrived, she saw another opportunity to apply pressure to Leigh. If she could convince *us* the inn was a dangerous place, we might pass our reservations on to her niece."

"And the skeleton Burton found in the basement? Was that another one of Inga's victims? I suppose you're going to tell me they're stuffed all over the house."

"Cordelia!"

"What?"

"This is serious."

"I agree! Who the hell was that guy down there anyway?"

"Really, I suppose you could say that was the crux of the matter. The man buried in the boat was Inga and Violet's father—Ruthie's grandfather, Harlan Svenby. His own son Daniel accidentally shot him. Ruthie was four years old at the time and witnessed the whole thing. But she must have repressed it. It appears Daniel Svenby took his own life about a year later. He couldn't deal with what he'd done. Inga and Violet tried to keep the suicide from Ruthie, but she's known all along."

Cordelia groaned. "Poor kid. What a thing to have to live with all these years."

"To be honest, I think Inga was also pretty terrified the skeleton would be found behind the wall and traced. She couldn't afford to have that happen. She was the one who set the fire right after Leigh bought the house. She wanted to burn it to the ground so no one would ever find her father's remains. When it didn't work, she was going to try it again. Before she had a chance, Leigh invited her and Violet to come live on the island. Inga decided to hold off. If she stayed here, she could at least keep an eye on things. Make sure no one messed around in the basement. I'm

afraid Burton screwed everything up. I suppose you could
say she was racing against time because of the wine cellar
installation. She apparently tried to talk Elmer into locating
it someplace else. When he refused, she had to slow him
down."

Cordelia snorted. "Seems like she did a lot more than
slow him down."

"She never intended for him to die. Leigh was beginning
to waffle about selling the inn. Stephen had let that little
tidbit drop one afternoon. Inga hoped once Leigh declared
the house up for sale, she and Violet would be able to convince Ruthie to leave. Even Ruthie would see her precari-
ous position. No money. No real job. If her aunts left, she'd
be destitute and totally alone. Both aunts had pretty much
agreed to stay and help Leigh as long as she needed them.
But if Leigh put the inn on the market, that absolved them
of any further commitment."

"So what happened to Elmer?"

"Pokeweed."

"Pardon me?"

"Don't you remember? It's an herb. Inga sent some to
Leigh the day we arrived. It was the little solstice present
she received in the mail."

"Ah yes, the tea. But I didn't think it could *kill*."

"Well, that depends. Let me explain. When Ruthie
worked in town at Bo Dierdorf's store, she used to bring it
home for Inga. It's used as a home remedy for rheumatism.
Inga's suffered from it for many years. The thing is, pokeweed is also quite poisonous. If you take too much, it reacts
like a slow, violent emetic. It can cause vomiting and even
convulsions as little as two hours later."

"Sounds like the cafeteria next to the theatre."

"Inga didn't realize she had built up a tolerance over the
years. The only problem she'd ever experienced was an upset stomach when she took too much. She knew her own

proper dosage, but that didn't mean the same amount would
have the identical effect on someone else. She gave it to
Elmer hoping to merely cause him a bad case of stomach
cramps. It would keep him out of action for a couple of
days, putting his recovery right in the middle of Christmas
weekend. She knew he had asked for the next week off to
go visit his daughter in Pittsburgh. That would delay any
further work until the new year. If Leigh still hadn't made
a decision about selling, Inga would simply have to think of
something else. But for now, a case of stomach cramps
seemed a small price to pay."

"Ha!" shrieked Cordelia. "Easy for her to say! God save
us from the single-minded."

"She mixed the pokeweed into a glass of cranberry juice
and waited until Michael Paget left the basement. When the
coast was clear, she brought it down to him. He drank most
of it right away. About an hour later he spent a pleasant
few minutes having a sandwich with Violet. He seemed totally normal. No one noticed anything wrong. After filling
his thermos with coffee in the kitchen, he went back downstairs to work. In less than an hour he was dead."

"But what about Violet?" asked Cordelia. "Was she in on
it?"

"She knew nothing about Elmer. But, in general, she did
know what Inga was doing—and why. Violet agreed something had to be done. She just took a more passive, wait-
and-see attitude. I'm sure the wine cellar made her terribly
nervous. She was the one who insisted Ruthie come away
with them on a cruise. And later she suggested they all
move to a warmer climate. In her own way, Violet was trying to find a solution. She simply wasn't as inventive as
Inga."

"Lucky Leigh."

"True. Inga said she was terrified Violet would discover
what she'd done to Elmer. Even though it was an accident,

when Violet questioned her about it, she lied. She convinced her it must have been an accident. Of course, Violet knew Inga had taken the skull. She heartily approved. It bought them more time. That is, until Dylan discovered it and we threatened to take it to the police. She was desperate to get it back."

"No doubt. But how did she do it?"

"When I talked with Henry Gyldenskog the night after Elmer's death, I inadvertently tipped him off to who might be responsible for Elmer's death. I asked him if he knew who the other person was who was trying to get Elmer to relocate the wine cellar. He knew that person was Inga. So, next day, he confronted her. She broke down and told him the whole story. They're good friends, you know. He told her he understood and would help her in any way he could. After we finished talking on Friday afternoon, she buzzed his room from the back office downstairs. Told him where he'd find the skull and asked him to get it. Then she came out and took her seat behind the front desk.

"Simple."

Jane nodded. "He grabbed it while I was busy with that bogus phone call."

"And she locked you in the freezer?"

"She did. She said she was going to let me out just as she saw Stephen opening the door. This is an awful thing to say, but I'm not entirely sure I believe her."

"Lucky you." Cordelia shuddered, watching Jane pick up one of her new high-top tennis shoes. "Dressing for success again are we? I can tell this is going to be a formal occasion this morning. Otherwise, you'd be wearing your *old* sneakers."

"That's right. I'm glad you understand my costuming subtleties. And you better start getting ready yourself. Winifred wants everyone down in the parlor by ten o'clock." She looked at her watch. "You have half an hour.

By the way, what's your chosen costume going to be today? Something from *Camelot?* Perhaps a unicorn from *The Glass Menagerie?*"

"I shall ignore your tasteless hyperbole. And don't change the subject so fast. How is Leigh taking all of this?"

"All right, I think. It's just that there's so much happening in her life right now. She and Stephen have split up. I can't say that I'm totally surprised."

"I'm sure you're saddened by the news."

"Knock it off, Cordelia. I'm sorry to see anyone in pain. Leigh *or* Stephen."

"Well, at least Leigh knows now who was behind all the goings-on around here."

"I wish her problems ended there. Her family is pretty messed up right now. Violet left earlier this morning. She's taken a room in town. She refuses to even talk to Inga. She says she can't forgive her for what she did to Elmer. Ruthie is staying on for a bit, but I think she's planning to move back into town too. Get a job somewhere. There's a therapist over in Cambridge she more or less trusts. She wants to finally make some sense of her life. And Inga . . . I don't know what's going to happen. There's a good chance she may go to jail for Elmer's death. There may be some kind of investigation into Harlan Svenby's death too."

Cordelia rolled onto her stomach. "Well, not very neat and tidy, but at least you were able to help Leigh get to the bottom of things. We can leave today knowing she's safe."

Jane found it strangely difficult to smile. "Yeah. I suppose that's true. It's just, she's going to be so alone now. No family support."

Cordelia hooted. "With a family like hers, she should pay them to stay away. And besides, she knows she can always bend your ear when she needs a little love and understanding. You're good at that."

"I am?"

"Well of course you are. Why do you think I keep you around?"

"I thought it was my good looks. My wit. My charm."

"No, dear. Remember? That's why *you* keep *me* around."

36

Jane paused in the front foyer, looking out at the dark, gray morning sky. The weather perfectly mirrored her mood. She'd just finished a short phone conversation with Peter and Sigrid. Peter had called to ask when she and Cordelia would be returning home. Jane had briefly filled them both in on last night's events. Interestingly enough, Sigrid mentioned a psychological term Jane had never heard before. It was the concept of the *vital lie*. Those lies so necessary to a person—or an entire family system—that living without them becomes impossible. What had Sigrid said exactly? A vital lie was the maintenance of emotional and psychological equilibrium at the expense of the truth. Jane reached up and closed the blind, cutting out the dim light. Somehow, a dark room seemed more tolerable today.

"What's this?" asked Burton, stepping out of the dining room doorway. "Playing with the shades, are we? Kind of a gloomy day out there. I suppose we don't need any reminders."

"I hope the snow holds off until Cordelia and I get back to Minneapolis."

"Are you leaving today?"

Jane nodded. "Right after lunch."

"Well then." Burton stuck out his hand. "It was good seeing you again, Jane." He moved in a bit closer. "I wanted to apologize for some of the things I said about Leigh. They were out of line."

"No problem," Jane assured him. "I understand."

"Well, anyway, okay. Enough said. Will we see you up here again sometime soon?"

"I don't know. I was just talking with my brother and his fiancée. They're going to be married in the spring. I told them to check this place out. It would be a beautiful spot for a wedding. Have you had one here yet?"

"No. But Tess and Winifred both came to me this morning. They asked if I'd do the food for their rededication."

"What do you mean?"

"It's a ceremony they want to have. They're going to rededicate themselves to each other in front of friends."

"You don't know what great news that is." Jane smiled.

"Burton?" called a man leaning out of the dining room door, "you're wanted in the kitchen."

"Thanks. Be there in a second." He turned once again to Jane. "Well, let me know about your brother's wedding plans. We'd love to have them here."

"Will do. And give my love to Dylan. You have a fine son."

"I know." Burton twinkled. "He's the spitting image of his old dad! Have a safe drive home."

Jane smiled her thanks, watching his back disappear through the doorway.

"Would you mind trying that number again?" said Jane, standing at the front desk. "If you get through, I'll be in the parlor."

The young woman behind the counter nodded.

Jane moved into the archway, the sweet smell of sandalwood incense greeting her as she peered into the parlor. Everyone was gathered together around the great hearth, sipping coffee and orange juice that the kitchen staff had left on the sideboard.

"Could I have everyone's attention for a moment," said Winifred, holding up both hands. She smiled warmly, her eyes lingering a moment on Tess. "I think it's about ten. We should begin. I've asked you all here this morning because I believe we need to come together one last time before we go our separate ways. We've been through a lot this week. We've felt the destructiveness of lies and past rationalizations. The lies we thought we needed to live, have, in the end, only caused us pain. But we'll go on. That's in our nature. And so, I'd like to offer a prayer to the Goddess, a benediction, if you will. Please," she said, reaching for Tess's hand, "join me in this."

Except for the crackling of the fire, the room was still. Reverently, Winifred raised her head and closed her eyes. "Great Goddess," she said, her voice echoing in the large hall, "you who have seen us through this time of turmoil, listen to our morning prayer. We ask you once again to bless and purify this house. May those who come to stay find peace and shelter within its walls. This is a special place. Let it always be so.

"Great Goddess, we ask that you would bless Jane and Cordelia during the coming year. May they both find the love and meaning for which they are searching. Bless them with health and happiness, and hold them in your arms, safe and secure in your love.

"For Per we ask that you would bless his journey south."

"Miss Lawless," whispered a soft voice, "I have your party on the line."

Jane turned. "Thanks." She backed out of the archway.

"You can take it here at the desk or in the phone cubby under the stairway."

Jane tiptoed in back of the stairs. Seating herself on a small stool, she picked up the receiver. "Aunt Beryl?"

"Jane dear! What a wonderful surprise. Are you home already?" Her voice was once again strong and robust.

"No. I'm still up at the inn. Cordelia and I are leaving this afternoon."

"Did you have a nice Christmas? I do hope my little call didn't spoil anything."

"Not at all. We had a fine Christmas."

"And Peter? Did he make his secret announcement?"

Jane could hear the curiosity in her voice. "He did. Since he's such a terrible lump when it comes to letter writing, he asked me to give you the good news when I talked to you next. He's getting married."

"Oh the dear boy! How perfectly splendid! Is it the young woman he sent me the picture of recently? Very pretty she was. A foreign sounding name. Sigmundo. Frieda. I have no memory anymore."

"Sigrid," said Jane.

"Ah, of course. Sigrid. When is the happy event?"

"This spring."

"Wonderful. I shall have to put on my thinking cap. I want to send them something they'll be able to use. Young couples need to watch their finances, you know."

"I think I know what they'd like more than anything else, Aunt Beryl."

"What's that, dear?"

"They want you to be at the wedding."

"Oh!"

"You'll be here anyway, right?"

"Well, I don't know. It's in the spring, you say? That's a long way off. I merely proposed a visit. You wouldn't want an old pudding like me to overstay my welcome."

"That's not a problem. I'm inviting you to come for as long as you want. You can stay for a week, a month, or the rest of your life if that's what you'd like. My home will always be open to you. Peter and I both want you to stay."

"Jane! I don't know what to say. I never expected this. Have you spoken to your father?"

"Yes. He knows."

"I will need an armed guard at the train depot, then."

"No. We're going to work this out. You'll see."

"God bless you," said Beryl, her voice cracking with emotion.

"When will you know what your specific plans will be?"

"I'll ring you next week. Jane, this means the world to me."

"Me too."

"Give my best to Peter and Sigfried."

"I will." She hesitated. "I love you Aunt Beryl. Goodbye."

"Goodbye, dear."

The line clicked.

Jane sat for a moment, staring at the phone. Well, she'd done it. She'd finally made the decision. And the funny thing was, she no longer had any doubt that it was the right one.

She stood and backed out of the closet, returning to the archway. Everyone was still gathered, holding hands, their eyes closed. Silently, Jane listened to the last words of Winifred's prayer.

"Great Goddess, Mother of us all, you have shown us that winter is truly the time for the germination of the soul. Grant us all a rich harvest. Bring us back together next year in celebration of the return of light."

Winifred raised her hands.

*"Blessed be your spirits, Harlan and Daniel Svenby.
Blessed be your dreams.*

Sleep in bliss and never know darkness or fear, only the peace and love of the Mother.
We are a circle.
No beginnings.
Never ending.
Blessed be.
Blessed be us all."